Praise for *Neu*
and #1 intei........
bestselling author Anna Todd
and her After series

"Todd [is] the biggest literary phenom of her generation."
—*Cosmopolitan*

"I was almost at the point like with *Twilight* that I just stop everything and my sole focus was reading the book. . . . Todd, girl, you are a genius!!!"
—*Once Upon a Twilight*

"The Mr. Darcy and Lizzy Bennet of our time. . . . If you looked up 'Bad Boy' in the fiction dictionary, next to it would be a picture of Hardin alongside Beautiful Bastard and Mr. Darcy."
—*That's Normal*

"The one thing you can count on is to *expect the unexpected*."
—*Vilma's Book Blog*

"Anna Todd manages to make you scream, cry, laugh, fall in love, and sit in the fetal position. . . . *After* is a can't-miss book—but get ready to feel emotions that you weren't sure a book could bring out of you."
—*Fangirlish*

"A very enter_____ na. . . .
This book wi

Escape

"I couldn't put this book down! It went with me everywhere so I could get my Hessa fix every spare moment I had. Talk about getting hooked from page one!"

—*Grownup Fangirl* on *After*

"Be prepared to have an emotional explosion!"

—*Biblio Belles*

"*Before* is brilliantly written. . . . I found myself putting it down and then pondering what would happen next between Hardin and Tessa before coming back to the story."

—*Into the Night Book Reviews*

"I'm so grateful to Anna Todd for giving me all the Hessa feels. Thank you for the 2,587 pages of insane angst and emotional turmoil. But above all, thank you for giving us, the reader, the chance to take the journey of love with Hardin and Tessa."

—*YA Book Addict*

BOOKS BY ANNA **TODD**

After

After We Collided

After We Fell

After Ever Happy

Before

Nothing More

Nothing Less

SHORT STORIES IN *IMAGINES*

"Medium"

"An Unlikely Friend"

nothing less

ANNA TODD

G

GALLERY BOOKS

New York   London   Toronto   Sydney   New Delhi

G

Gallery Books
An Imprint of Simon & Schuster, Inc.
1230 Avenue of the Americas
New York, NY 10020

This book is a work of fiction. Any references to historical events, real people, or real places are used fictitiously. Other names, characters, places, and events are products of the author's imagination, and any resemblance to actual events or places or persons, living or dead, is entirely coincidental.

Copyright © 2016 by Anna Todd

The author is represented by Wattpad.

All rights reserved, including the right to reproduce this book or portions thereof in any form whatsoever. For information, address Gallery Books Subsidiary Rights Department, 1230 Avenue of the Americas, New York, NY 10020.

First Gallery Books trade paperback edition December 2016

GALLERY BOOKS and colophon are registered trademarks of Simon & Schuster, Inc.

For information about special discounts for bulk purchases, please contact Simon & Schuster Special Sales at 1-866-506-1949 or business@simonandschuster.com.

The Simon & Schuster Speakers Bureau can bring authors to your live event. For more information or to book an event, contact the Simon & Schuster Speakers Bureau at 1-866-248-3049 or visit our website at www.simonspeakers.com.

Printed and bound by CPI Group (UK) Ltd, Croydon, CR0 4YY

10   9   8   7   6   5   4   3   2   1

ISBN 978-1-5011-5296-2
ISBN 978-1-5011-3085-4 (ebook)

*For all the Landons in the world
who put everyone else before themselves,
even when they shouldn't.
Karma will work in your favor <3*

Landon's

Playlist:

"Without" *by Years & Years*
"Echo" *by Nelou*
"Ghost" *by Halsey*
"TiO" *by Zayn*
"Take Me Home" *by Jess Glynne*
"Crown of Love" *by Arcade Fire*
"Control" *by Kevin Garrett*
"Assassin" *by John Mayer*
"I Can't Make You Love Me" *by Bon Iver*
"What a Feeling" *by One Direction*
"Never Let Me Go" *by Emily Wolfe*
"War of Hearts" *by Ruelle*
"Edge of Desire" *by John Mayer*
"Chainsaw" *by Nick Jonas*
"wRoNg" *by Zayn*
"As You Are" *by The Weeknd*
"Something Great" *by One Direction*
"Unhinged" *by Nick Jonas*
"Death Has Fallen in Love" *by Mads Langer*
"Last Flower" *by Mads Langer*
"I Know Places" *by Taylor Swift*
"Cough Syrup" *by Young the Giant*
"iT's YoU" *by Zayn*
"Heavy" *by Emily Wolfe*
"Wolves" *by One Direction*

nothing
less

prologue

*D*ADDY?" A SMALL VOICE CUTS through the darkness of my bedroom.

I lean over and click on the lamp, and my eyes adjust to the light spreading throughout the room.

"Adeline? What's wrong?" I sit up, tugging the blanket up to my chest, remembering that I'm not dressed underneath. I glance over at my wife; her naked back is exposed and she's sleeping on her stomach, sprawled out the way she usually is.

A small hand rubs over little brown eyes. "I can't sleep."

Relief spreads through me. "Did you count sheep?" She often has trouble sleeping lately, and I'm trying not to worry too much about it. Her doctor says that she's just having a hard time shutting her wild mind off at night, which is pretty normal behavior for her age.

Adeline nods. "And ponies. I counted ponies, too. A blue one, a red one, and a grumpy yellow one."

I try not to laugh. "A *grumpy* yellow pony?"

"Yep. He stole the blue one's cookie."

My little girl's mom stirs in her sleep but doesn't wake. I pull the blanket up over her exposed back, just in case she decides to roll over.

I look at my daughter, whose eyes match my own, and can't even try to hide my amusement at her inventive imagination. She's so creative for her age, always telling tales of goblins and princesses and the fantastical.

With a smile, I reach for her hand, and she moves her teddy into her other arm and grabs my hand. The poor stuffed bear is close to falling apart. Aside from school, she doesn't go anywhere without it, and some days I even find the furry thing in my messenger bag when I get to the school.

"How about you meet me in the kitchen so you can tell me what happened next?" She nods, and I kiss her hand before she drops it to her side. "I'll be out in just a minute, sweetie," I add so I can throw on some sweats.

Adeline looks over at her mom and back at me before she makes her way to the doorway. She turns around. "Can we have a cookie while we talk?" my little negotiator asks. She's just like me, always wanting sweets.

I glance at the clock on the nightstand. It's twelve thirty, and she has school in the morning. Since I'm her first-grade teacher, I shouldn't encourage her to eat sugar in the middle of the night . . .

"Please, Daddy?"

I know I'm supposed to be responsible, and that I shouldn't be condoning a sugar rush six hours before she has to wake up for school. Her mom's going to kill me, but I know dang well she would cave, too. Those big brown eyes and that teddy bear in her arms remind me that she won't be a kid for long.

Adeline waits expectantly.

"Grab me one, too. I'll be out there by the time you pick out the *tiniest cookies in the jar* for us."

She smiles like she didn't have any doubt that I would say yes.

"The *tiniest* ones, okay?" I smile at her.

She agrees and walks out of the bedroom. I stand up and grab my sweats from the floor.

"Sucker," my wife's sleepy voice says from the bed.

I pull the pants up my legs. "You're awake?" I ask with mock surprise.

She rolls over and lifts her arms behind her head, the sheet dropping to her waist. "Of course." A sleepy smile spreads across her beautiful face.

"Coward," I tease.

"Pushover."

I try to keep my eyes on her face. If I allow myself to admire my wife's naked chest, I will never leave this room.

Once I'm dressed, I lean over, resting my knee on the edge of the bed, and gently press my lips against her forehead. Her eyes are closed when I pull away, her lips pulled into a comfortable smile.

I leave the bedroom, and when I reach the kitchen, Adeline is holding the hand of her teddy in one small hand and a big cookie in the other.

"That doesn't look like the smallest cookie." I open the fridge and grab the jug of milk.

Adeline smiles, and her tongue pokes out between her missing teeth. She's growing up too fast. "I thought you said the *biggest*," she fibs.

chapter

One

*E*LLEN'S BIRTHDAY CAKE is in my arms, ready to carry downstairs. Nora is standing next to the door, waving goodbye to
Posey and Lila. I watch Nora as she pushes her pizza-patterned
socks into a pair of plain white sneakers.

"You ready?" I set the cake down on the red entry table, and
she nods.

She's been quiet since our exchange in the bathroom, and
I don't know how to start a conversation with her now. I agreed
that I wouldn't try to fix her, that I wouldn't push to know her secrets or help her carry her baggage. She's warned me over and
over that she's not good for me, that she can't be what I need her
to be.

How can that be, when I have no idea what it is that I need?

All I know is that I enjoy her company and I want to get to
know her. I'm okay with taking it slow; the best presents usually
take the longest to unwrap.

Picking up the cake, I lead us to the elevator in silence and
press the call button. The swoosh of the elevator climbing floors
is the only noise in the quiet hallway.

When we step inside, Nora moves to the farthest side of the
small car.

I allow her space and try not to look at her while she looks at me. I can feel her eyes on me, but I can tell she's tapped out on talking today.

My arms feel empty despite the cake in them, like they're *missing something.* Nora, maybe? Each second with her, I feel like I'm losing control of my own body.

Nora touches her fingers to the end of her braid, and my eyes meet hers. The elevator hasn't moved since we stepped in. I couldn't even guess how long we've been standing in here; it feels like minutes, but it's possible that only a few seconds have passed.

Her eyes stay on mine, studying me, trying to unlock something.

I'm not the one with secrets, I want to say to her.

I think of Dakota and our time together last night. I think of how embarrassed and guilty I felt when I couldn't . . . perform. I think about the way I felt when I found the bathroom empty, my ex having left via the fire escape. It's only been one night, and here I am with Nora, wanting to be close to *her.*

I guess I have secrets, too.

"Is it broken?" Nora asks, and I have a moment of panic when I think she's talking about my cock.

When I realize she's talking about the elevator, I want to laugh.

"I don't know." I press the button for the ground floor again. In response, the elevator dings and the door opens and closes. The car begins to move, and I shrug my shoulders. Had I forgotten to press the button? I don't know.

When we reach the bottom floor, I wait for Nora to step out of the elevator first. Her elbow touches my arm, and I step away to give her space. My skin feels warm, and I wish for a moment I could live in a different reality. A dimension where Nora is mine to touch, mine to hold. In that world, Nora would trust me and share parts of herself that no one else can see. She could laugh without hesitation, and she wouldn't try to hide.

With each silent step through my apartment building, that perfect imaginary world fades.

"I didn't get Ellen another gift," I remember out loud.

Nora turns around and slows down until I'm next to her. "I'm sure this homemade cake and your time are gift enough." She takes a breath. "I would love such a gift." Then she continues to walk.

When she says things like this, confusion fills my already-crowded mind.

"You don't like birthdays, though?" I ask, not expecting, but hoping, for a sliver of explanation. Her birthday is next week, but she made me promise that I wouldn't do anything for her.

She's making me promise a lot of things lately. I've only known her for a few weeks and I've already promised her too much.

"Nope." Nora pushes the door open, holding it for me to pass through.

Instead of asking her why, I decide to talk about my favorite birthday memory. "When I was younger, my mom would always make a huge deal out of my birthday. The entire week was always a celebration. She made all my favorite meals, and we stayed up late every night."

Nora looks up at me. We're approaching the door to the corner store now. A couple passes, hand in hand, which gets me to wondering if Nora has ever had a serious boyfriend. It drives me crazy that I don't know anything about this woman. She's twenty-five. She must have dated in the past.

"She would always make these cupcakes baked inside of ice cream cones and bring them to my school. She thought it made the kids like me, but it only made them make fun of me more." I remembered my freshman year when no one in my class would even touch one of the sprinkled cakes she made.

No one except Dakota and Carter. The three of us tried to eat as many as we could during the walk home from school so my mom would think everyone in my class loved her gift and had celebrated my birthday with me.

We had five left when we got to our block. We ended up leaving them on a piece of lumber at the entrance to the Patch, a wooded area that was home to addicts and people down on their luck—with empty stomachs and empty lives—and we liked to think that we fed at least five of them that day.

"I would have eaten one." Nora stares past me.

She doesn't elaborate on her reasoning for hating her own birthday, and I didn't expect her to. That's not why I shared a piece of my past with her.

Nora opens the door to the store, and the little bell rings. I follow her inside, and I smile when Ellen regards us, cake in hand, and tries her hardest to fight off a smile.

chapter

Two

*W*E HAVE SO MUCH CAKE LEFT," Nora says, lifting a plastic fork to her mouth.

Small crumbs of white cake and green icing fall onto the table between us. Turns out, Ellen doesn't really like sweets. She cites being a teenager for not liking flowers when I lament that I should have just brought those. But not liking cake? I don't know what kind of devil she is, but I'll gladly eat this for her.

Despite hating most things, she did enjoy our company. Though she tried to fight the smile on her face, she failed, and the three of us had a good time. Nora turned the shop's OPEN sign to CLOSED, and we sang "Happy Birthday." We discovered that I'm a terrible singer. Even without melody or candles, we made sure she knew we cared that it was her birthday.

Nora streamed pop radio on her phone, and Ellen talked to her more than she's ever talked to me. Our makeshift party only lasted about half an hour. Ellen was getting anxious about the shop's being closed, and I got the feeling she was tired of talking about herself. Which is too bad. I've often found that the people who don't like to talk about themselves are the ones I want to talk to the most.

"More for us." I grab another fork from the counter and dig into the corner of the cake. Nora's sitting in the chair next to me with one knee propped up on the seat. The little pizza slices on her socks are equal parts quirky and adorable. I reach my hand out and poke at the top of her foot. "What's with these?"

She licks her lips. "Life's too short to wear boring socks." She shrugs, bringing a forkful of cake to her lips.

I look down at my own socks, white with gray on the heels and toes. Yikes. These are boring. And *tube* socks. No one wears tube socks anymore.

"Is that your life motto?"

She nods. "One of them," she says with her mouth full.

Icing is on the rim of her mouth, and I wish we were in a romantic-comedy movie so I could reach over and wipe it off with my finger. She would get all mushy and butterflies would swarm in both of our stomachs and she would lean into me.

"You have icing on your lips," I say, doing the exact opposite of a romantic gesture.

She swipes at her mouth with her thumb, missing the spot. "You're not going to wipe it off for me? It's the perfect setup for a kiss in the movies."

Her mind is in the same place as mine. I like the comfort of that, for some reason.

"I was just thinking that. If this were a movie, I would lean over and wipe it for you." I smile.

Nora grins, icing still messy on her lips. "You would lick it off your finger, and I would watch your lips, the way they part."

"I would look at you while I did it."

"I would sigh as you licked your finger clean, never breaking eye contact."

My stomach flutters. "You would have butterflies in your stomach."

"The wild, angry kind that make me feel like I'm going crazy." Nora's eyes meet mine. She's smiling, and she's just so pretty.

"I would tell you that I missed a spot and lean over again. Your heart would be beating so fast."

"So fast that you could hear it."

I repeat her words, lost in them. "So fast that I could hear it. I would touch your cheek."

Nora's chest rises and falls slowly. "I would let you."

"Your eyes would close the way they always do when I touch you."

Nora looks surprised at this, as if she wasn't aware that she does it.

I stare at her mouth as she talks, wondering what she's thinking.

"I would pull you closer to me and lick my lips," she adds to our little story.

My heart is pumping so wildly that I can hear the blood rushing behind my ears. I take a breath, and Nora has moved closer. I don't think she even notices.

"I would brush my lips against yours. So light at first that you would barely feel it. I would part your lips with my tongue and kiss you."

Nora's eyes are half-lidded now, and her eyes are on my mouth. "You would kiss me like I've never been kissed before— and I probably haven't, not the way you kiss me. It would be like my first kiss, even if it wasn't." Her voice is a whisper.

I can't not kiss her. I lean closer to her, leaving only a few inches between us. "You *haven't* been kissed before." She's so close now that I can feel her breath on my cheeks. "Not the way I would kiss you. You would forget every kiss that came before mine, every touch. Every single one."

I take a breath, and her lips are on mine before I can exhale. Her lips taste like icing. Her tongue is warm in my mouth, and her hands are greedy in my hair. She pulls me closer, her fingers tugging at the roots.

Both of my feet are on the floor, and I wrap my arms around her body, pulling her from her chair to mine. She settles on my lap, her thighs on either side of my legs. She's kissing me like *I've* never been kissed, and *I* want to forget every kiss that came before her, every touch.

Her soft body rocks against mine as she bites at my lip. I feel myself hardening under her, then am surprised that I'm not the least bit embarrassed. I know the moment she feels me. I taste her gasp as her arms wrap around my neck. She adjusts her body on mine so she can feel me rubbing against her. Her pants are so thin, and my sweats aren't exactly hiding anything.

When she rocks against me, her pussy rubbing against my hardness, I groan. I can't help it. She feels so good against me, even fully clothed.

Fuck, my mind is racing, *she's kissing my neck now.* Her mouth knows exactly where to kiss, where to lick, the exact spot on the base of my neck to suck. I reach for her hips and gently squeeze them, guiding her to rub exactly where I need her.

She moves her hips in the sexiest way. She's a goddess, pure and simple. She's a goddess, and I'm a lucky bastard to be here with her right now. There really is something about this kitchen that makes us insane for each other. This is definitely not how I thought the night was going to go.

Not that I'm complaining at the turn of events.

Nora pulls her mouth away from my neck, still rocking her pussy against my cock. "God, I wish you weren't Tessa's roommate." She sucks at the skin again, then stops. I squeeze her hips, and she speaks again. "I would fuck you—*fuck*—I would fuck you right now if you weren't."

The familiar tingle of an orgasm creeps up my spine at her words. She's so sexy, she's so open, and she makes me crazy. Absolutely freaking crazy for her.

"We can pretend I'm not," I say, only half joking.

She laughs and slides against me. "I'm going to come, fuck, Landon. This . . . doesn't . . . count . . ." Her words are throaty and sensual, and I can barely breathe as she rides me, thrusting her hips against my body.

I move my hands to her back to steady her quick movements. Before I can stop myself, I'm on the brink of joining her. I don't want to think about it; I don't want my mind to ruin this moment. I just want to feel her—I just want to make her come and join her in bliss.

"Me, too. I'm going to, too," I say into her neck. I wish I were as good with words as she is. I kiss where her neck meets her shoulder, not exactly knowing what I'm doing, but the sounds she makes as she comes against me tell me I did something right.

My mind goes blank. There's only sensation now. I'm only sensation, and she's so good at silencing my mind, and this feels so good. She feels so good, on my body, inside my hectic mind.

As she comes down, her body slows and her breathing relaxes. She lays her head on my shoulder, and I can feel the wetness between our bodies, but neither of us seems to care.

"That was . . ." she begins. "I—"

Her words are cut short by the noise of the front door closing.

"Landon?" Tessa's voice comes from around the corner, cutting through our heavy breaths, slicing through our euphoric thoughts.

"Shit," Nora mutters as she climbs off me, then loses her balance. I grab her elbow, keeping her from falling to the floor.

I stand, and Nora's eyes move to my crotch. The wet spot there. "Go."

I move quickly toward the bathroom. Tessa walks into the kitchen as I reach the doorway, and I try to bolt, but she stops me. At least my back is turned toward her.

"Hey, I tried to call you," she says.

I don't want to turn around. I can't turn around.

"I wanted to see if you could bring my other shoes to my

work. Someone dropped a bowl of salad dressing on my shoes, and I have to close tonight." Tessa's voice is strained.

I can tell without even looking at her that she's stressed, and I'm not exactly in a position to console her, or anyone, right now. I look around for something to grab so I can cover myself and turn around, but there's nothing aside from a box of Lucky Charms.

"Anyway," Tessa begins, her voice lightening, "what are you guys up to?"

I grab the cereal box and cover my crotch and turn to Tessa. Her eyes shoot straight to the box. I hold it tight.

"We were . . ." I search for excuses and words and try not to let my nervous fingers slip from the corners of the box.

Tessa looks at Nora, then back to me. "Oh, hey—what are you doing here?" Tessa asks innocently.

I search for help from Nora, but she's silent. I'm going down on this sinking ship, with only the leprechaun on the cereal box for an ally.

"Well," I begin, still without a clue as to what the heck I'm gonna say. Tessa is standing in the doorway with white globs of dressing covering her shoes. She's not the only one with white stains on her . . .

"We were cooking," I say, and mentally thank Tessa for buying the family-size box of Lucky Charms.

"Cooking?" Tessa looks at Nora, her expression unreadable.

Nora steps forward. "Yeah, chicken and . . ." Nora looks at me. "Lucky Charms?" Her tone is so unsure that I'm positive Tessa will catch it. "As the breading. You know how we have those Frosted Flake–covered tenders at work? I wanted to try with Lucky Charms," Nora explains.

I almost believe her, and, more importantly, Tessa seems to, too.

Nora continues, "You have to go back to work? Here, let's get your shoes."

With Nora's distraction in place, I scamper off, saying "I'll be right back" over my shoulder.

This is so awkward. Why is everything in my life so dang awkward? Thankful that Nora is a better liar than I am, I disappear into the hallway, cereal box in tow.

"What's with him?" I hear Tessa ask Nora. I don't stay around to hear her response.

chapter

Three

*M*Y BEDROOM IS SILENT.

It feels so small.

Or maybe it's me who feels small after yet another embarrassing moment with Nora? This time was better because we shared the awkward scene.

We caused it.

I can still feel her body against mine, moving with need, with purpose. I can hear her moans in my ear and feel her hot breath against my skin.

Now my room feels warm.

Too warm.

I move away from the back of my door and walk across the room to the window. My desk is messy; stacks of books and Post-its clutter the wooden surface. Well, it's from IKEA and cost less than a hundred bucks, so it's probably not "wood" at all. I tap my finger on the dark brown potential wood, and it sounds hollow. I knew it wasn't real.

My fingers are shaky as I push my hand through my blinds to pull open the window. The windowsill is covered in chipped paint and dust, even a dead fly. Tessa would cringe at that. I make a mental note to clean it up this week. I pull at the stubborn wood, and it finally cracks open.

I lift it higher, welcoming the calm sounds of the city into my room. I love the noise level here in Brooklyn. There are cars and usually some voices of people walking down the sidewalks, but nothing too crazy. The amount of random taxi honking is significantly less than in Manhattan. I'll never understand the whole angry-honking thing. It doesn't make any sense to me why people think it helps traffic in any sort of way. The only thing the rude gesture does is piss people off and create even more tension.

Random thoughts are doing a good job of keeping my mind off what Nora and I just did. Well, not now that I'm thinking about it again. How did we go from creating a little movie scene to her straddling me on a chair? I pull my pants and boxers off and toss them into my dirty-clothes hamper by the closet door.

I change my clothes and sit down on the edge of my bed, close to the window. My phone is plugged into the charger sitting on my nightstand. I reach for it.

Hardin answers on the second ring. "It's too late to talk me out of coming—I'll be there this Friday."

I roll my eyes. "Hi, I'm good. Thanks for asking."

"Noted. What can I help you with on this fine evening?" Hardin asks over a car alarm beeping in the background.

"Nothing. I'm having a weird thing . . ." I don't know how to explain what's going on or why I called Hardin to talk about it.

He laughs. "You're going to need to explain much more than that."

I sigh into the phone and listen to my surroundings. I can faintly hear Tessa's and Nora's voices in the kitchen.

"Okay, so you know Tessa's friend Nora? Well, Sophia was her name when you met her, but Tessa says she likes her friends to call her Nora. I mean, you probably won't get either name right anyway."

He's silent for a moment. I wonder if my voice was too loud.

I can't make out anything the women are saying, so I hope they can hear even less of my voice.

"Yeah. I think so."

"Okay, so we just had sex." I tug at the blinds, pulling the string to raise them. "Well, not really sex, I guess. But really, really close to it."

"And?" Of course Hardin's response would be *And?*

I make sure my voice is only slightly louder than a whisper. "This is the thing. Nora has told me so many times that we have to stay friends, and we were just talking, like usual, and then two seconds later she's straddling me and having an orgasm and then Tessa walked in right after, and now I'm in my room and I'm kind of freaking the hell out because I don't know what to do or say now."

"Wow. Tessa walked in? The chick was straddling you on a chair? Well, there's no denying that, then. Wait—so you fucked her on a kitchen chair? Or she just rode you until she came?" he asks in a casual tone, like his mouth isn't as dirty as a public toilet.

"Um, the second one. We didn't have sex—well, like the sex where something goes into something else . . ."

"Really?" His voice is calm, amusement playing at its edges. "Did you really just say that? I might as well ask you to show me on the doll where she touched you."

"I don't know why I called." I sigh. Leaning back, I stare at my weirdly colorful ceiling fan.

Hardin seems to notice something in my voice, so he eases up a bit. "So, do you like her? I mean, why else would hooking up with her be a problem? You're single, she's single. Right?"

I contemplate this for a moment. *Am* I single?

Yes. Dakota and I have been broken up for months.

The looming fact that she was here just yesterday waves its hand in my face.

Man, I'm an asshole. I should tell Nora about Dakota's being here. It's only fair. That's what a nice guy would do, and I'm a nice guy.

"We are both single. Except Dakota was here last night."

I hate to admit it.

I'm not that kind of guy.

I'm really not.

"Yikes. Delilah, too? What the hell is going on there?"

I don't bother to correct him on Dakota's name. "I don't know. But don't tell Tessa. Seriously, she's got enough going on, and Nora is really freaked out about Tessa finding out. I mean it. I don't care if Tessa's naked and asks you to tell her what's up—you better pretend you know nothing."

"If she's naked, there's no promising anything."

"Ugh."

"Fine. Fine. I won't say anything. Did you talk to her about her schedule yet?"

No. Because I'm too big of a chickenshit. "Not yet. She's been working a lot lately. Oh, and I need to warn you about something, but you can't freak out." I pause. "Seriously, you can't. Promise me," I say softly. I don't want Tessa or Nora to hear me gossiping about them to Hardin.

"What? What's going on?" he asks, and I can tell his mind is going to the worst of places.

"Promise me," I repeat.

He huffs in impatient frustration. "Yeah, sure, I promise."

"You know that waiter guy from the lake that weekend? When you and Tessa were fighting the whole time?"

"We weren't fighting the *whole time*." His voice is defensive, but lightly so. "But, yeah, what about him?"

"He's here."

"In your apartment?" Hardin raises his voice, and I start to think maybe this wasn't the best idea to tell him right now, like this.

"No. In New York. They work together."

He sighs, and I can only imagine his expression right now. "Have they been . . . you know? Like, dating or something?"

I shake my head even though he can't see me. "No, nothing like that. I just wanted to tell you because I think, for your sake, it would be better if you don't make a big deal out of it. You know, show Tessa you're maturing and all."

Also because I don't want my apartment to be burned to the ground in Hessa World War Two. Of course, if it did burn down, I wouldn't have this issue between Nora and me every time we're in the kitchen together . . .

"Maturing? I'm very mature. Fucker."

"Yeah, I can tell by your extensive vocabulary, *fucker*," I tease.

"Listen, man. I'm proud of you for cussing and for half fucking Naomi or Sarah or whatever she's going to change her name to next week, but I have a call in one minute."

I can't help but laugh at his way with words. "Thanks for the help."

He's silent for a second. "If you really want to talk about it, I can call you back after?"

His voice is so full of unexpected sincerity that I sit up. "No, it's fine. I need to get out there and face the music."

"I hope it's a death-metal band."

"Shut up."

The line goes silent.

Four

*B*Y THE TIME I LEAVE MY ROOM, Tessa has already left to go back to work, and I find Nora sitting alone on the couch, her feet propped up in front of her on a stack of my couch pillows. Her back is leaning against the arm of the leather couch, and she's holding the remote in her hand.

"Tessa left already?" I pretend that I didn't wait to hear the front door close before I came out of my bedroom.

Nora nods. She presses the arrow on the remote, scrolling through the guide. She doesn't look at me. I notice that she's changed her pants, too. Did she bring extra clothes with her, knowing that I was going to make a mess of the ones she was wearing? I hope so.

The thought makes my heart race, and I try not to think too much about what Tessa almost caught us doing.

"Do you think she knows?" I had planned on being a tad subtler when I brought up the subject, but I guess my big mouth has other plans.

Nora's thumb keeps pressing on the remote, but she glances at where I stand in the doorway of the living room. "I hope not." She pauses and draws a breath. "Look, Landon—" Nora's voice is full of the beginning of a goodbye, and I've barely heard her say hello.

"Wait." I cut her off before she can talk herself out of giving me a chance. "I know what you're going to say. Your tone and the fact that you won't look at me kind of gives me a pretty big hint."

Nora's eyes meet mine, and I walk farther into the living room and sit on the chair next to the couch. She lifts herself up and crosses her legs beneath her body. Her hands grab for a pillow, the pillow that Ken's mother gave me last fall, and place it on her lap. "Landon," she says softly, and I love the way my name blends with her breath. "I'm not—"

"Don't." I'm rude to cut her off again, but I know what she's going to say, and I want to change how this is going to go. "This is where you warn me off and tell me that you aren't good for me and all that. But not today. Today we talk about why you think that and figure out where to go from there."

I feel high when I finish. I feel good that my thoughts became words, and I think I just grew a chest hair or two.

Nora's eyes lock onto me with a calm intensity. "There's nowhere to go from here. I told you that we couldn't date . . . We could never be together in a real way. I'm not looking to get into another relationship."

I'm surprised by her boldness. Usually when these types of awkward conversations happen in books or movies, the one doing the rejecting looks away or picks at their fingernails or something.

Not Nora. Bold Nora is staring straight at me, and it's making me a little nervous. My high is gone, my chest hairs have shriveled up and disappeared, and my mouth is dry.

Nora said *another relationship*. What was her last relationship? I'm 99.9 percent sure she won't elaborate on this for me, but I ask anyway. "When was your last relationship?"

Her eyes narrow but she doesn't look away. "It's complicated."

"Everything is."

She smiles at that.

"Tell me about it. I want to know about you. Let me," I encourage her.

"I don't want you to know about me."

I can feel the conviction in her words. She means them, and that kind of stings. I can't help but frown. "Why not?"

The pillow is covering her chest now, and her fingers are gripping its top corners intensely. I remember when Gran, Ken's mom, gave me the pillow. She told me that she'd bought the same one for Hardin, but when Ken took out the trash that same day, he found the blue-and-yellow pillow in the can. I kept mine, and I'm convinced that when Ken gives Hardin the pillow back someday, he'll finally be ready to keep it.

When Nora doesn't respond, a hint of anger bubbles in my chest. "Why? Tell me why you don't want me to know you. You like me, Nora. I'm not really as suave as all the other guys out there, but I can see *that*. Why can't you just let me get to know you?"

"Because you won't like me anymore. If you keep digging around, you won't like what you discover."

Nora stands up and tosses the pillow onto the couch. It falls to the floor, and neither of us moves to pick it up. "I told you from the beginning that this isn't going anywhere."

I stay in the chair. If I get up, she's going to slap me or kiss me, and as much as I would like either of those options right now—some kind of connection—we need to have an actual conversation for once.

"You say that"—I keep eye contact with her—"but then we kiss or . . . well, you know. If you just told me the reason you're trying to keep me at a distance, we could figure it out together."

When she just looks at me, my frustration makes me braver. "This is the thing I don't understand about humans. I'll never understand why people can't just say what they feel and talk about shit. I don't get it. Nothing can be that bad. Nothing is too bad to figure out. I'm not some asshole guy who will pretend to be here for you and then disappear." I stand up. I want to be closer to her.

She takes a step back.

"Nora, I don't have any intention other than getting close to you. Believe me. Or at least allow yourself to try to."

"You don't even know what you're saying. You don't know anything about me. You barely noticed I existed until two weeks ago." Nora's hands are balled at her sides, and she takes two steps closer to me.

"Barely knew you existed?" It's an absurd claim.

Nora lets out a huff. "You were so wrapped up in Dakota that nothing else mattered. I don't know why we're talking about this. We're friends. Nothing more."

"But—"

"No fucking *but*s," she hisses. "I'm tired of people telling me what I'm supposed to do or how I'm supposed to act or feel. If I say we're friends, we're fucking *friends*. If I say I never want to see you again, then I won't ever see you again. I'm capable of making my own decisions, and just because you think you're a damn therapist doesn't mean I have to talk to you. Not everyone wants to sit down and spill their fucking guts to a stranger."

"I'm not a stranger. You can try to convince yourself that I am, but you know I'm not." I try to break through the wall that she's so adamant about keeping between us. I'm no therapist; I just don't have a problem with saying how I feel.

"Oh, *really*?" Nora says, almost shouting.

"Yes, really!" I try to mock her anger, but it doesn't work. Any anger I had been feeling disappeared when I saw how vulnerable she was through *her* anger. There's something at play in her that I don't understand.

"How many times did you see me before you moved here?" she asks.

What does this have to do with anything?

Before I can speak, she adds, "Think about it before you answer."

I'd seen her once or twice. Ken knows her dad somehow. "You were at my mom's house. We had dinner once," I tell her, proving her wrong.

She laughs, but not from amusement. "See?" Her hands move in front of her like she's pushing the air toward me.

I keep my eyes on hers even though I want to look away.

"Eight times," her voice breaks through the silence. "Eight times is how many times we saw each other. It doesn't surprise me that you don't remember."

"There's no way. I would remember that."

"Really? Remember when we were talking about Hardin and how I didn't know him? I kept hoping you would remember. I was there when he slammed you against the wall at your parents' house. I remember when he raised his fist to you but he couldn't hit you because he loved you. I remember sitting at your kitchen table a few days before that and you were talking to me about college and how you hope Tessa got into NYU. I remember the blue of your shirt and the honey flakes in your eyes. I remember the way you smelled like syrup and blushed when your mom licked her finger and wiped your cheek. I remember every detail—*and you know why?*"

I'm stunned into silence.

"Ask me why!" she demands.

"Why?" The word is a pitiful sound from an idiot's mouth.

"Because I was paying attention. I've always paid attention to everything around you. The sweet and sexy, sort-of-dorky boy who was in love with a girl who didn't love him back. I memorized the way your eyes close when you drink good coffee, and I loved cooking with your mom and hearing you and your stepdad cheering at some stupid sport on TV. I thought"—she pauses and looks around the room before zeroing back in on me—"well, I had half a thought that you were paying attention, too, but you weren't. I was nothing but a distraction from Dakota, *who is a freaking bitch,* by the way."

"She's not a bitch," my idiot mouth says.

Nora's eyes widen. "All of that . . ." Her eyes close and open slowly. "I say all of that, and all you can do is defend Dakota? You don't even know her like you think you do. She's been spreading her legs for every guy who even smiles at her since she moved here, and you're so obsessed with her that you don't even try to see how awful she is."

Her words hit me and my heart drops. Too many thoughts are going through my head to process anything that's been said in the last five minutes.

"She . . . she wouldn't do that," I mumble.

Nora sighs. She shakes her head with angry pity. I watch as she walks to the door and pushes her feet into her sneakers. She doesn't speak, and I can't find words for her.

I stand in the middle of my living room and watch her walk out of my apartment. If this were a movie, I would run after her and explain myself. I would be brave and find words to ease her pain and frustration.

But life isn't a movie, and I'm not brave.

chapter

Five

I'T'S BEEN FIVE DAYS since I've seen or heard from Nora. Five days, but she's been on my mind more than ever. And what she said about Dakota. It just can't be true, but it keeps playing over and over in my head. Why would Nora say that? And with such venom?

Tessa mentioned that she worked a shift with Nora last night and that Nora seemed distracted and was barely speaking. Tessa didn't know why, but she thought it was weird.

Distracted by me?

Doubtful.

I realize that I do barely know Nora. Maybe she's right—getting to know her would mean I wouldn't like her. She turned so aggressive so quickly. For a moment I decide to call Nora *Sophia*. I didn't know Sophia, not the way I was starting to know Nora, and if I separate the two of them, my life will be easier, so maybe I should admit I don't know this girl and go back to Sophia.

Still, a big part of me hates that she felt like I wasn't paying attention to her, that I ignored her for Dakota. It wasn't like that. Not intentionally. I was already in love with Dakota when I met Nora; I didn't know that I was supposed to be paying attention.

I didn't know her attention was mine to have. I thought of her as Sophia, the older, beautiful chef who would never give me the time of day. But now in this city she's become Nora, the stunning and mysterious friend of Tessa's who said all those hurtful things about Dakota . . . and who's doing a good job of making me fall for her.

Falling for may be too dramatic, but I've certainly been interested in and very, very attracted to her. And in turn, she's gone off on me and basically told me to fuck off. Along with her revelation about me needing to mind my own business, she told me that Dakota cheated on me, more than once.

My head still hurts at the thought, and I haven't made up my mind whether or not I want to ask Dakota for the truth. Part of me thinks that Nora was just mad and in the heat of the moment started spewing out whatever she thought would hurt me the most. That being said, that part of me isn't big enough to ignore that it takes a lot of effort and emotional gymnastics *not* to believe Nora. She might just be playing to my worst fears, but what she said *feels* true.

Tessa's voice surprises me. "Did you really do another load of laundry?"

I set the stack of towels down on the ground and turn to her. She's standing in the hallway, her lime-green tie bright as ever.

"Yes. It's time I start helping more around the house. Well, *apartment*."

I open the closet, and Tessa leans against the wall. She's wearing makeup today; her eyes are lined with black and her lips are shiny. It's been a while since she's worn makeup. She's beautiful without it, but today she looks a little less sad than she has the last few months.

Hardin's flight lands any minute, and I'm wondering if the two are related. I thought she would be more upset when I told her, more zombielike than usual, but that doesn't seem to be the case. She seems to be brighter, her steps lighter.

"You help just fine. I like to clean, you know that."

"Sure," I halfheartedly agree.

This little hallway closet is impossible to use for anything. The three shelves are really small, and the bottom section is taken up by the vacuum and the broom. I shove the towels in, hoping they won't fall before I can close the door. But fall out they do, and I reach down and pick them up.

"Is it weird that I'm nervous?" Tessa asks softly. "I shouldn't be nervous, right?"

I shake my head. "No, not weird at all. I'm nervous, too."

I laugh, not joking at all, and shove the towels back into the closet, trying to keep them as folded as possible this time.

"You're sure you're okay, right? Remember, Sophia said you can stay with her for the weekend if you aren't comfortable." The name *Sophia* feels odd in my mouth, but calling her Sophia helps me not ache at the sound of her name.

Tessa nods. "It's okay, really. I have to work most of the weekend anyway."

I can't begin to guess how these next couple of days are going to go. It's either going to be a relief, the two of them holding hands and skipping down the road of reconciliation, or one of them is going to burn the place down. It's Hardin who's known for burning buildings, but that's another story for another time, and I feel like Tessa's learned a few new tricks, so she's not out of the running as the arsonist.

"He's taking a cab from Newark, so he'll be here in about an hour, given the traffic." I close the door and look at Tessa. Panic bubbles in my chest.

It's not fair for me to ask her to be okay with him coming here. I should have told him to stay in a hotel; there are hundreds in the city. Tessa is my best friend, and I should have made Hardin make other arrangements. Then again, the burning flames of hell can't keep that man away from her, so why should I try so hard?

I rub the stubble budding across my chin. "I feel like this isn't going to go well. I shouldn't have agreed to it."

Tessa pulls my hands away from my face. "It's fine." Her eyes are on mine. "I'm a big girl; I can handle a little Hardin Scott."

I sigh. I know she can handle him. She's the only person in this universe that can. That's not the problem. The problem is that handling him usually comes along with a war. I try to think of this situation as if it were a battle. Tessa on one side, her sword drawn, Nora and her army of cupcakes behind her. Then there's Hardin, stone-faced and alone, his tank ready to roll over anyone in his way. I find myself in the middle, waving a puny little white flag but preparing for carnage.

I follow Tessa out into the living room to finish putting away the rest of the clean laundry.

"Will you-know-who be around this weekend? I don't know how that will go over . . ." I picture Robert, the pretty-boy waiter, crushed by Hardin's tank. If Tessa is working, will Robert be there, too? If so, I'll just keep Hardin far, far away from the restaurant.

Tessa grabs her black apron from the top of the pile. "No, he works all weekend, too."

I don't know if that will make things better or worse. That means, in fact, that he *will* be around her all weekend. Should I offer to send Robert to Mars while Hardin's here?

Maybe.

I hate being stuck in the middle between them, but I do my best to be as neutral as possible while still being a good friend to both of them. Tessa is working all weekend anyway. Working with Robert. Oh, so maybe it *is* for the worse, then. They'll be together, and Hardin will be thinking about that.

Between Dakota's possibly cheating on me for the entirety of her life in New York, the city I moved to for her, and Nora's storming out of my apartment, my life has turned into a teen drama. No, not teen. I'm a grown-up now. Well, sort of. So it's a

New Adult drama. Is New Adult a thing? I heard two women debating this the other day at Grind, the coffee shop where I work. One of them, a short woman with curly brown hair and a two-hundred-thousand-word manuscript, was livid that a twenty-year-old got a publishing deal writing something called New Adult.

"What the hell is New Adult, anyway?" the other one asked her, clearly intent on getting her riled up.

"Some shitty subcategory that publishers created to help put out their shittiest work. Too young for romance, but not young enough for YA," the aspiring author barked.

As I wiped up the coffee rings on the table next to them, I thought that I would like to read some New Adult books. A lot of what I love to read is considered Young Adult, but what about those of us who want to read something a little more serious, more relatable to our actual lives? Not every underdog can save the world, and not every love is magical and life changing. Sometimes even the nice guys get the short end of the stick—myself included. Where are *those* books?

"Do you guys have any plans for the weekend?" Tessa asks. She's struggling to tie her apron around her back, but just as I move to help her, she ties it.

"Not that I know of. I think he's just sleeping here and leaving Monday afternoon."

Tessa does her best to maintain a neutral expression. "Okay. I'm working a double shift today, so don't wait up for me. I won't be home until at least two."

Tessa has been working nonstop since she arrived in August. I know she's doing it as a distraction, but I don't think it's helping. I know she's going to stop me, but I start my lecture anyway.

"I really wish you wouldn't work so much. You don't have to help pay anything. I got enough money from grants, and you know Ken refuses to let me pay for much anyway," I remind her for the tenth time since she moved in with me.

Tessa fusses with her hair and looks over at me. The smile on her face indicates she's about to tell me to shut up. "I won't go over this with you again," she says, shaking her head.

I decide to save my energy for the weekend and let her have her way. "Text me when you're off, then?" I grab Tessa's keys from the hook and drop them into her palm.

"I'm fine," she says.

We both study her shaking hands.

When she leaves, I jump in the shower and shave my face. Sometimes I want to grow my beard out, but once I do, invariably I shave it off. I can't make up my mind. If I let my beard take over my face, maybe I'll be invited into the hipster secret circle in Greenpoint. Then again, am I ready for that type of commitment? Hardly.

I wrap a towel around my waist and brush my teeth. I don't know if I like being an adult so far. Why does New York have to be so far from Washington? I should call my mom today . . .

A knock at the door echoes through the apartment.

Hardin; it must be Hardin. Why do I feel so anxious about his arrival?

I pull the door open, wishing I had put some clothes on, because he's going to talk crap to me the moment he sees me in my towel.

My eyes meet Dakota's, and I step back more out of surprise than to let her inside. She's the last person I expected to see; I'm not sure I'm really ready to see her.

"What's going on? Why are you here?" Our last meeting wasn't exactly pleasant, and since then Nora showed up at my apartment with a box of her belongings.

Dakota looks at me, through me almost, her eyes deep wells

of black. "It's . . ." she croaks. Her bottom lip shakes with anxiety. "My dad. He's . . . he's going to die." She covers her mouth as the words come out.

A little cry escapes her lips. "It's worse now that I've said it. He's dying, Landon; my dad—he's going to die. I'm not even there, and he's going to be dead soon. I—"

Instinctively, I reach for her and pull her into my chest. Her cheeks are wet against my skin, and her body is shaking as sobs take over her.

I don't know which thought of mine is worse: that I'm not sad about him, or that Dakota feels like a stranger in my arms. "What happened?"

Her hands move up my bare back, and I rub my hand over her curly hair.

"His liver—it's failing. They said he has alcohol hepatitis; I don't know what that means, exactly, but his liver is full of scars. I knew the bottle would kill us off one by one. Carter, my dad . . . I'm sure I'm next."

I hug her tighter to try to halt her dark thoughts. "Tell me everything they said."

I guide her to the couch while I close the door and then join her. She's still shaking when we sit, and she molds her body to mine, holding on to me as if she'll lose ground if she lets go.

She explains that the nurse didn't say much aside from medical terms Dakota didn't understand or remember. His body is failing fast, and he hardly has enough money to live, let alone pay these expenses. It deeply bothers me that a man, no matter how unpleasant and downright mean he's been, can work his whole life and barely have enough insurance coverage to save his life.

"Do you want to go visit him? Are you planning on it?" My fingers trail up and down her arms, comforting her.

"I can't. I owe rent still, and I'm barely scraping by."

I look down at her face, but she turns it away, burying herself into my chest.

"Is that the only reason? Money is the only reason you can't go?"

Despite their history, I wouldn't be surprised if Dakota didn't want to see the man before he died. I wouldn't blame her.

"I don't want you to pay for it," she says before I can offer. Dakota lifts her head and looks at me. "I'm sorry I came here. I didn't know where else to go. My roommates won't understand, and Maggy isn't really that great at listening to other people's problems."

"Shh." I stroke her back. "Don't apologize." I tilt her chin up to my face.

"Should I even be sad? I can't decide if I'm sad or relieved. The only reason I think I'm sad is because he's the last of my family. If he dies, do I even exist? I have *no one*, Landon."

I don't tell her that she hasn't really had him since she was a little girl. I don't tell her that deep in my heart I'm not at all sad that he's dying. Instead, I tell her that it's okay to feel however she feels. I tell her that she doesn't owe anyone an explanation for those reactions.

"If I don't go, no one else will. He won't even have a funeral. How do people pay for funerals?" Dakota's voice cracks, and I continue to hold her.

I think about the members of Dakota's family I've met in the past. She has an aunt somewhere in Ohio, her dad's sister. Her grandparents on her dad's side are dead, and her grandparents on her mom's side don't speak to her anymore. They used to call every week after her mom left, but the calls slowly stopped coming, and we concluded that they gave up hope that Yolanda would ever return from Chicago. Talking to Dakota must have reminded them of the loss of their daughter, and, selfishly, they withdrew from their grandkids.

Carter's funeral was nearly empty. Only Dakota and I were in the front row. A few teachers from school came and stayed for a couple of minutes, and Julian made an appearance, of course. He left in tears almost immediately. Three assholes from our school came and were chased out by Dakota before they even took a seat on a pew. Forgiveness was not to be found in that small church that day. Everyone else was gone before the service even started.

Dakota's dad didn't bother to show up. Neither did Yolanda. No one cried; no one shared happy stories. The pastor pitied us, we could tell, but Dakota wanted to stay for the entire hour to remember her brother.

"Do you think he'll go to heaven? My dad says God doesn't let people like him into heaven." Dakota's voice was as blank as her eyes.

I tried to keep my voice down so the preacher wouldn't hear my reply. *"I don't think your dad has any idea who God lets into heaven. If there's a heaven, Carter's there."*

"I don't know if I believe in God, Landon," Dakota said, and not in a whisper. She wasn't embarrassed to say that in a church.

"You don't have to," I let her know.

I held her tighter, and after ten minutes of silence I went up to the podium and recalled our best times with Carter. With only Dakota in the church, I told an hour of stories, our crazy adventures, the plans for our future; I didn't stop talking until the pastor politely indicated I should wrap it up.

The funeral for her father would be similar, only this time Dakota would be alone. No one to relive memories for her. I can only think of one positive memory of the man. I hate him more than I knew was possible, so I'm not sure I could bring myself to give him a respectful word or two. Not even in death.

"Come with me. Can you come with me? I'll help pay. I'll figure out some way to help pay for some of it," Dakota says suddenly.

Come with her? To Michigan?

"Please, Landon. I can't do this alone."

Before I can answer, there's a knock at the door.

"Hardin," I say. "Hardin's here for the weekend."

Dakota peels her body away from mine and finally seems to notice my lack of clothing. "I'll go." She leans over and presses her lips to my cheek. "Please think about it. I would leave Monday. I'll use the weekend to scrounge up some money. Please consider it and let me know by Sunday."

"Okay." Too much is going on in my brain for me to say anything more.

Dakota follows me to the door, and when I open it, Hardin's standing in the doorway, a black duffel bag hanging from his shoulder. His long hair is messy, and he's taller than I remember. His eyes scan Dakota, then me, and he raises an eyebrow.

"Well, hello, Landon. Delilah." He walks past us into the apartment.

Dakota's eyes are swollen, and she doesn't bother responding. Without another word, she hugs me tight and leaves me standing in the doorway. After a moment of watching her go, I walk inside, closing the door behind me.

A little too loudly for my liking, Hardin asks, "Why was she here? I thought you were fucking the other one?" He tosses his bag onto the couch and walks around the living room, studying every inch like it's a crime scene.

"I need some advice," I say with a sigh.

Hardin stops at the chair and touches a pair of Tessa's pajama pants. His fingers run over the fuzzy material, tracing the edges of the clouds.

"Put some clothes on first. I don't give advice while someone's naked. Not with you, at least."

I roll my eyes and walk back to my bedroom to get dressed and deal with the storm coming my way.

I CAN'T TELL IF I'M A SLOB OR NOT. I wear sweatpants a lot, but mostly because they're comfortable. If I were a woman, I could never wear heels and tight dresses. I would be like Tessa: yoga pants and tank tops all the time. I grab a blue T-shirt and gray sweatpants and decide to shelve the issue for later thought.

When I return to the living room, Hardin is sitting on the couch, his laptop open and a pen held between his teeth.

"Already working?" I ask. What the hell is he working on, anyway?

Sitting down on the chair, I watch him ruffle through a stack of papers on the table. A cup of coffee, half-empty, is sitting next to his shiny laptop. There's a sticker—for a band, I assume—covering the Apple logo. I glance to my laptop on the edge of the coffee table and compare the two of them. His with a metal-band sticker, thorns and roses, and mine emblazoned with a HUFFLEPUFF FOR LIFE sticker. In my defense, mine is pretty damn cute, and also funny because I'm not a Hufflepuff. Some silly on-line quiz told me I was, so I tried to own it. I bought the sticker and everything, but deep down I know I'm a Gryffindor through and through.

"Yeah. It took you long enough to get dressed," he complains.

Hardin complaining? Such a surprise.

I toss a pillow at him, and he grumbles something under his breath. "Where's Tess?"

"Working. She's staying busy while you're here."

He lets out a huff but otherwise stays quiet. I can see the pain haunting his green eyes. I can hear the quickness of his breathing at the mention of her.

"How busy? What time does she get home usually?" he asks.

I hesitate. I need to keep my feet on neutral ground here. "Tonight she'll be home around two."

Hardin closes his laptop and leans toward me as if he's going to stand up. "Two? In the morning?"

"Yeah. She's closing tonight. And working a double shift during the day."

"Two in the morning is *ridiculous*. There's no reason for her to be working until the fucking morning." Hardin gathers the loose pages and shoves them back into his binder.

"I can't control how much she works. Neither can you."

He sighs and nods, clearly not wanting an argument. "So, what's up with you? Why was Delilah here looking like someone killed her puppy?"

Such grace Hardin Scott has, let me tell you. "Her dad's dying."

I watch his face fall slightly. "Oh, my bad."

I shake my head and lean back against the chair. My hair is messy under my fingertips. "She's going back to Michigan and wants me to go. Monday."

Hardin crosses one leg over his knee and brushes his hair back. He hasn't gotten it cut since the last time I saw him. "What about Nora? Are you guys still hooking up?"

So he *does* know her name . . . "No. She stormed out of here about a week ago saying that I was too wrapped up in Dakota to see that she liked me. She hasn't been here since."

"So you have the clearance there. If she hasn't been here or talked to you, you're free to do what you want. If you feel guilty, ask yourself why."

Okay: *Why do I feel guilty?* Nora got upset with me over something I couldn't help. Would she have rather had me cheat on Dakota with her? I couldn't pay attention to Nora's feelings for me because first, in Washington, I was in love with Dakota, and then, since I've moved here, I've been mourning the end of my relationship with Dakota. I understand why Nora felt embarrassed and angry. I would feel the same way if I was ignored, but it's not like I was upsetting her on purpose. I still can't believe someone like Nora would even give me the time of day, and yet she did; and somehow I managed to mess that up, too.

"Maybe I should just stay away from both of them. Being single isn't so bad."

I close my eyes and consider this. Maybe I should be alone. Someone like me is good alone. I already have too many people to worry about. Tessa, my mom, my baby sister (who will be here in just a few weeks), Hardin, Dakota . . . Can I add another name to the list?

"Being single fucking sucks, dude," Hardin chimes in. "Trust me, it fucking sucks."

I open my eyes and look at him. "You could have lied to make me feel better."

"Nope. I cannot tell a lie." He raises his hand into the air as if he were swearing into the military.

This makes me laugh. "Liar."

He shrugs and wears a wicked smile. "I've turned over a new leaf."

A few hours later, Hardin returns from a meeting that he won't tell me anything about. He says he'll fill me in next week, when they call him with a follow-up. I'm curious, but part of me doesn't want to know anything that I'll just have to hide from Tessa anyway.

Thinking that I have to work in the morning, I start to wonder what Hardin's dinner plans are, and just as the thought crosses my mind, he walks into my room, without knocking.

"I'm going to eat; want to come?" He smacks his hand against my foot.

Before I sit up, I ask him where he's going.

"The Lookout," he says matter-of-factly.

"Tessa works there," I remind him.

He shrugs his broad shoulders. "I know."

Okay . . . ?

"She's keeping her distance from you for a reason. I don't think—"

He holds up a hand to interrupt me. "Look, I'm going whether you come or not. I just wanted to be nice and invite you. I know she works there, and I want to go. I'm going. Are you coming or not?"

I groan and roll off my bed. "Fine. But that Robert guy works there, the one who—"

"I know who he is. Even more reason for me to go."

The thing about Hardin is that when he makes up his mind, his mind is made up.

Wow. The thing about me is that I'm great at explaining things.

Seeing no other solution, I nod. "Let me put my shoes on."

He looks at my clothes, his eyes moving up and down. "You're wearing that? Doesn't Nadia work there?"

"Yes, *Nora* works there. And, yes, I'm wearing this."

If Nora *is* working, I highly doubt she's going to speak to me anyway, and my clothes are comfortable. Not as slick as Hardin's all-black ensemble, but at least my pants let my dick breathe, unlike his tight jeans.

Ten minutes later, I've changed into dark jeans and a plaid button-up shirt. My sleeves are short and my pants are a little too tight, but Hardin sat on the couch refusing to let me leave wearing "pajamas," and I'm too hungry to argue anymore.

During the walk to the Lookout, Hardin asks about my classes, my job, and every other non-Tessa topic under the sun. He's much more talkative now than he was when I first met him. He's come a long way.

We spot Tessa before she spots us. The Lookout is a modern restaurant with industrial-themed décor, and as we hit the hostess stand, Tessa is standing just behind a big metal tree that has clockwork on the limbs instead of leaves. The dessert display is right next to the hostess stand, and I can't help but search for Nora's dark hair. I see a flash of that gorgeous hair and olive skin as Hardin asks Robert for Tessa's section, but she's gone before I can get a good look.

Ironically, Hardin acts as though he doesn't have a clue who Robert is.

"I'll be right back," Robert says, glancing at Hardin and then back to the other side of the restaurant. It's not a big place; only about twenty tables line the walls.

"What a fucking prick," Hardin says to Robert's back. I ignore Hardin's annoyance.

Nora appears from behind the counter, a tray of small cakes in her hands. Her hair is tied up high; messy strands frame her face. Her eyes are unfocused as she stares straight ahead.

Does she know I'm here?

Does she care?

"Tessa," I hear Hardin say.

I keep my eyes on Nora. She opens the large display case and begins unloading the tray of cakes, lining them up neatly. She doesn't look away from her task. It's on the darker side in here, but I can tell she's exhausted. I can see the low set of her shoulders from here.

Out of the corner of my eye, I see a Tessa-shaped figure approach, and when I turn my head to her, I say preemptively, "Hardin wanted to come here." Just in case she's uncomfortable, I want her to know this isn't my doing. I'm just following along to keep the peace.

Tessa doesn't reply; her eyes are locked on Hardin.

"We don't have to stay and eat here if you're busy," I offer.

I can't read the energy between these two maniacs.

Hardin's fingers are wrapped around Tessa's wrist and her eyes are bright, brighter than they've burned in months.

"No," Tessa breathes out. "It's okay, really." She pulls away from Hardin's grip and grabs two menus from behind the hostess stand.

I follow Tessa to the table and glance back at Nora one more time. She still doesn't look at me. I can't tell whether she's ignoring me or just doesn't see me. How can she not notice me staring at her?

Hardin and Tessa make small talk while I scoot into the booth, and Hardin pretends he doesn't know how late Tessa works. He pretends that it doesn't drive him crazy knowing she's walking home that late. He tries to be normal around Tessa.

"Is Sophia busy?" I ask when we order our food.

Tessa nods. "She's busy. Sorry." Tessa doesn't correct my use of Nora's name. Does she know something's going on? Am I a bad friend for hiding it from her?

Tessa frowns, and Hardin leans toward her. Does he even notice the way his body moves in response to hers? When her fingers move to write down our order, his eyes watch intently; his shoulders rise and fall to match her breathing.

These two make me sick. I'm a lonely schmuck, and these two are magnets drawn to each other. They will always be together. I know this is the truth. I can't be a magnet; to be a magnet you have to have someone to latch onto.

It's a sad day when one wishes to be a magnet.

When Tessa tells us that Nora wrote off our check, Hardin leaves an enormous tip that Tessa shoves back into my pocket as we're leaving. During the meal, I couldn't think about anything other than Nora's proximity. I watched the walkway leading out of the kitchen the entire time. I didn't even notice when I cleared my plate. The food was great, I'm sure.

It drives me crazy that Nora knew I was here but didn't come out to the table. I didn't mean to hurt her, and I deserve the chance to explain myself. She had over an hour to at least walk by, wave, or smile politely.

When we reach the door to leave, I pull on Hardin's sleeve. "I'll meet you back at my place."

Hardin doesn't ask any questions, doesn't offer to stay with me. He just nods and walks away. I'm glad for it.

I sit down on the bench outside the restaurant and check the time on my phone. It's ten minutes past nine, and I have no idea when Nora's shift is over. I'll wait outside until she's off, I decide. Even if it's two in the morning.

I look around the street and lean back against the cool brick. The fall air is calm and holds a slight chill. The sidewalks are nearly empty, which is not common for Brooklyn on a Friday night in September.

While I wait, I try to think about what to say to Nora. How will I begin the conversation?

Two hours later, when Nora emerges from the Lookout, I still haven't decided. She walks right past me, her long hair bouncing down her back. When she stops at the corner of the street, she unbraids her hair and shakes her head. She's stunning, even beneath the unforgiving streetlights.

I should make my presence known; I should call her name and face her instead of silently following her. But something inside stops me. Where is she going, anyway? Is she back at her apartment with Dakota?

I don't know, but I have a feeling I'm about to find out.

Nora walks through the quiet blocks, turning down the smallest side streets. It worries me that she doesn't notice she's being followed. She hasn't looked back once. She put earbuds in and seems to be content roaming Brooklyn at eleven at night without paying attention to her surroundings.

She crosses to Nostrand Avenue, and I assume she's going to take the subway. Should I be following her? Why doesn't this feel creepy, watching her and shadowing her like a psychopath? Either way, I find myself crossing the street and following her down the steps of the subway entrance.

I stay at least twenty feet behind her, and allow a group of people to come between us. Nora bobs her head to her music while she waits in line to scan her MetroCard.

The train car is nearly empty when I step inside, and if Nora even glances around, she'll see me. I take a seat next to an elderly woman reading a newspaper and hope that it will block me from Nora's view a little bit. The car is eerily quiet, and when I cough, I decide that I'm not that great a stalker.

Nora pulls her phone from her pocket and stares at the screen. She swipes and sighs and swipes again. Ten minutes later, she stands to get off, and I follow. We transfer to another train and forty-five minutes later are at Grand Central Terminal; I have no freaking clue where this woman is going, or why I'm still following her.

We board a Metro-North train, and another thirty minutes pass before we arrive at Scarsdale station. I have no idea where

Scarsdale is, or why we're here. When we get out of the station, Nora stops at a bench and unbuttons her work shirt. She's wearing a black undershirt made from a meshlike material. Her bra is showing, and I try to not stare at her figure as she shoves her shirt into her bag and zips it back up.

Nora takes out her earbuds and pulls her phone out of her purse, and I hide behind a sign for an insurance company. "I'm here; I'll meet the driver outside the station. How was his dinner? Did he eat at all?" she asks whoever is on the line.

A few seconds pass. "Well, I'll help. I'll be there in fifteen minutes."

She hangs up the phone and puts it in her pocket, then turns toward where I'm hiding. I duck down farther.

What was my plan here? Whose driver is picking her up?

Just when I think I'm in the clear, I hear Nora say, "Your feet are sticking out from under that sign, Landon."

chapter

Seven

I PEEK AROUND THE SIGN to see Nora walking toward me. Her dark hair shadows her face. She looks like a villain under the fluorescent lighting in the station parking lot. She's wearing tight black jeans with a rip in one knee, and her black bra is showing through the mesh fabric of her tank top. Is she even allowed to have a rip in her jeans while baking things for customers to consume? More important, why am I thinking about that right now?

I stand still as she approaches me, her prey, in the middle of nowhere. To be honest, the train systems here still freak me out. I can't read the signs, I can't stand people packing in around me like sardines, and I hate being trapped underground, but when I'm aboveground sometimes I get a little motion sick.

How the hell am I going to get back if I can't even read the signs?

Where the hell is Scarsdale, anyway?

Nora waits for me to walk out from my "hiding" spot. "You didn't think I knew you were following me since Lookout?" She raises a brow, studying me.

I wouldn't have been surprised if she'd pulled out a whip, or a sword, with the way she's commanding her surroundings. She's not timid, she's enchanting, and being out in the dark night with her here only adds to the mystery of her. I feel like I'm in a movie, and her dark green eyes look nearly black instead of their normal brown-green.

Nora stops two feet in front of me and pulls her cell phone, not a sword, out of her back pocket. She quickly checks the screen and puts it away.

"I've taken two self-defense classes," she begins, highlighting how terrible my spy skills are. "I saw you as soon as we turned on Nostrand. I was waiting for you to approach me." She pauses, and her full lips turn up in a smile. "But you just kept following me. What's up with that?"

Her hand touches my arm briefly.

She officially thinks I'm insane, or maybe she's a little insane herself.

I rub my hand over the back of my neck and try to think of an explanation. "Well"—I nervously clear my throat—"well, I wanted to talk to you after your shift."

"Then why didn't you stop me? You know, instead of following me?"

"I don't know."

She smiles. "Yes, you do. Just say it. Just say why you followed me. I have this special ability to tell when people are lying. It's my greatest talent, really." Her eyes square with mine. "So, let me ask you again. Why did you follow me an hour and a half from Brooklyn to Scarsdale?"

Without even a second thought, I just begin speaking: "I wanted to talk to you hours ago when I was at your work, and I know you knew I was there, but you didn't say hi or anything. You haven't come by in a week. You haven't called me or anything."

"I don't have your number."

She licks her lips, and I remember what she tastes like. Her hands on me, her tongue gently caressing mine. I'm glad she can't read my mind.

"You texted me the day we went out."

"Oh, yeah. I forgot."

She contemplates. Her fingers are steady as she tucks her hair behind her ear. "Okay, so what did you want to talk about?" Nora leans back against a wall and bends her knee. She's getting comfortable before she calls me out for being creepy.

What exactly *did* I want to talk about? Should I tell her that I wanted to check on her? That I missed her? She claims she'll know if I lie.

The words tumble from my mouth—"I missed you"—and Nora's back straightens against the wall.

"Where were you going? Where *are* we?" I ask after a few seconds of silence.

Before Nora responds, she tenses. She looks over at me, then past me.

When I turn around, I spot a guy in a suit walking toward us. "Ms. Crawford," he says, this man who is massive, a real-life giant.

Okay, maybe not a giant, but he looks huge as he steps up next to Nora.

"Chase," she says, and smiles. It's a strange smile, unreal. "I'm coming. I was just saying bye to my friend. He helped me get here all the way from Brooklyn. Such a nice guy, he is." Her eyes dart to his and then back to mine.

I have no idea what's going on.

Nora gives me a small wave and follows the man, who I assume is the driver she mentioned a few minutes ago on her phone call.

"That's it? You're not going to talk to me after I came all the way here?" I lift my hands in the air. I stare at Nora's back.

She doesn't turn to face me. "I appreciate you coming!" she calls back.

She disappears around the side of the building, and I groan in frustration.

Why the heck did I come here? Now I have to find my way back to Brooklyn at close to midnight. I should have gone after her instead of just standing here and letting her walk away with her bodyguard friend.

Who the heck was that guy, anyway? She changed her shirt and took her hair down—*why?*

Does she have a secret boyfriend here?

Is she a stripper?

Is she in a cult?

Does she possess multiple personalities?

Who freaking knows.

When I get back to my neighborhood, two hours later, my door is locked. Since I gave Hardin my key when I sent him back to my apartment alone, I hope he answers the door. At first I knock gently, but when that doesn't work, I pound a little harder, and a few seconds later Hardin opens the door, shirtless and half-asleep.

He rubs his hands over his eyes. "I thought you were in your room this whole time, Ninja."

"I was with Nora." I decide to save the pathetic details for later.

Hardin raises a brow and flops back onto the couch, which looks so small with his long body lying on it. His feet hang over the edge. I'm surprised he's on the couch and not in Tessa's room, but I don't have the energy to ask about it, and it doesn't look like he has the energy to explain, either.

"Good night," I tell him, and go straight into my room.

My head pounds for hours as I try to sleep.

• • •

I wake up ten minutes before my alarm and have to force myself to get out of bed. I can't believe I slept until eleven. I have work at noon and get off at four. Not too long a shift, considering that six to two is my usual on a Saturday morning, so today will be a breeze. More of a breeze if I get to work with Posey instead of Aiden.

One can only hope. Four hours with Aiden feels like eight. But with Posey, four hours will feel like thirty minutes.

During my shower, I force myself to put on my happy face. I can't mope around work all day. I go through the motions of my morning routine. Shower, lotion, face lotion, because Tessa tells me I need to use that. Clothes: a white T-shirt and black jeans. Coffee: black and strong.

En route to the kitchen I see Hardin isn't alone on the couch anymore. His arm is tightly wrapped around Tessa's body, and Tessa's face is buried in his chest. I'm not one bit surprised.

I need to eat something small before work, but I don't want to wake either of them. The bananas on the counter look rotten, and I shouldn't try to cook anything. I open the cabinet and grab the first box of cereal I see.

Just when I stick my entire hand into the box, I hear the un-mistakable shuffle of feet on the hardwood floor. It must have been the coffee machine that woke them, or the crunching of the bag of Frosted Flakes. I don't remember the box being here yesterday, but anyone who brings food into our place has to know that it's fair game. I chomp on the dry cereal quickly, regretting trying to eat a fistful in one bite. I grab my coffee from the counter and walk toward the hallway. I find Tessa. As my smile grows, her cheeks bloom a deep red.

"What?" Tessa asks, not meeting my eyes.

I lift my coffee to my face. "Nooooo-thing." I take a sip, and Tessa gives me a signature eye roll and retreats back to her room, where apparently Hardin has scampered off to as well.

• • •

When I get to work, Aiden is behind the counter. Great.

"Hey, man, rough night?" He bro-fives me, and I cringe.

"You could say that."

I clock in, wishing I had one of those remotes from that Adam Sandler movie that freezes time. I'm not saying I would punch him or anything, but I'm also not saying I wouldn't.

"Me, too, man. Me, too." The bell on the door rings, and I look away from the hickey on Aiden's neck.

Why does he always have a hickey? Who does that anymore?

"Whoa. Look," Aiden's bro-voice whispers, and I look toward the door.

Nora walks in, her hair down and messy about her shoulders, and she's wearing a light denim shirt tucked into white pants. The whole effect is stunning.

"Hey." She smiles at me, and I hear Aiden suck in a surprised breath.

"Hey." I wipe my hands on my apron and turn to her.

Aiden quickly asks Nora if she wants anything to drink. She smiles at him, and I can see him straighten his back and tuck his shirt in. Just for her. Never mind that he has a hickey on his neck; that must not bother him.

"What do you recommend?" she asks him, and it annoys me. It shouldn't annoy me.

"Hmm, well, you look like an experienced coffee cond-i-saur."

God, I hope she recognizes that he said it wrong. I'm going to go out on a limb and assume he meant *connoisseur*.

"What is that, like, a dinosaur?" I say suddenly.

Why did I say that? What's wrong with me? I even did the awkward chuckle at my own lame attempt at a joke.

Nora smiles, her fingers pressed to her lips. Aiden laughs, but I have a feeling he's either annoyed or doesn't know why we're all chuckling.

"I would recommend trying our new coconut-milk latte," Aiden says, grabbing a paper cup and his Sharpie.

Nora steps forward, toward the counter. "I don't like coconut milk."

I bite back a smile. Aiden pauses.

Nora looks at me. "What's that drink you make Tessa? The one with banana?"

I can feel Aiden's ego deflating next to me.

The resultant breeze feels amazing.

I take the cup and the Sharpie from Aiden and scribble Nora's name on the cup, mostly because it's fun to write. "It's a macchiato with hazelnut and banana. I can make you one."

Nora pays for her coffee, and Aiden continues to try to make small talk with her while I pump the flavoring into the cup.

"When does your shift end?" Nora asks when I hand her the custom drink.

"Four. I just got here a few minutes ago."

Nora takes a cautious sip, blowing into the cup first. "Okay. I'll wait here."

Maybe she heard me wrong. "Wait here? It's four hours from now."

"Yeah, I know. It's not that busy. I'm sure it's fine if I take a table in the back?" Nora stares at me without even glancing toward Aiden.

The way she's looking at me makes me feel important, and I think I like knowing that it's driving Aiden crazy that someone like Nora would choose to stare at me and not him.

"Yeah, of course," I say.

She smiles, knowing damn well that I wasn't going to send her away.

chapter

Eight

*D*ESPITE WHAT NORA SAID, Grind ends up being unusually busy for a Saturday afternoon, and Aiden's body is moving slower than usual. He's forgotten two orders, written the wrong name on three cups, and dropped a bottle of mint flavoring on the floor. I was the one who mopped it up.

With Nora watching silently from the back corner, I was too impatient to wait for him to fill the mop bucket and ever so slowly swipe the bundles of yarn across the slippery stain. Besides, the smell was awful, the heavy aroma of the mint syrup giving me an instant headache, and I knew I could have the area mopped before he even finished filling up the bucket. He didn't thank me, of course; rather, he snidely reminded me not to forget the WET FLOOR sign.

I had hoped the constant line in the shop would keep my mind off Nora sitting there, watching me. But it didn't. I feel anxious with her here, and I can't help but look over every few seconds at where she's sitting. Still, I'm working fine despite the distraction, unlike Aiden. Apparently, he can't handle the pressure of the line of caffeine zombies. I can't remember when my brain switched from being annoyed by him to setting him up as competition in my head. Weird.

I hand a woman named Julie her triple skim-milk latte and glance at Nora again. She's writing something down in a notebook. Not looking at me. I can't tell what it is she's writing. It makes me feel a little like she's a cop on a stakeout.

I take this moment to enjoy the view of her. She's relaxed, her pen between her fingers. She taps the pen on the paper a few times and recrosses her legs. I love the way her lips pout. The feminine bow of her top lip sticks out a touch more than the bottom.

"Dude!" Aiden's voice barges into my obsessive thoughts about Nora's lips. When I look at him, I notice that the line has calmed: only two more guests are waiting on their drinks . . . but my feet are wet. Why?

Aiden's pointing to the pitcher of green tea pouring onto the floor, and my feet. I grab the handle and yank it up, replacing the lid. The puddle isn't too big; only half the pitcher is gone. I look over to see Nora watching me now, a smile on her face. My cheeks heat up, and I grab the mop. I force my busy brain to only think about mopping. Swipe, wring, swipe, dip into water. Wring again, swipe.

By the time the lobby clears out, only two hours have passed. My shirt is dirty, covered in espresso-bean dust, and my shoes are still damp from the green-tea spillage. On the bright side, we haven't had a customer in close to ten minutes, and Aiden has that look on his face that tells me he's going to start whining soon.

"I'm superhungry and I need to read some lines for an audition," he says, right on cue. His shoulders are slouched, and his white shirt is stained with brown streaks. We both look like we've been through the Great Battle of Caffeine and lived to tell the tale. Nora would be the queen we're fighting for, one of us getting to take the crown and be her king.

Before my imagination can carry me to a land far, far away, Aiden takes another step toward me and waves his hand. "So, I'm gonna take a break, 'kay?"

"Sure." I glance to Nora and nod. "That's fine with me—we're empty out here anyway."

I need to sweep the trash from the floor and wipe coffee rings and muffin crumbs off the tables. I need to fill up the ice bin and wipe off the countertops. The list goes on and on.

Nora gets up from the table and runs her fingers through her hair. I grab a rag and walk out from behind the bar.

"He's nice, huh?" Nora points her thumb to the back room, toward Aiden.

"He's okay." I shrug, not wanting Aiden to hear us talking about him. He's obnoxious, but I wouldn't want to hurt his feelings or anything. I know how it feels to have people talk about you as if you aren't listening, and it sucks. I wouldn't wish it on anyone. Well, maybe a few people, but Aiden isn't one of them.

"He reminds me of King Joffrey." Nora laughs, covering her mouth.

"Who's that?"

Nora's eyes widen. "King Joffrey, the little blond twat."

Huh?

"You really don't know who I'm talking about, do you?" She's staring at me in disbelief.

I shake my head.

"You've never watched *Game of Thrones*?"

"Oh. No, not yet."

"No way!" Nora rushes toward me, grabbing hold of my wrists. She smells like coconut. "Please tell me you're joking. I had you pegged soooo wrong. Which rock do you live under, and how do you stay away from spoilers online?"

The college and job rocks, I want to say. But that would be rude . . . and also lame.

"I haven't had time yet. I plan on watching it. Everyone talks about it, but I don't have the right online accounts." I sound like a robot.

I do have that one Facebook page that I always forget the password to and have to reset. I have about ten Facebook friends, half of them my family. My mom's Facebook page is full of baby updates and belly pictures, and Tessa's is full of Pinterest posts. My mom is obsessed with tagging me on stuff. Pictures, quotes, images of puppies. The last time I logged on to my account, she had posted pictures of us from her wedding and tagged me. Soon enough, all of my mom's friends were commenting things like:

"I remember pinching those cheeks when he was just a baby!"

"Little Landon has grown up to be such a handsome young man!!!"

"When can you expect Landon to marry, Karen?"

To that last one, my mom responded, *"When him and Dakota finish college!"*

Things were so different last year. Even a few months ago, my life was completely different from the way it is now. I was supposed to be living with Dakota by now, starting our future together.

Enough about Dakota.

"You have to watch it," Nora insists.

I half agree with her. "I might." I don't know if I even have time to watch a TV show between school and work and Nora and Tessa and Hardin and Dakota and my mom and baby sister and Ken.

Between her fingers Nora rolls a paper straw-wrapper. "What shows *do* you watch?"

I tell her that I've been watching whatever Tessa watches lately. Nora sits down at the table closest to me and tells me that I'm doing myself a disservice by not watching *Game of Thrones*. She tells me that she loves to hate-watch the *Bachelor* shows. I tell her, truthfully, that I've never seen an episode. I see the stars' faces plastered on the gossip magazines, all lined up in the magazine kiosks that I pass on the way to class, but I couldn't tell you any of their names. She tells me that someone named JoJo is a fool for sending home a cowboy from Texas last week.

I listen to Nora talk and decide that I like the way her words feel as they fill my ears. She talks with her hands, and so gracefully that I don't ever want her to stop talking. She's one of those people who take words and make them important. She gives them a meaning they couldn't even dream of having without her lips giving them life.

"So, how about you?" she asks finally, and I can't even remember what she was going on about. I was too focused on her animation and how full of words she is to hear what she actually said.

"Um . . ." I fumble with my words, pushing my memory to do me a solid.

"Plans for tonight?" she asks, half-smiling.

Nothing. Absolutely nothing. I shrug. "I'm not sure yet. Hardin's here in town until Monday."

She nods. "I know."

"So I guess it depends on what Hurricane Hessa is doing."

Nora smiles at this, and I notice she has another straw wrapper in her hand. The way it's folded, it's like a sword, and two small piles of sugar are on the table. Nora's holding an empty brown-sugar packet in her hand. I recognize the sugar hills from the day I first met Posey's little sister, Lila. A piece of napkin is stuck in the top of one pile, folded like a flag, just like the last time.

It has to be Nora who made them before. How did I not notice she was here?

"Tessa has to work all night," Nora says. She cups her hand at the edge of the table and swipes away her little fortress.

I leave my rag on the table and walk to the bar. Lifting the partition, I grab a small trash can and carry it over to her. She shakes her hands over the plastic bin and wipes them across my apron.

"I wanted to take you somewhere," Nora says, her voice low.

"I want to go somewhere," I respond immediately.

I look at her. She looks at me.

I clear my throat. "I mean, I want to go with you, wherever you want to take me."

Nora asks where the broom is and doesn't say anything else about where she wants to take me.

Nine

*S*O, DO I HAVE TIME TO CHANGE before we go to this place?" I ask Nora as I clock out. Posey is standing in the break room, tying her apron. Lila isn't with her today, so I hope that means her grandma's health is improving. Posey smiles at us as we leave, and I'm happy to know that Cree, the newest employee at Grind, is coming to relieve Aiden in an hour. Posey can tolerate Aiden better than anyone else, but Cree is much more pleasant.

Nora's eyes rake over my stained gray T-shirt. "Nope. No time to change."

I follow Nora out the door and onto the sidewalk. The sun is out today. It's not warm, but it's not as chilly as it will be to-night. September weather in New York is my favorite—hockey season and good weather, what more can I ask for? To be honest, I haven't watched any games so far this season. It's different now that Ken's not around. We watched the games together. Sports were the bricks that built our father-son relationship. Well, the closest thing to a father-son relationship I've ever had.

"I want to give you the proper welcome to Brooklyn. Have you been to Juliette in Williamsburg? Or the flash-frozen-ice-cream place?"

I shake my head. I haven't done much of anything since I moved here. I've walked and jogged around my neighborhood plenty, but I haven't been inside many places or looked for the cool hangouts. Who would I go with, anyway? Tessa is too busy working, and I haven't had the chance to make any friends here yet. No one on campus talks to me much. Every once in a while I get a random person asking me for directions, but that's it. Washington Central University would probably have been the same if Tessa hadn't introduced herself to me.

"I haven't heard of either," I say, which seems to make Nora pleased and eager to take me wherever she has planned.

"Where were you going last night? When I followed you?" I ask while we wait for the light to change.

She laughs. "Well, straight to the point."

I wait for her to answer, but her lips stay closed. "You're not going to tell me, are you?"

She shakes her head and touches her finger to the tip of my nose. "Nope."

I should care that she's hiding something from me. I should ask more questions about the secrets she hides, I know I should.

Instead, I ask, "So, Juliette? What is it, exactly?"

Nora smiles a little with my transition of topics. I promised her before that I wouldn't try to fix her, and it's easier to keep that promise if I don't pry into her life.

This plan is awesome, except for the small fact that I want to know everything about this woman. I want to know how many sugars she puts in her coffee and what her favorite song is. I want to hear how it sounds when she sings mindlessly, and I need to know how long it takes her to get out of bed in the morning. I have an obsessive, overpowering need to know everything about her, and she's going to drive me completely insane by not giving me what I need.

When we arrive at the French bistro named Juliette, Nora is bursting with excitement. "This place is the best. Everyone says

that Le Barricou is better, but don't let them fool you. Just because Yelp says so doesn't make it true."

"What's Yelp?" I ask, trying to keep up with Nora's quick feet.

The chalkboard sign on the sidewalk says TRY OUR TUSCAN
KALE SALAD. A little green leaf is drawn next to the words. Oh, so
the French have adopted the California Leaf-Eaters way of life,
too. Okay, so that society doesn't exist . . . Well, it probably does,
I just don't have any proof. And isn't Tuscany a region in Italy?
Some French bistro . . .

Nora walks in front of me and passes through the doorway.
She turns around to face me just before she reaches the hostess
stand. "You have so much to learn, young one." She smiles, then
turns back around.

I glance around the restaurant, and Nora tells the hostess
that we need a table for two. The young woman grabs two menus
and begins to explain the specials of the day while leading us to a
small circular table near the back of the room.

"Is your rooftop open?" Nora asks before she sits down.

The hostess looks around the room. "Not yet. Opens at five.
We do have the terrace you can sit in."

Nora smiles at her and nods. "Yes. Please."

The woman leads us up a set of stairs to a space that looks
like a garden. Potted plants hang from the ceiling, nearly touching the tabletops. The terrace is practically empty, only one table
occupied.

"Perfect. Thank you so much," Nora says.

I really like that she's so nice to people in the food industry.
It reminds me of my theory that everyone should have to work as
a server at least once in their life. It also reminds me of the time
Dakota had a meltdown at Steak 'n Shake in Saginaw because her
burger came with onions when she had asked for none. I was embarrassed, but sat quietly as she raised her voice at the manager
pretty intensely before asking for her food to be taken off the bill.

She felt like a jerk after we left.

I didn't disagree with her.

I sit down across from Nora. The metal chair makes a loud noise when I scoot it closer to the table. The menu is small; lunch only. There are more cocktails than meals printed on this thing.

"I always get the same thing." Nora reaches across the table. She points to some kind of peppers and then to cauliflower something. I only recognize a few things on the entire menu. Is the menu in French?

"I'm getting the shishito peppers and cauliflower and leek gratin, and *pommes frites*. I love everything here." She laughs and tucks her hair behind her ear. "I always order way too much food."

"I . . . I'm going to get . . ." I see the word *burger* and point to it. "I don't think I know what anything on the menu is." I laugh in an attempt to hide my embarrassment.

Nora sets her menu down and moves her chair closer to the table. It doesn't make an awful noise like mine did.

The hostess walks back to our table with a pitcher of water. Sliced cucumbers and ice are inside the pitcher. What is this place? Can I even afford to eat here? I'm definitely not in Saginaw anymore.

Nora thanks the hostess again, and she tells us that someone named Irene will be with us shortly. The more I look around, the more I see the terrace is pretty cool. Green leaves pouring out of wicker baskets hang over nearly every inch of the place.

"Which things don't you know?" Nora's hand is on my menu between us.

I look over the menu. Words like *croque-monsieur* and *pommes frites* laugh at me from the pages. "Basically everything except the burger."

Nora is a trained chef. She probably thinks I'm an idiot.

Though if she does, she isn't showing it. Her face is relaxed, her lips ample and pink. Her eyes look up to mine, and she runs her tongue over her lips. I look away quickly before I forget my own freaking name.

"Most of these dishes are pretty simple. Restaurants just use fancy words so they can charge us twenty dollars for a ham-and-cheese sandwich. That's what this is." She taps her finger on the *croque* thing. "And this"—she looks up at me again—"these, *pommes frites*, are literally just french fries."

Either I'm really damn hungry or Nora's culinary lesson is incredibly hot. She's so smart—too smart for me, I think.

"You should get the burger. I'm going to order a couple of things that I want you to try—but don't read about them on the menu, because they sound disgusting." She smiles when she notices the worried expression on my face. "I won't get you anything too out there." Her finger taps the tip of my nose.

Why does she always do that? And why is it so adorable?

Irene, our pretty server with dark lipstick and a Spanish accent, takes our order. Nora does me a favor and orders all of our food. Her voice changes into a beautiful lilt as she does so. I sit enchanted into silence until the server leaves and Nora begins a new conversation.

"Have you been to France?" Her eyes scan the French-themed décor on the walls.

I shake my head. *Have you been to France?* she asked so casually, like she was asking if I had been to the grocery store on the corner.

"No. I haven't been. You?" My voice is shaking.

Why can't I just be calm and cool, even for a little bit?

"I have. I've been twice with my family on vacation. But I've only seen the typical touristy things. I want to see the real France. I want to go where the French people go. Not where you pay thirty dollars for a glow-in-the-dark Eiffel Tower statue.

I want to eat real crepes and try my best to speak French. I want to have coffee that doesn't need a packet of sugar." Nora takes a breath and covers her mouth. "I ramble a lot." She laughs.

I take a drink of my water and try to think of something smart to say. I'm fresh out of smart, well-traveled words, so I ask another question. "Does your family travel a lot?"

I know very little about her family. I know that her parents live down the street from my mom and Ken, and that her dad is a surgeon and wanted her to be one. She doesn't share much, and when she does, she only gives me tiny clues that I have to piece together.

"Yeah. They do. My sister is pregnant right now, so we aren't going on our usual trip for Christmas, but we normally take one or two a year. I didn't go on the last one because of the wreck—"

Nora pauses for a moment. She feels as if she's said too much. I can tell.

"But now that Stausey is pregnant and due a week before Christmas, my dad thinks it's best to stay here."

There's a hint of frustration in Nora's voice again, but I don't know enough to know where it stems from.

Wreck?

Pregnant sister?

"How old is your sister?" I ask, walking on eggshells.

"Thirty. Five years older than me. It's her first child with her husband, Todd. That baby is going to be the most spoiled little thing." Nora's smile is soft now. I can tell she likes the idea of being an aunt. "Speaking of"—she runs her fingers over the con-densation on her glass—"you'll have a little sister soon. How's your mom doing?"

Nora is so good at redirecting conversations that by the time I noticed she had, we were nearly done eating. Turns out, she was right about the food. Every single thing was delicious. The cauliflower-and-leek casserole was my favorite, and I'm not even 100 percent sure what a leek is.

I felt guilty while shoving the burger down my throat, knowing that Nora doesn't eat meat. The thought had slipped my mind when I ordered it. Not until I offered her a bite of pretty bloodred meat did I remember. Even still, it was too good to not eat. I just made sure not to talk with my mouth full.

"You have to try this last thing and then I'll leave you alone," Nora tells me when I clear my plate. I don't like the sound of that, of her leaving me alone. "Only for now," she clarifies, and I bite back a smile.

She dips her spoon into a bowl with burned cheese crusted around the edges. "Close your eyes."

I do just that. Something mushy and warm touches my lips when I open my mouth.

"Keep your eyes closed," Nora instructs.

I smell onion as I use my teeth to pull the food from the spoon. I chew the soggy bite in my mouth, and the taste is good, despite the texture.

"This is just onion soup, nothing too special. Do you like it?" Nora's voice sounds even better with my eyes closed.

I nod and open my mouth for more. I keep my eyes closed, and she feeds me another bite. I don't think about the other table near us. I don't even consider that the server could come back at any moment. Right now, all I can focus on is Nora's ability to make eating onion soup sexy. I swear, she could touch a tree and I would find it appealing.

Seconds pass, minutes maybe, without interruption. "Have you traveled anywhere, Landon?"

I shake my head and open my eyes. "I went to Florida once when I was younger. My aunt Reese and her husband took me to Disney World. I got food poisoning on the second day, though, so

I was sick the entire time. I ended up watching Disney movies from my bed in the hotel."

My aunt Reese felt so bad for me, she even brought gifts from the gift shop and decorated my room. On the nightstands were two Mickey Mouse stuffed animals, and the table was covered in a beach towel with Cinderella's castle printed on it.

"That's awful." Nora's sitting so much closer than I remembered her doing before I closed my eyes. Her elbows are on the table, and she's leaning forward enough that I wouldn't even have to lean over to touch her face.

She's so beautiful.

"If you could go anywhere, where would you go?"

Just before I answer, Irene comes back to our table and clears the plates in front of us. "Can I get you anything else? Would you like to see the dessert menu?"

"I'll have an espresso," Nora says. "Do you want one?"

"Sure?"

Irene smiles at me. "Two espressos. Got it."

"It's a thing people do in Europe. They sometimes have coffee after their meal," Nora tells me.

"I really like how smart you are."

Nora smiles at me from across the table. She leans back, distancing herself from me. "I really like how smart you are, too."

"*I* couldn't read the menu." I laugh, reminding her.

She lowers her eyes, keeping them on mine. "You know a lot of things that I don't know. You're a good student and have read ten times more books than I have. Just because you can't read a fancy menu or haven't traveled the world doesn't mean you aren't smart."

I hadn't expected the conversation to take such a serious turn, but I notice that with those last words Nora seems upset. Her lips are pursed, and her brows are crumpled together.

"Did I say something?" I ask.

"No."

I look up at the basket of leaves, sort of hoping it will fall on my head so this conversation will end.

"Well, yes. You do this thing where you put yourself down all the time. I don't even know if you notice that you do it, but every time I compliment you, you try to find holes in it. Who told you that you weren't good enough? That's what I want to know." She lowers her voice. "So I can have a nice long talk with them."

Irene drops off our espressos, along with the bill, which Nora and I reach for at the same time.

"Let me." I half expect her to fight me over it. She surprises me when she doesn't.

As we drink our coffee in near silence, I think about how nobody has ever said to me what she just did. Not that I can remember. I'm not the most confident guy in the world by any means, but I didn't realize just how much I put myself down, and I don't know how to fix it.

When we leave the bistro, Nora takes a picture of the outside of the building. I don't ask her why, and she doesn't share.

"So, I think we should skip the ice cream place." She pats her stomach. Her denim shirt is buttoned all the way up, and I can see the crease of her bra now that we're back in the sunlight.

Nora's phone rings, and she stares at the screen. Her face falls. "Damn. I have to go."

Right now? In the middle of my Welcome to Brooklyn Tour?

"Now?" I step toward her, taking her hand in mine. I worry that she may pull away, but she doesn't. Her hand is warm in mine. I straighten my back and look down at her. "You have to go now?"

She nods. "I need to go to Scarsdale. I shouldn't be gone too long."

"What's in Scarsdale? Is that where you're staying now? You never told me what happened with Dakota and Maggy."

Nora squares her shoulders and threads her fingers through mine. "And you never told me why you two broke up."

She's changing the subject again. "I don't want to talk about Dakota." I would rather be doing at least a hundred other things than talking about Dakota right now, after our amazing afternoon together.

Nora leans up on her toes, her lips only inches from my ear. "And I don't want to talk about Scarsdale," she whispers. She leans into me, and I melt, warming to her body against mine.

"I want to know you. Let me," I say softly.

Nora lifts her face to mine, and I forget that we're on a crowded sidewalk. "I'm trying."

Her lips are soft as they brush over mine. "I'll come"—Nora's words are delicate, and she speaks with her lips still on mine—"by your place in a few hours. Okay?"

I nod, unable to say much of anything, and she disappears.

chapter

Ten

WHILE I MAKE MY WAY BACK to my apartment, I can still feel Nora's lips on mine and I can still smell the coconut scent of her hair. She's so confusing, so frustrating and addictive. While I'm in the elevator, I briefly consider turning around and heading to the subway. I could find my way to Scarsdale, now that I've been there.

Would she be upset if I did?

Yes, I'm positive that she would be.

My apartment is empty when I get there. I know Tessa's at work, but I assumed at least Hardin would be here. Still, I'm sort of glad that I can have some time alone to think about Nora and who she is, what she's hiding.

Would our meal today be considered a date? I paid for it; she fed me. Nora literally fed me, and the memory of it is still scorching through me. I need a distraction. If I sit here thinking about Nora feeding me, Nora kissing me, I'll go insane.

I walk into the kitchen and grab a Gatorade and sit down on my couch. Hardin's binder is smack-dab in the middle of the table. As I move it over, a few pages fall out. I grab one and don't even bother trying to decipher his scratchy handwriting. What is all this? My curiosity gets the best of me, and I find myself flipping through the pages. It looks like some sort of diary that I should most definitely not be snooping through.

From that day on, his words bled from his veins. It was unstoppable, no matter how much pressure he applied to the wound. The words bled from him, staining page after page with his memories of her.

I put the page down and shove it back into the binder. I don't know what this is, but I'm positive Hardin wants to keep it that way.

I've been watching episodes of *Arrested Development* on Netflix and staring at the clock on the TV since I got here.

My apartment is quiet. No matter how many random thoughts I try to focus on, time barely moves. Time is one of those inevitable forces that humans can't control. One of the few things, actually. As humans, we are obsessed with time and the idea of manipulating it. Some of the most incredible stories focus on the idea of time. Usually the idea is that if someone had a time machine, they could change their past and their future. They could become rich and famous or even rule the world. Right now, if I had a time machine, I wouldn't go all crazy and try to change my entire life, or the world. I would simply fast-forward a few hours so I could see Nora.

Well, if she still plans on coming, that is.

Jason Bateman is on my screen trying to keep his dysfunctional family together, and I'm trying to keep my mind off Nora. She was more open today than usual. She told me about her family trips to Europe and her sister, Stausey. It's weird to think about her family in Europe, sunbathing and eating strange foods and drinking tiny black coffees while I was running around my plat, hanging out with Carter and Dakota, eating Mikesell's potato chips and drinking water from our faucet. Sometimes I would get a Mountain Dew, and it was a treat. Her reality was light-years from mine.

A tapping at my door has me on my feet in seconds. When

the door opens, beautiful Nora is there, grocery bags in both hands. Since she left me outside Juliette, she's changed into a black T-shirt and wiped some of her makeup off. Her shirt is so long that I can't tell whether she's wearing shorts . . . not that that it would be a problem if she wasn't.

Her hair is braided now, and draped over her shoulder. She's wearing black sandals, with two straps covering the span of her feet. The buckle reminds me of a Pilgrim's belt.

My words come before I can stop them: "You are so beautiful."

I don't mind, and she doesn't seem to, either. Her eyes fall to the floor, and she smiles. For the first time since I've met her, her smile is unguarded. It's completely natural, like walking or speaking, and it's beautiful and I love her.

Well, I don't *love* her. I barely know her, but she has a smile that would make any man believe he loves her.

"Hi, Landon." Nora walks past me and into the apartment. The energy inside my place changes with every step she takes. She makes things brighter. The ceiling even seems higher when she's around.

Instead of sharing that information, I respond with a simple "Hi" of my own.

We're both quiet as we go into the kitchen and I help her with the bags. She grabs one from me and puts it on the counter closest to the stove, a few feet away from me.

I start pulling things out of the brown paper bags: an onion, a bottle of olive oil. "What is all this? Did Tessa have you stop by the store or something?" I pull out a wheel of cheese. Goat cheese, to be exact.

Nora opens the fridge and sets a half gallon of milk on the top shelf. "No. I'm going to make cupcakes."

I lift the next item up to my face. Fig spread. "With figs?" I point to the onion on the counter. "And an onion?"

She nods, closes the fridge, and walks over to me. "Yes, and yes."

Doesn't sound like a very good cupcake, but, sure.

As she moves around my kitchen, I'm fascinated by the way she moves, so self-assured, so comfortable in her own skin. When she lifts her arms to open the cabinet, a pair of dark denim shorts peeks out from beneath her oversized black T-shirt. So there *is* something under there. Which is . . . fine.

She hasn't made a peep in a few minutes now. She turned on the oven in silence; she wiped butter across the bottom of my cupcake pan without saying a word.

I'm going to have to start the conversation, it seems. She's standing in front of the stove, the cupcake pan resting on the burners.

"How was Scarsdale?" I ask.

She turns her cheek so that I can see her face. "It was Scarsdale," she responds flatly. "How's Brooklyn?"

I smile. "It's Brooklyn."

Nora turns back around to the stove, but her shoulders move up and down ever so slightly as she quietly laughs to herself.

I don't know what to talk about. I want to talk about so many things, but it's hard to walk a tightrope and talk at the same time. I think about the last time we were in this kitchen, her hands squeezing my biceps as she moved her body against mine. The taste of her mouth when she moaned into mine. I reminisce about the curve of her luscious hips as she rocked them on my lap.

"Is something wrong?" Nora asks as another wave of memories hits me. I think back to the first time she touched me. She was so forward, running her finger down my bare stomach. The air in the kitchen has become so thick with awkward silence and tension that I can barely find my breath.

I shake my head, lying.

I sit down at the table, and Nora moves around me to grab

the carton of eggs from the fridge. The oven beeps, giving notice that it's reached the temperature needed to make Nora's mystery cupcakes.

She sighs, and I want to scream because I have so many things to say but no way to say them. I want to touch her, but I don't have the strength to do it.

"Are you sure?" Nora's voice is quiet, her shoulders squared. "Because you're being weirdly quiet, and it sure *seems* like something's wrong."

I don't say anything. I don't know what to say without risking her fleeing. "If I say anything, you'll disappear. Remember?" My voice has an edge that I didn't mean to include.

Nora turns around to look at me. She wipes her hands on a towel and walks over to where I sit at the table. "What makes you think that?"

This woman is insane. "You said it. You told me if I try to fix you, you'll disappear. It's frustrating." I pause to make sure her eyes are on mine. "It's frustrating that I want to be around you, but I feel like I'm walking on eggshells while wearing cleats. I don't know how to talk to you, or what to say. I know that you aren't ready to let me in yet, but you have to at least crack the door, because I'm out here reeling, hoping you'll at least *consider* letting me in."

Nora studies my face. Her eyes move from my mouth to my eyes and back to my mouth again. Her eyes are softer now, her brows slightly furrowed. "Landon"—she takes the seat next to me—"I didn't mean for it to be like this. I don't want you to hide the way you feel or be afraid that I'm going to run at a moment's notice."

My finger runs across the wood sticker on the table, which is peeling off. Another IKEA fail, but this time I'm grateful to have it as a distraction.

"Landon, look at me." Nora's fingers are warm when they

touch my chin, lifting my face. "Let's play a game. Okay?" She moves her chair toward me. I want her fingers on my skin once more. Before I agree, she starts again. "The only rule in this game is that we tell the truth, okay?"

I like the sound of this game, but it seems too easy. "The whole truth?"

"And nothing but the truth."

"So help you God?"

She gives me that smile that makes me think I love her. "For as long as you both shall live?" Nora says, and we both laugh. "I think those are wedding vows." Her laugh is natural, like her beauty. "Oops." She smiles humorously.

I try to stop my laughter. "I like the idea of this game. But what's the prize?"

Nora licks her lips and pulls her pouty bottom lip between her teeth. I watch her suck it for a second. "The truth," she says.

I can't think of anything I would rather be doing than touching those lips. With my lips, with my tongue. Even with my finger. I just want to touch her. I need to.

I need to touch her like I need to breathe.

"Whose truth? Mine or yours?" I know that they aren't the same.

"Both," she says with certainty.

I stare at her with steady eyes. "And when do we begin?"

The braid on her shoulder is falling loose, tiny hairs sticking out of the bundle. She runs her fingers over it as if she can hear my thoughts. "Now. I go first."

I nod in agreement. That's fine with me.

She takes a deep breath and tugs on her hair tie. Her fingers pull through her dark hair, unknotting the waves. "When we were at the station in Scarsdale, you said that you missed me. Was that true or not true?"

I don't hesitate. "Yes. True."

She smiles. I watch her fingers weave her thick hair back into a braid.

"My turn." I continue to pick at the chipped edge of the table. "Did you miss me? Truth or not truth?"

She nods. This feels an awful lot like Katniss and Peeta's Real or Not Real game. I stare at Nora, waiting for her to actually say the words. She doesn't.

"Words aren't real until you say them."

She stares back at me appreciatively. "Not true." Watching her say so, I can feel my chest ache. She holds her hand up. "I meant that what you just said isn't true. Words are real when we write them down. Taking the time to make them permanent makes them real."

I shake my head to disagree. "Words can still be erased if you write them down. But if you say them, they always exist."

Nora leans away, resting her back on the chair. "The words only exist until you don't mean them anymore."

I study her, and I'm cautious with my response: "I promise not to say things that I don't mean."

My hand reaches for hers, but she pulls away.

She hesitates, then says, "And I promise not to say things I'll want to erase."

chapter

Eleven

NORA GESTURES TO THE BUTTER and the carton of eggs she's placed on the countertop. "Do you want to help me make the cupcakes?"

"If by 'help' you mean 'emotionally support you through your baking process,' then, yes, I would be happy to help."

She's amused by my answer, and I love the way her soft laughter fills my small kitchen. I'm no help in the kitchen—my mom can vouch for that. Nora stands on her toes to grab more ingredients from the cabinets. I begin to wonder why she put all the groceries away if she knew she was going to use them. Women are weird.

"Let's play my game again," Nora suggests.

I go and stand next to her. Her hands are busy measuring white powder in a cup. Flour, maybe?

The fact that she wants to play her truth game again means she's willing to share more truths. This makes me happy. I've never felt so desperate for information about someone in my life. She says so little, yet I feel so much for her. How is it possible? She makes me question everything I thought I knew about relationships. With Dakota, everything was pretty simple. It took months, maybe even years, for me to realize that what I felt for Dakota was more than friendship. Dakota confessed her feelings for me first, which made it easier to share mine with her.

"Let's play my game instead." I'm not exactly sure what my game *is*.

Nora turns to me and licks her lips. It's like she knows how sexy she is and she uses that knowledge to torture me. This woman is going to make me crazier than I already feel.

"My game . . ." I search through the pages of my cluttered brain. "My game is that I get to ask you three questions. You have to answer at least two and can pass on one. Then it's your turn and I do the same."

Nora raises an eyebrow and leans against the counter. "And what's the prize for your game?"

I look at her and hope that my excitement doesn't show through my words. "The truth, just like yours."

She nods and stares at me, taking me in. "You didn't change." She points to my coffee-stained T-shirt.

I look down and wonder why I didn't change when I got home. I had time. I lay on my couch for almost three hours. I definitely could have changed.

Wait . . . I look at her and shake my head. "No distractions." I take a step toward her. I know her tactics, and this time I'm not going to let her distract me. "Are you scared to play a silly little game with me?" I lower my voice and notice the way her neck moves when she swallows.

She has a faint cluster of freckles on her chest, climbing up the base of her neck just above the collar of her oversized shirt. I follow the curve of her neck up to her face. Her eyes are on mine, and this time I'm not looking away first. I want to be in control of this game.

"Nora." I take one more step closer to her. Electricity hums through me, straightening my spine, steadying my voice. "Are you?"

She swallows again. Nora's eyes are wide, and her hands are behind her, gripping the countertop. Her heart is pounding. I swear I can hear the blood rushing through it from here. I reach out. My fingers graze the skin of her shoulder, and I trace a line down her chest, across where her heart lies and back up to her neck. She's breathing heavily, her chest rising and falling under my touch. My heart is racing, just like hers. I wonder if she can feel my pulse through my fingers.

I close the rest of the space between us, and Nora's body leans into mine. She's so close. Her eyes never leave mine, and I want to kiss her for the rest of my life.

Nora blinks, and my heart stops. *Did I say that out loud? Please, please tell me that I didn't actually say those words.*

"I go first." Nora blinks again and pushes past me. Relief floods me. My mouth can't be trusted to stay quiet when she's near.

She pulls open one of the bottom cabinets and grabs a mixing bowl. "How long do you plan on living here, in New York? What's the last song you listened to? Where's your biological dad?" Nora's first round of questions are solid, to say the least.

I don't want to answer about my dad, but I can't expect her to be open with me if I don't do the same.

"I don't know. I thought about moving back to Washington, but I'm starting to like it here. The last song I listened to was . . ." I pause, trying to remember. "It was 'As You Are' by The Weeknd. And my dad, he's dead."

Nora's expression changes, and I get the feeling she thought I would skip the last question. If she were me, she would have. I wanted to.

"My turn," I say before any condolences can be expressed. "How long have your parents been married? What's the last book you read? How long was your last relationship?"

Nora's eyes turn to me. I look away. I know which question she's going to skip.

She takes a deep breath and pretends like she's completely focused on her baking. With another breath, she speaks. "My parents have been married for almost thirty-two years. Their anniversary is in just a few weeks. The last book I read was called *Marrow*. It was so good and so fucked-up. And I'm skipping the last question."

I nod, taking in her answers. I wish she would have proven me wrong, but I'm not going to complain. Not yet, at least.

Nora doesn't waste any time before taking her next turn. "What do you like more, sports or reading? What's your favorite memory from your childhood? And how did your dad die?"

I stand a few feet away from her and lean against the counter.

"Reading. Though I love sports almost as much. My favorite childhood memory is really hard to choose." I skim through the happiest memories I can pull up. "The first that comes to mind is when my aunt and her husband used to take me to baseball games when I was younger. We went a lot; every time was my favorite. My dad died from natural causes."

"No one dies from natural causes in real life."

The smell of onions fills my senses, and I back away slightly. Nora chops the onions like those chefs on TV. It's pretty cool to watch.

"My dad did. He had a heart attack when I was little."

Nora regards me quietly, and her hand moves the spoon in quick circles to mix the batter.

"My turn. How did your parents meet? If you weren't a pastry chef, what would you want to do? Why did Dakota kick you out of the apartment?" I slide that last question in pretty gracefully, I would say.

Using a spoon, Nora drops her mix into the cupcake pan. "My parents met while my dad was on a business trip in Colombia. He does a lot of work with charities, and he had a team in

Bogotá to train surgeons at a local hospital there. My dad is from Kuwait, but was already living in Washington State. My mom worked at the cafeteria in the hospital in Bogotá, and my dad fell in love with her."

I look over at Nora, taking in her features. What a beautiful mix of ethnicities she is.

"If I wasn't a pastry chef, I would open up a food truck, like the ones that park on the streets in Williamsburg. Dakota kicked me out of the apartment because she felt threatened by me. She told me to stay away from you, and I didn't listen." Nora smiles, laughing lightly. "So now I'm homeless."

I frown in frustration. "It's not funny that you were kicked out of your apartment."

Nora rolls her eyes at me and walks to the oven, pan in hand. I move over to her and open the oven door. She sets the pan on the center rack and closes the door.

She turns to me. "My turn. How many people have you slept with? How did you meet Dakota? How often do you think about fucking me?"

I can't begin to describe the noise I made when she asked her last question. My body tenses, and blood flows through me, straight to my cock. I push and push the thoughts away, but the mental images of Nora straddling me are so hard to battle.

"I've only had sex with one person. I'm sure you can guess who that is. I met Dakota when I was just a kid. She was my next-door neighbor . . . And I'm skipping the last question."

She shoots me a dirty look. Dirty as in pissed off, not as in she wants to rip my clothes off.

"Hmm . . ." Nora hums, and taps her index finger on her lips.

I clear my throat and pray that my jeans can hide what I'm thinking.

"My turn." I can hear the change in my voice. It's thick with longing and need, and I really just want to push her soft body against the counter and lift her shirt over her head and taste her skin.

I ask the first questions that pop into my head without screening them. "How did you meet your last boyfriend? Does it bother you that I've only slept with Dakota? And how often do you think about fucking *me*?"

Her eyes dart away from mine, and she carries the mixing bowl to the sink and turns on the water. "I met him through my parents. My dad has some business with his. Yes, it bothers me like you wouldn't believe. I think about fucking you nearly every minute of every day."

My voice gets caught in my throat, and I can't breathe. My stomach flutters like a thousand angry moths are swarming inside me.

I don't know what to say to Nora, the twenty-five-year-old woman who for some reason wants to fuck me. Her words hit every nerve in my body, and I'm not sure I could actually handle her. Inside my head, she's already naked, spread out on my bed and calling for me.

Gah, she actually wants me. And thinks about fucking me. And has no problem telling me. I'm so out of my league here, yet my fingers are twitching, wanting to touch her.

"Oh," I say. I ball my hands into fists to keep them from reaching for her.

Nora doesn't look at me, and I don't trust what my body would do if she turned around. She washes the bowl and pats it dry with a kitchen towel.

"My turn. Do you trust me? What's your favorite TV show? And . . ." She tilts her head back and forth, thinking. "If Dakota came here right now and begged for you to take her back, would you?"

Why did I create this stupid game, anyway?

Instead of calling it quits, I suck it up and continue with the next round of answers. "I do. I don't know if I should, but I do trust you. My favorite TV show is *Arrested Development*. And no, I don't think I would."

Nora finally turns around to look at me. After making brief eye contact, she looks to the floor quickly. "Don't *think* you would? Or *wouldn't*? You don't sound very sure."

I grab a rag from the counter to busy my nervous hands. "I wouldn't."

Nora nods and stands still, leaning her back on the counter next to the fridge. I jump into the next set of questions, intentionally keeping my body a few feet away from hers.

"Do you trust *me*?" I steal her question and she notices, regarding me with an eye roll. "Did your last relationship end on a good note or a bad one? And lastly, do you have feelings for me? Beyond sexual attraction?"

Nora's fingers tug at the loose pieces of her braid. Her long, almond-shaped fingernails are painted black, and she has flour dusted on her knuckles. "I trust you. I don't trust anyone else in the entire world the way I trust you, and that frightens me, because I barely know you—and you don't know me at all."

I want to interrupt her and tell her that I know her better than she thinks. I want to tell her that I'm going to know her even better than she can fathom. I'm going to know her better than she knows herself, and I'm willing to play this game every day until I do.

On paper, I couldn't write her down. I could make a bullet-point list, but I couldn't draw her in the vibrant colors she deserves. I'm learning more of the depths of her each time I'm with her, and it's not an easy feat, breaking down wall after wall, but I will learn her soul. I will study every page of her until I can recite them from memory.

"My last relationship ended on a bad note. Worse than that,

really. And I'm skipping the last question." Nora's hands are still fidgeting with her hair, and she shuffles her feet.

I look down at them, and she moves again. She's restless, and so am I.

"I want to go again. Then you can go twice. Okay?" I say.

She nods, staying silent.

I step closer to her. She seems so small now, in my kitchen. With blushed cheeks and downcast eyes. She's still the warrior I met, but she's without her weapon.

"Do you have feelings for me, aside from attraction?" I ask her again, taking a wide step to her. She tugs on her hair but doesn't move. She nods her head unconsciously, and I move to stand in front of her body.

She looks up at me, and I touch her chin with the tips of my index finger and thumb. She sighs into my touch.

"Next question." I bend my neck just enough so that my face is positioned just above hers.

She waits patiently, her eyes on mine. Her eyelashes shadow the tops of her cheeks when she blinks. I keep my fingers on her chin so she can't look away from me.

"Does it scare you, the way you feel about me?" My question is heavy, and I feel the weight of it pass to Nora.

She nods.

I cup her cheek now, gliding my hand over her skin to rest on her neck. I lean closer, so close that I can hear each breath that passes between her lips. I can see so many things from here. The worry in her eyes, the set of her mouth. I try to keep my nervous hands steady as I take her into them. I slide my free hand behind her back and grab the counter. She's intoxicating, so sweet and addicting that I can't look away from her. I have her cornered now, caught between me and the counter.

Fire is burning up my spine, through my chest.

"What's your last question?" Nora whispers, and I taste her breath.

I move my hand down her arm, touching her just enough to tickle her skin. Bumps form in my wake, and a shiver moves over her body. "Do you want me to kiss you?"

chapter

Twelve

Nora

I KNOW THAT IF I NOD, all bets are off. Landon will press his mouth to mine, and there will be no more talking. That can't happen. Not that I don't want it to, *because, boy, do I.*

"Skip," I say into his mouth.

His eyes drop, ever so slightly, and I hate the look in his eyes. I saw it in Scarsdale and when I left outside Juliette. Sadness should never touch Landon, not him.

"I'm skipping the question. If I don't, we will never talk like this." Each word burns like bleach down my throat. I want his hands on me more than I would ever be stupid enough to admit.

I kept on telling myself to keep my distance from this boy. *He's too young for you, Nora. Too young.*

I look at the dark stubble on his chin. He was freshly shaven yesterday. I can't believe that's something I pay attention to, but I can't help but notice. The hair grows thicker around his chin. He doesn't look so young now, standing in front of me with his eyes on me. His eyes aren't as young as his body. Something older, wiser, is inside them. I don't know what it was, but something hurt him deeper than just a breakup with Dakota.

"You're skipping the question?" His lips turn up, forming a shy smile, and his arms close tighter around me. He's still gripping the edge of the counter, but the safe space between us is getting smaller and smaller.

I nod, and his smile grows. Barely moving, he shakes his head, just slightly.

My God, he's convincing.

And too nice.

He's too nice for you, Nora.

Way, way, way too nice.

Fuck, I've turned into that woman I always thought I despised. I hate women like that; they are the literal worst.

This is how that woman works:

Phase One: She sits around with her closest friends, drinking wine in their pajamas. "I've dated too many assholes. Why are all men assholes?" she cries into her cheap Moscato. "No more assholes for me." She raises her coffee mug full of wine.

Phase Two: She shows up for coffee with her friends. She suddenly likes bitter coffee because her new beau does, and he's nice and smart, and she's never dating an asshole again. "He's so sweet," she tells her friends. And she's right—you won't find him at a bar on a Friday night, or nursing a hangover on Saturday morning. You'll find him walking the aisles of Anthropologie, holding her coffee while she tries on everything in the store.

Phase Three: She sits with her friends at a nightclub, wearing a new black dress, and has curled her hair for the first time in a month. She's wearing full makeup, not for her nice guy, not even for herself. "I'm kinda not sure about him anymore. He's kind of boring," she complains, and shares a smile with a hot guy in the crowd.

Phase Four (last and final phase): She sits on her couch, watching reruns of *Grey's Anatomy*. Her friends sit around her with wine in their hands. "Men are such assholes," she says, because the hot guy from the club cheated on her and now she's back to Phase One.

I am that woman right now.

"I don't think skipping that one's very fair." Landon's mouth touches my ear, and I shiver.

My God, this man.

This man is Tessa's best friend.

I have to remind myself of this. This is one of the thousand reasons I have to end this mess between us now. He's her best, best, best friend in the world, and if I fuck that up, I would never forgive myself.

Tessa has dealt with enough this year, between Hardin's ruining her life and her not getting into NYU yet. She lost her dad and the love of her life, and I've seen the way she leans on Landon for support; if I take Tessa's rock away, I wouldn't deserve him anyway.

"Nothing in life is fair." I bend my knees and duck out of his cage.

I can't think clearly enough to be anything close to productive when Landon's this close to me. Every time I step into the elevator in this building, I tell myself, *Keep it together. Don't stare too long, don't ask Tessa too many questions about him.*

I knew I had a problem when, every single time I went to their apartment, I found myself hoping he was inside. The flood of disappointment I felt when he wasn't there scared the shit out of me, and still does.

"How do you like NYU? Are you excited for your mom to have little Abby? Where would you go if you could fly anywhere, right now?" I ask in a feeble attempt to change the course of the conversation before I end up on my knees in this kitchen.

He glares at me, and I take an extra step away from him. "I like it just fine. Yes, I am. Spain, to go to a Real Madrid game."

Landon is clearly not amused by my bland questions, and I'm clearly not doing a good job at keeping things platonic. Landon walks over to the refrigerator and grabs a blue Gatorade. I make a face at it, and he smiles at me.

He twists the top open and continues to stare at me. He's watching me intently, and I can tell he's concocting something.

"There's a bonus round to my game."

Oh, sure there is. "Is there?" I try not to smile at him, but I can't fight it. "Do tell."

He leans back against the counter, and I keep a safe space between us. Five feet; that's safe enough. I back away at least ten more, pretending to need a glass of water.

From this distance I can't see as clearly how he looks at me. I can't stare as closely at the masculine curve of his broad shoulders. I can't obsess over his strong hands and thick fingers. If I keep my distance from him, he won't be able to tell that I'm itching to touch him.

It's more than an itch. Itching can be cured by scratching, and my need for him doesn't have such a simple solution. The feelings I have for Landon will have to be burned from my body to be calmed. A thousand yards of bandages will be needed to dress my wounds.

Landon takes a long drink before he answers. He sets the bottle down on the countertop and faces me. His kitchen feels so damn small.

"Okay, so it goes like this. You have to answer one of your skipped questions, or you lose."

"Hmm." I consider this. *Lose* what, *exactly?* I look at Landon. This kind, caring, sexy, stained-T-shirt-wearing guy has crept his way into me, and I try to remember which questions I skipped. I skipped the stuff about my last relationship, but that was for Landon's own good. Okay, it was mostly for my own good, but a little for him, too. I don't want him to know that side of me.

I also skipped the question about my feelings for him. I really, really shouldn't answer that.

"You only skipped one question," I point out.

He nods, knowing damn well that this "bonus round" is designed to work in his favor. He smirks and lifts his drink to his mouth again.

I have to consider that I want him to get to know me. I want him to feel like I'm not going to run if he asks the wrong question at the wrong time. But honestly, I probably would. It would be easier, and for once in my life I would like to take the easy way out of something. We're playing a dangerous game here, and I'm not ready to lose.

"I'll answer one," I tell him.

He nods. "I get to choose which one."

"Don't be greedy."

He smirks again, and my first instinct is to moan. My body is screaming for him, and I can picture him perfectly, on top of me, pushing into me, that stupid smirk still on his innocent face.

"Rules are rules, young lady."

His words make my brain fuzzy. His smile is bigger now, braver. It's fascinating the way he shifts from teenager to man, being submissive one second and commanding the room the next. He steps toward me, further shedding the teenage boy, and reaches for my hand. I let him take it. I'm mesmerized.

I straighten my back as he approaches me. His hands are cold when they wrap around mine. I love how he makes me feel so small, even though I'm close to his height. My height used to be such an insecurity of mine. I remember when my *abuelita* told me that men loved women they could put in their pockets. She was tiny herself, hence we called her *abuelita*. Every woman on my mother's side of the family is tiny: small frame, small hips, small feet. But not me.

At five foot seven, I'm taller than my mother and her mother.

I'm taller than Stausey, and my big hips were a topic at many family dinners. Legend has it that I get my frame from my mother's *abuela*. She was said to have to make her own pants because her backside was just that big.

"Why so quiet now?" Landon asks.

He has me cornered again, but has let go of my hand. I can touch him; just one little touch won't hurt.

I lift my hand to his face and caress the curve of his cheek. His cheekbones are prominent, which sometimes reminds me of a frat boy somehow. Landon has the looks of an asshole and the heart of a puppy.

I tell him that he needs to answer the question first. I want to know how often he thinks of taking me. I run my finger over his pink lips, tracing the soft shape of them. The curve of his nose is slight, and his eyes close under my touch.

"How often do you think about fucking me?" I repeat.

His eyes flutter under the lids, but he keeps them closed.

"Is it as often as I think about you?" My words are as audible as a sigh, but I know he can hear them. I continue to touch him, to admire the sharp line of his jaw. "Because I think about you fucking me in so many ways. I touch myself while thinking about you, and I don't mind admitting that." I lean closer to him, and his chest rises and falls.

The tension in this room will choke us both.

"Do you do the same, Landon? Do you think about how it would feel?"

I cup his face in my hands, and his eyes open halfway.

Under hooded eyes, his body calls back to me. He shifts his legs and pushes one thigh between mine. He lifts his leg up, so his thigh presses against me. The ache in my stomach tightens.

"I do." A hint of rasp coats his low voice. "I think about you all the time. The last time . . ." He looks toward the kitchen table and back to my face, and rests his eyes on my mouth. He's so close that I can smell the sweetness of his drink on his tongue.

"The last time was . . ." I trail off. I feel drowsy under him.

Landon's eyes open farther, and his hands grab my hips. His mouth is on mine before I can push through the fog in my brain.

chapter

Thirteen

*L*ANDON'S HANDS THREAD THROUGH MY HAIR, pulling me closer. His mouth is so soft, yet his touch is hard, commanding. I'm in awe of him, and my mind is swimming with lust for him. His hands move to my hips and he lifts me onto the countertop. His body is between my thighs, and I close my legs around his back. I wish the counter were lower, so I could feel his cock press against me.

How do we always end up here? With our mouths and hands all over each other?

"Nora," Landon says into my mouth. The way he says my name, so tenderly, makes me want to moan. I fight the urge, but my body is almost out of my mind's control.

I wrap my arms around his neck, pulling him as close as possible.

"Don't try to fight it," he says, as if he knows that my mind is pushing hard against him.

I nod and pull my mouth away from his. I move my lips to his ear. "I want you to fuck me, Landon." I drag my lips slowly across his cheek, down to his jaw.

He trembles under my touch, and I pull at the bottom of his shirt and lift it over his head. His body makes me ache. The muscles on his abdomen aren't too overworked; the lines are faint and soft, but strong. The trail of hair on this stomach is just another part of his body that I want to have my mouth on. My hands look so small as my fingers find the buttons of his jeans, and I pop them open quickly.

He's wearing black briefs that fit snugly. Why does he have to be so hot? Why does he have to make me forget my judgment and rip his clothes off? I've read my fair share of romance novels, and I've always rolled my eyes at the way a man's body supposedly has the magic ability to turn a woman's brain to mush. But here I am, with my very own shirtless man—in a *kitchen*, of all places—and I can't form a single coherent thought.

My thoughts are plenty, but none of them pure.

My mouth moves lower, to suck on the smooth curve of muscle just where his shoulder meets his neck. He moans and I suck harder, not caring if I leave a mark. If I mark him, does that make him mine? If Dakota saw proof of my lips on him, would she do everything in her power to destroy me?

Probably.

Do I care?

Not right now.

My hands find their way down his chest to the line of his briefs. The elastic is tight, but I push my hand through and grip him. He's hard for me, so hard for me.

Landon lets out a heavy breath and drops his head to my shoulder. His hair smells like pine and soap, a stimulating mix. I rest my free hand on the back of his head and hold him to me as I stroke him with the other. I move my hand slowly, pumping him.

He feels so heavy in my hand, and all I can think about is that I want to watch his face change as he grows closer to his orgasm. I love the way he closes his eyes when he comes. I've thought—many, many times—about how he came in his boxers as I straddled him.

"This is better than imagining, isn't it?" I ask.

I barely recognize my own voice.

Landon lifts his head slightly, and his hands move to my hips. I feel his fingers tug on my shirt, and I lift my body so he can take my shirt off. The second it hits the floor, his mouth is less than an inch from my chest. His eyes are wide on mine, asking for permission.

I nod and reach behind my back to unclasp my bra. My bra falls away, and Landon's eyes blink in anticipation. He makes me feel so wanted. He makes me forget the years of insults in my past and those I inflict on myself in the present.

He eagerly cups my breasts, and I notice that his hands are shaking as his fingers rub circles around my nipples. They harden under his gentle movements, and I moan when he pinches one between his thumb and index finger. Landon's eyes stay on my chest while his hands play with me, exploring my pleasure. I stop stroking him; my body can't possibly handle both sensations at once.

"You . . ." Landon's breath is hot on my breasts. "You're so— there isn't a word for how beautiful you are."

His words fall over me, coating me, and I watch him bend down farther. His lips wrap around my nipple, and he sucks it. When I moan his name, he sucks harder. His other hand is rubbing my other breast in slow circles, and my entire body aches painfully for him.

I've never had a man touch me with such reserve. Landon's touch is both steady and gentle, claiming and freeing. No one has ever taken the time to admire me the way he is now. His cock is out, pressing solidly between us. I want to take every second of this in so that I can think of him later, when he's no longer mine to touch.

His mouth moves to my other breast. It's overwhelming, watching him and feeling the vibration of his moans on my skin.

"I want to take your shorts off," he says, his voice low.

I nod barely, I think.

He grabs me and lifts me off the counter with ease. His hands are no longer shaking when they unbutton my jean shorts. He tugs at them, and they don't fall. I help him, pulling at the fabric, and once they're over my ass, they drop to the floor.

Landon's fingers hook around the strings of my panties, and he kneels in front of me. I put my hands on his head and stroke his soft hair. Slowly, he moves his head back and forth over my panties. I can feel how wet they are already. I'm throbbing.

He inhales a long breath, and my knees nearly buckle under me. How can someone so sweet possibly be so sensual? Landon is so much more unpredictable than he thinks he is.

His nose rubs over my clit, oh so gently, and I moan for him. His hands trail down my body, taking my panties with them as they skim over my legs, and I tremble.

Landon looks up at me, nerves clear in his eyes. He's nervous. Of course he's nervous—he's only been with one woman before. He doesn't have the same experience that I do. He's pure, and I'm covered in mud. I need to guide him a little more.

"I want you. I trust you," I assure him, and his eyes soften. "Taste me." I tug gently at his hair. "I know you want to taste me on your tongue, Landon."

With that, he wraps his arms around the back of my legs, and I spread them just enough for him.

My head rolls back the moment his tongue touches me. My wetness mixing with his warm, wet tongue has me holding on to the counter for support. The pleasure I feel is crippling, and the way his tongue glides over my sensitive nerves has me biting down on my lip, trying not to make a sound.

My stomach tightens, and I feel my orgasm climbing up my spine. I'm convinced he's going to drive me too crazy; he's too much.

Landon Gibson is the definition of too much.

He draws small circles with his tongue; he doesn't stray from where I need him. His name falls and falls again from my lips, and his arms are strong, holding me up when my body melts into him. As I come on his tongue, I can't hold my own body up. He grips me harder, and I let go of his hair and dig my nails into the countertop.

When I finish, he slowly rises from his knees. His cheeks are flushed and his lips are a deep pink, a little swollen and wet from me.

"Let me touch you. I need to touch you," I whine, needing him. *Now*.

Landon's eyes are intense, pouring into mine. "Come to my bed," he instructs. It's a foreign voice, a voice so full of command that I immediately nod and follow him to his room.

The walk down the hallway to his room is a long one. Between my thighs, I ache. Between my ears, I throb. My doubt is threatening to sweep down the hallway and take me with it. I'm taking it too far, I know I am, but I can't stop this any more than I could stop a barreling train.

Landon's room is simple. His bed rests against the wall and has a plain gray bedspread with just two pillows. I stand in the doorway, completely naked, and try to focus on the décor of his room and not my thoughts. I'm not sure what to do. I know what I *want* to do, but I want him to lead what happens. I want to be able to feel less guilty when this ship wrecks, knowing he was my co-captain.

Landon walks over to me and leans behind me to close the door. He turns the lock, and it clicks into place. My heart races.

Without a word, he wraps his arms around my waist and pulls me to him. He's wearing only briefs, which he's pulled up since we left the kitchen. His hardness presses into me, and I kiss him. I can taste myself on his tongue, and he moans when I grip him through his briefs.

"Lie down. It's my turn to taste you," I tell him.

He hesitates to pull away, like his mouth doesn't want to leave mine. The idea warms me, and I welcome it with open arms.

My body is growing impatient. I look down at Landon's nearly naked body, and I can't fight the crushing need to see the rest of him. I push at his shoulders, and he moves to his bed. Grabbing the smooth fabric of his briefs, I pull them down his legs. They pool at his feet, and he kicks them away.

I press my hands against his bare chest to push him onto the bed. He's breathing so heavily that I search his eyes before I continue. Sensing my wordless question, he nods and lies back on the bed. His brown hair is a mess on his pillow, and I climb onto the bed. Moving up his body, pressing my naked skin to his, I want to tease him.

My mouth finds his and I kiss him, hard. I kiss him and I kiss him until his shoulders relax and I taste him sigh. I press the wetness between my thighs on his hardness and he moans, his hands balling into fists in the blanket.

I rub him again, sliding myself over him, coating him. I want him to feel how much I want him. He groans, my name tumbles from his mouth, and he moves one hand to my bare back. His fingers find my hair, and I bend down to press my mouth to his ear.

"Pull it," I tell him. He blinks at me in surprise, and I put more weight on his body. If I move, ever so slightly, he will be inside me. "Pull my hair, Landon."

His throat moves when he swallows, and he tugs at my hair. I let my head fall back, and he shifts his hips under me. He moves one hand to my hip, keeping me in place. His cock is pressing against me, at the exact point of contact I need it to.

Fuck, this man will kill me. He tugs my braid again, and I watch desire ignite in his eyes.

He tests me, tugging harder, and I lower my head to his chest. I kiss him there, just below the dip of his collarbone. "You don't have to be gentle with me. Not when we're both feeling anything but gentle."

I kiss his neck, just under his ear.

"You make me crazy," he tells me.

"I know." I kiss his mouth.

He pulls on my hair again, and I moan into the kiss.

"I've never felt like this before," he confesses. His mouth is touching mine. "The things I want to do to you are things I've never even thought about before." The honesty in his voice makes my chest sting.

"You can be whoever you want with me, Landon. You can try new things." I bite at his lower lip and feel the shift of his hips again. On cue, he pulls my hair. I knew he would catch on quickly.

I climb down his body, kissing my way down, and his hand releases my hair.

"You don't have to be shy." I kiss him just above his navel. His muscles retract. "If you want to do something, just say it. Like right now, I want to take your thick cock in my mouth and taste your come."

His hips jump at my words, and his eyes are burning into mine.

"Is that what you want?" I kiss lower.

He nods furiously, and I smile. I follow the trail of hair with my mouth and kiss him one last time, in the sensitive spot between his thigh and his cock. It jerks next to my face, and I take it in one hand. I want to admire him, the way he admired me.

I try to be patient and place a kiss on the tip of him, but the noise he makes when I do cuts through my patience. I take him in my mouth and he comes instantly. My name has never sounded better than it does when he moans it while filling my mouth.

When he's finished, he reaches for my shoulders and pulls my body to his. I lay my head on his chest, and it moves with each rise and fall of his breath. His fingers caress me, tickling my skin as he drags them down my arm to my hip, and then back up.

Landon's hands are strong yet soft on me, and I can't remember the last time I was held this way. It's been, what . . . at least two years. Even when I was with him, he never held me like this. Quiet time was sparse in our house, and I never realized just how rare it was until it was too late. Landon's fingers move up to my hair and gently rub my scalp. I let my eyes close and soak in the contact.

The harsh pang of loss that's been throbbing inside me for years feels as if it's dissipating with every stroke of Landon's fingers in my hair. I love how gentle he is, how untainted his soul remains. I've never met anyone like him, and I can't help but wish for more of him. More time, more kisses, more of his fingers leaving their marks on my skin. Dakota is so lucky to have been with him for so long, sharing so many memories with him. I'll never understand why she took him for granted. I will simply never, ever get it.

A loud crashing sound comes from the living room, and we both jump. I climb off the bed and search for something to cover my body. Landon already has gray sweatpants hanging from his hips, and he's pulling an NYU T-shirt over his head.

Another crash. Landon looks at me. "You stay here." He seems slightly panicked, but not afraid.

When he opens the door, the sound of shattering glass fills the room.

chapter

Fourteen

Landon

*W*HEN I HIT THE HALLWAY, a string of curse words fly into the air. The voice is too low to recognize at first, but I have an idea . . .

If Hardin is breaking things in my living room, his ass is going right back where he came from. It takes my brain a few seconds to process what's happening when I finally see the living room. My grandma's table is knocked over, one leg broken, and the vase that was once atop it is on the floor, fractured into glass shards around some stranger's feet. Hardin is kneeling down with a trickle of blood at the corner of his mouth and his arm wrapped around the stranger's neck.

The man's face is red; a thick trail of blood flows down his face and has stained his mouth. The blood adds to the drama of the whole scene. When I pay close attention, I see that he's small-framed, and probably pissing himself because he thinks Hardin's going to kill him.

I stop a few feet from them. *What the hell is going on? Who is this guy?*

I search his face again. He looks a little familiar, but where do I know him from?

"If you don't plan to kill him, you should let go," I caution

Hardin. Going to jail would definitely throw a wrench into his weekend reunion with Tessa.

He looks down at his new friend and then back up to me. "Fine." He pulls his arms away from the man.

Gasping, the stranger falls over onto his side and cups his hands around the front of his neck.

"What's going on?" I demand. Whatever it is, it happened really, really fast. I didn't even realize Hardin had come in.

Hardin stands up. "Don't move." The stranger moves to hold his nose with one hand while his other is on the floor, open palmed.

Hardin doesn't take his eyes off the intruder. "When I got here, he had his ear pressed against your front door. I don't know what the fuck he was listening for. He was probably going to try to break in or some shit. I would know."

"Well, why did you bring him in here?" I look back at my grandma's ruined table.

Hardin stares at me like I've asked him why the sky is neon green. "So he wouldn't leave?" he says with an eye roll.

The man tries to sit up, and Hardin crushes the free hand under his boot. "I said *not to fucking move*." Hardin raises his hand and casually pushes his hair back over his forehead, completely ignoring the shouts of the man on the floor in front of him as he steps on his hand.

"What were you doing here?" I ask the stranger.

Hardin pulls his phone out of his pocket. I assume he's calling the police. I feel like I'm inside a movie.

"If he calls the police, you're going straight to jail," I point out.

The man moves his arm when Hardin takes a step away. Gripping his hand, he lifts himself to his knees. When Hardin returns, the man promises not to move and rests his back against my wall. He looks more and more familiar the more I stare at him.

"I was looking for my friend's apartment," he says. "That's all."

I don't know if I believe him. My apartment did get broken into a few weeks ago, so I can't be too sure. When my eyes register his black coat, his dark eyes, and his gray jacket, a memory pricks at my brain. I've seen him before in the hallway here, that's it.

"I think he's telling the truth. I've seen him here before," I tell Hardin.

The man stands up, and Hardin puts his phone back into his pocket.

My bedroom door opens, and Nora walks into the living room wearing a pair of my briefs and one of my white undershirts. Her dark nipples show through. I see Hardin and the random guy looking at her, and my chest flares.

"You can go back in my room." I hope she listens. I hate the two of them looking at her so exposed.

"What the hell?" She looks at Hardin, then at the other man. "Cliff?" Her eyes harden suspiciously. "What the hell are you doing here?"

"You know him?" I look between the two of them.

"She knows him?" Hardin asks me, knowing that I have no idea what the hell is going on.

Nora's eyes dart to me, but she doesn't respond.

"I was looking for my friend's place. He just moved into the building," this Cliff says.

Nora stares at him for a few seconds, and I watch them exchange communication without any words.

Who the hell is this guy?

"He's leaving; it's fine," Nora says at last, pointing toward the door. She's so calm and casual about all of this. So calm it's disconcerting.

Cliff rubs his neck and stands in the doorway. He doesn't say another word before disappearing into the hallway.

Hardin turns to Nora and raises his hands. "You just let him leave? You didn't find out why the fuck he was here in the first place!"

Nora walks farther into the living room, her eyes on Hardin. "Yes, I did. You heard his reason for being here." She rests her hands on her hips, and I consider walking up and pulling the hem of the briefs she's wearing down a little, just to cover a little more of her luscious body.

We just had a scene from a *Fast and Furious* movie go down in the living room, and I can only focus on the curve of Nora's thighs. I need help.

"He was lying!" Hardin shouts.

Nora moves closer to him. "First off, don't yell at me again," she says through her teeth, challenging him. "And second, you don't know that he was lying. You don't know him."

Hardin tilts his head back. "Oh, that's right. You do. How about you explain that little gem?"

"Guys." I walk between them. "Hardin, he's gone. Nora, go to my room." I feel like a dad with two temper-fueled children. Nora turns around and opens her mouth. Before she speaks, she closes it and turns to walk past me and down the hallway. I expected a fight from at least one of them.

"You better make her tell you who the fuck he is," Hardin demands.

And here we go . . . "Shut up and get the broom." I point to the closet next to the entrance to the kitchen. "I'll figure it out. You just clean that glass up."

Hardin glares at me. "I mean it. This isn't just about you. Tessa lives here, and if anything happens to her—"

The oven beeps from the kitchen, and I remember Nora's cupcakes. I had completely forgotten about them. Has it only been twenty minutes since we went into my room?

Heading into the kitchen, I grab an oven mitt and pull the

pan from the oven. The tiny cakes smell delicious and are perfectly browned at the top. My mouth waters, and I rest them on top of the stove and go back into the living room with Hardin.

So many questions are running through my mind. Is the intruder Nora's last boyfriend, whom she refuses to talk about? Is he just some regular thief, the one who broke into my apartment before? What would he have done if no one was home or if Hardin hadn't shown up when he did?

I need to get the mess the brawl made cleaned up so I can get back to my room and talk to Nora. Hardin's sweeping without complaint, and I grab one side of my late grandma's table and turn it upright. I'm going to have to fix this before my mom comes to visit again. She would be heartbroken if she saw it like this.

"I know," I reply to Hardin's silent reproach. I'm going to find out who he is and whether Nora really believes that he was just looking for his friend.

Hardin gripes at me while sweeping the rest of the broken glass into the dustpan. Just before I open my bedroom door, his voice trails down my hallway: "Don't tell Tessa about this. There's enough going on."

I let him assume my silence means that I'm agreeing with him and step into my bedroom. Nora is sitting on my bed, still wearing my clothes. I push my back against the door and wait for it to click shut. To be safe, I lock the door behind me and stride toward her. Her phone is in her hand, and when she looks at me, her eyes stare into mine but they don't connect. She's withdrawn already.

I keep my voice timid. "You know we have to talk about who that guy is."

Nora looks down and shifts, pulling her legs beneath her body. "Do we?"

I'm not letting her shoot this down. "Yes. We do."

I walk over to the bed, sit down next to her, and listen for sounds from the living room. It's quiet. Hardin either left or is being nosy, listening to our conversation from the hall, just like this Cliff guy.

"Is he your ex-boyfriend?"

Her body jerks at my question, and she shakes her head. "No. No, he's not."

I scoot closer to her and take her hands in mine. "Then who is he? This isn't a small thing, Nora." I gently squeeze her hands. "The guy was listening at my door. Do you know him well enough to believe that this is all a big misunderstanding? Truly?" I look into her eyes and wordlessly beg her for the truth.

I would like to believe that the last hour we've spent together has taken us to a new level of trust. I need her to trust me enough to be honest with me about this. The voice in my head is shouting doubt at her, but my mouth stays silent.

"Yes" is all she says.

I scratch my hand over the stubble on my chin, and she stands up from my bed. "Where are you going?"

She reaches the door before she responds. "I'm going to go grab my work clothes and come back. I have to work early in the morning."

I move off my bed, but I stay across the room from her. "I'll come with you."

Nora shakes her head. "I'll come back. I promise. I'll be back, and I'll stay the night with you. In your bed." Her voice is shaky, uncertain.

She walks back to me and reaches for my hands. I pull her into me.

"I will come back." Nora presses her lips to mine. I kiss her back, wrapping my arms around her as she melts into me.

I stay quiet, and her tongue feels so good on mine. I love the way she kisses me: slowly and thoroughly, full of cautious passion. Her fingers bury themselves in the fabric of my T-shirt.

After a few seconds, she pulls away from my embrace. "I'll be back in a little while." She kisses my cheek. "I'll hurry." Her words sound so certain.

I feel as if I'm in a trance. I nod and drop my arms to my side. "Your clothes are in the kitchen," I remind her.

Heat fills my cheeks, and she pulls her bottom lip between her teeth.

"I'll change in the bathroom." Nora eyes me. "You don't like these on me?" A gleam of mischief is sparkling in her eyes.

"I like them a little too much."

"I'll come back to you," she promises, although it sounds awfully ominous.

When she walks out of my room, I lie back on my bed and close my eyes. What the hell did I get myself into with this woman?

chapter

Fifteen

Nora

*T*HE SIDEWALK IS HARD under my feet, and each step on the pavement brings another memory of Landon. The crinkle by his eyes when he smiles that sweet, shy smile. The way his hands feel on me.

I've made such a mess. Why do I always make a mess everywhere I go?

The last few weeks have made me feel things I'd forgotten how to feel. I've felt happy. It sounds simple, to feel happy, but it's an accomplishment for someone like me. Living my life for other people, living in a prison of worry and deference, made me forget how it feels to be simply happy.

"Hey!" a woman's voice shouts behind me. The familiarity of the voice creeps through me, and my scalp prickles.

I turn around to see Dakota near the window of an art-supply store. Her curly hair is pulled back from her face, and she's dressed like she's going to a funeral. Her black skirt hits just above her knees, and her navy blazer is too big on her small frame. It's odd to see her in these clothes when I'm used to seeing her in gym or ballet clothes.

I don't have time to deal with her, not today. I don't have the energy to waste on her. "I'm on my way somewhere," I say as she approaches me. I look up to Landon's building, to be sure he didn't follow me. The idiotic part of my heart wanted him to, even though it wouldn't have ended well if he did.

"So am I. We need to talk."

I shake my head and push past her. We definitely don't need to do that. "We have nothing to talk about, Dakota."

"You know that's not true." A hint of a threat is in her tone.

I whirl around to face her. I raise my hands in the air in frustration. "What? What do you want to talk about?"

"You just came from Landon's apartment. I thought we had an agreement."

I roll my eyes and drop my head back. She can't be serious. I'm too old to play this game with an immature brat who wants to dominate a toy she's already thrown away.

"Are you kidding me? We are fucking *grown*, Dakota. I'm twenty-five years old. I'm too old to play these games with you. Landon is old enough to make his own choices, in life and love." The last word tastes weird in my mouth.

I should have just walked away from her when I saw her, yet I couldn't.

"Love?" she chokes out. "Love? You think that Landon loves you?"

I shake my head. No, I don't think that. I know he doesn't love me. We won't get that far before everything explodes in my face.

"Good. Because he doesn't. You can't come into his life and weasel your way in. He's too good for you." Dakota pushes her hand out and rests it on her hip.

I step toward her, keeping my face neutral. "I don't care."

If she thinks I don't care, maybe she will go away?

Dakota's lips turn into a fake smile. She's tiny, but she scares me a little sometimes. Like the night she came back to the apartment with liquor on her breath and wild eyes. She kept asking for my phone to call her brother, saying she needed to see him. She never opened up to me enough to tell me how he died, but that night I knew better than she did that he wouldn't be answering that call. She was out of it. Gone. She cried and cried in the kitchen, hiding under the table. She screamed at me when I tried to give her a glass of water and threw the glass across the kitchen. She didn't even flinch when it shattered against the wall.

The next morning I pulled her from the floor, and Maggy helped me carry her into her bedroom. From that day on, I knew something inside her was broken.

Dakota's eyes are feral on me. "Good. Neither does he. He likes to fix things and people." Her eyes take me in, try to swallow me whole. "And he saw *you*—"

"I get it. Now leave me alone." We don't have time for her to list all the ways I need saving.

I begin to walk away from Dakota, but she grabs my arm and jerks me back. I take a deep breath, shake her off, and keep walking. My fingers itch to lash out at her, but I keep them at my side.

She follows. "Why did you do it? Can you at least tell me why you pretended to be my friend to get close to my boyfriend?"

"That wasn't a part of it. I didn't—"

"*Yes*, you *did*. Stop the lies, Nora. Does Landon know that you knew the whole time?"

I grit my teeth. "Shut up."

It's much more complicated than this. This is all too complicated to discuss on the sidewalk. Of *course* he doesn't know. I led him to believe Dakota didn't talk about her feelings for him or even mention him. He knows nothing, about anything. I feel so close to him, even though he doesn't know anything.

Dakota is still walking with me, but at least I'm almost to the subway station now. She won't follow me all the way to Scarsdale. She's not that bold.

"I think if he knew how calculated this whole thing was, he

would run from you. He doesn't like liars, or stalkers. And I'm assuming he has no idea what's in Scarsdale." Dakota's words cut little slashes into me, and the air burns them as we walk. "I trusted you, Sophia. I thought we were friends. We let you live with us."

I glare at her. I don't do well with threats, a little fact about me that Dakota will learn very, very quickly if she keeps talking to me the way she is. "I posted an ad on a website and ended up living with you. You weren't doing me any favors."

Dakota lifts her purse higher onto her shoulder.

What am I doing arguing with her? Still?

"Yes, and when we met, I saw you hold that picture frame for a few seconds too long. You knew the entire time who he was." Dakota blinks, and her eyes focus on the building next to us. "All those questions you asked about him, about our relationship. I was nice to you, Sophia. So was Maggy."

Maggy, who would spend two hours putting on her makeup in our small bathroom, but pleasantly talk to me all the while, was the nicer of the two. Still, from the day I arrived at the apartment, I felt the division between the three of us. Me versus them.

"What is it that you want, Dakota?" I finally ask. I take the steps down to the subway slowly, and she's right behind me.

It briefly crosses my mind that she could push me down the stairs.

"I want to know what's happening with you and Landon, and I want to ask you—well, *beg* you—to leave him be. He's the only thing I have." Her words float around me, envelop me from behind. I wish Brooklyn subways were more crowded so I could slip into the crowd and disappear.

I wait until we reach the bottom of the stairs before I respond. Dakota wants me to stay away from Landon, something I can't do. Even when I tried, I couldn't.

She doesn't stop talking. "Don't you have enough? Your rich family, your big houses all over the country. The money you get every month from—"

"Look, Dakota." She has no idea what she's saying. My family's being wealthy has nothing to do with my wanting Landon. That she sees the two as parallel says a lot about how she sees him. I can't tell if she views him as an object or equivalent to riches. "I don't know what to tell you. You broke up with Landon months ago, and you've been seeing—"

Dakota shakes her head vigorously at this. "I was *confused*. I see that now. I needed attention, and Landon wasn't here. I felt lonely, and Maggy said I should be single my first year of college. Everyone always says that. All those stupid movies say it, too."

I never understood this idea of being single during college. Yes, it's important to be independent, and college is when you figure out who you are, and what you want. But if you already have an amazing man, why would you ruin that just to party and hook up with random guys?

"So you want me to stay away from Landon so you can get back with him?" I ask finally.

"If he will take me back, yes. He was mine from the beginning. Since before he even knew you. Before you saw that picture of him."

"I met him before that. My parents know his, remember?" Dakota is good at making me feel crazier than I am.

She nods slowly. "Yes, I remember. But I also remember the hours we spent talking about him, the many, many times I told you how much I love him and miss him—and I also remember about that time you told me to sleep with Aiden."

"I was trying to help you, as a friend. You kept saying you wanted to experience life in the big city!" I try to keep my voice down, but I'm doing a horrible job at it. "You told me how hot Aiden was, that you wanted to sleep with him." I narrow my eyes at her. "You already had your mind made up—I was just giving you that extra push to make you feel like less of an asshole when you fucked him."

Dakota's nostrils flare, and for a very, very short moment, I'm almost afraid of her.

"Are you kidding? I had my mind made up? And who the hell are you to judge me anyway, *mis-sus*?" she says, exaggerating the last word.

My entire body is covered in small slashes now. With every word, I feel more and more like a monster. Dakota may as well be pouring salt water into the cuts. Hearing her say she loves Landon is the equivalent of that to me, and her blaming all of this on me—possibly rightfully so—makes it much, much worse.

"Can you stop walking and just talk to me, please?" Her voice is soft, sad even.

I face her. "What will make you happy? If I stay one hundred feet away from him at all times? Tessa is my friend, too, and he lives with her. And Landon is happy with me. Dakota, let him be happy."

Her lip quivers, and she swallows. "How do you know he's happy?"

What a loaded question. *Because I can feel it,* I want to tell her, but I won't.

"How do you know he's happy, Nora?"

So now it's back to Nora. Tears prick my eyes. "I just know he is. Maybe I'm wrong; I don't know him like you do."

Her eyes stay on mine. "No. No, you don't."

I sigh and look around the station. A man and a woman are holding hands while they wait for the train. They have to be at least sixty, and when he leans down and kisses the top of her gray hair, my heart feels heavy. *How is it possible for my heart to feel so heavy when it's so empty?*

Dakota stops and frowns. "I don't have anyone, Nora. I thought I had you, but a friend wouldn't do what you did."

She's right. I was never a friend to her. I never wanted to be. I only wanted *him*. I should feel guilty, but it's hard to do so when I know how she treats him: like a lapdog. He's not a fucking lapdog. He's so much more than that. More than either of us deserve.

"I'm sorry for how things went down," I tell her, half meaning it. "I didn't mean to hurt you. Things just happened this way."

Dakota regards me, and I see a tear roll down her cheek before she can wipe it away. I know it will kill her that I saw her vulnerability, so I choose to show her kindness and ignore it.

"Landon and I have something real, Nora. We've loved each other since we were kids. He's been there for me through everything. Through my dad's abuse, my brother's death—we've suffered together in ways you would never understand. He's my person, Nora. He's my person, my only person, and I know I haven't treated him the way he deserves, but I was being stupid, and now I see that. Now I know that I have to do everything I can to make sure he knows how much I love him and appreciate him."

Her words make me shudder. I'm going to throw up, I can feel it coming. Acid burns the base of my throat. I can't listen to her talk about him like this. I physically can't handle listening to her say his name or explain the depth of their connection.

I stay silent, unable to offer her any words.

She starts talking again, and I wish I could press a button and turn my ears off.

"To you he's a piece of a game. You're just having fun with him, and he's just having fun with you. Fun, that's it," she says matter-of-factly. "But to me, he's my other half. He's the one person I can count on in this world. I have years and years with him, and even though you may think you can, you can't compete with that." She pauses. "I don't want to hurt you."

For some reason I believe her. That doesn't make it hurt any less.

"I've lost my mom and my brother, and my dad is going to die any day now. I can't lose Landon, too." Her voice breaks into full sobs, and she covers her face with her hands. Strangers stare at us as they pass.

When did I become such a shitty person?

"Please, Nora. Give me another chance to be who he needs me to be." She wipes her hand across her nose and looks back up at me. Her shoulders are shaking with sobs, and I can't help but feel for her.

Who am I to come into their life and tear them apart? She may be awful, but there's a soft part of her that always drew me to her. I don't hate her; I never have. I just knew she didn't deserve Landon. But now that she's in front of me, sobbing into her shaking hands, who am I to decide that?

She's right, I don't know him.

She does.

I don't love him.

She does.

I don't deserve him.

And, maybe, she does.

"Fine." I pull her hands away from her face.

She wipes her eyes again and looks at me. I don't know what else to say to her.

"I'll go away," I promise, and walk away, blending into a pool of strangers before she can stop me.

chapter

Sixteen

Landon

*I*T'S BEEN TWO HOURS since Nora left my apartment to get her work clothes. Well, her excuse was that she needed her work clothes, but I'm not completely ignorant of the coincidental timing. A stranger shows up in my apartment, and Nora just happens to know his name? And then she needs to leave for a bit, when she could easily just wake up earlier tomorrow and get her clothes then?

What a day I've had. Nora showed me a side of her I hadn't seen; not only is she mind-blowingly sexy, she managed to turn off all the noise in my head with the sound of her voice. I felt comfortable, and as stupid as it sounds, I felt confident in my inexperience with her guiding me, telling me I can be who I want to be when I'm with her. The thought of being able to spin a completely new version of myself is strange. With her I can be more than the nice guy; I can be more than someone's best friend. I don't have to solve everyone else's problems and neglect my own when I'm with her.

My head is throbbing, and my living room is finally put back together. Hardin argued with me for a little bit before he disappeared and came back twenty minutes later with an extra chain lock to put on the door. Luckily for him, he caught Ellen just as she was leaving, and she was nice enough to reopen for a moment to let him buy a lock. I don't think he would have slept tonight without one, and given that he *is* Hardin, I could even see him breaking into the store downstairs to get one himself. I think of what he said about Tessa, and how nervous she was after our break-in, and go to the closet to grab my small toolbox to install the lock.

Ken gave me this toolbox when I decided to move to New York. It's nothing too special, but it meant something to him, so it means something to me. I could see it in his eyes when he handed me the small red box, and I noted the way his voice changed when he explained the function of each tool inside. I didn't let on that he was telling me things I already knew.

I didn't tell him that I've been fixing things my whole life, that I'm an expert. Instead, I let him explain each thing to me in great detail. I even asked questions like *"What's the difference between a Phillips head and a flathead screwdriver?"*

I had a feeling he needed these simple moments with his stepson, to make up for lost times with his actual son.

When the lock is on and sturdy, I sit down on the couch and turn on the TV. What can I watch to distract me from staring at the clock? I turn on Netflix and scroll.

And scroll.

And then, scroll.

Nothing sounds distracting enough to keep my mind off Nora. While I read the titles of the movies recommended for my account, I curse the irony.

Julie & Julia and *Chocolat* are the top two: cooking-related movies, of course. The selections make me think of Nora in her work uniform, and then, out of it. It's possible that the movies are recommended because of her and Tessa's history, but I decide that it's some sign from somewhere. I keep scrolling. Nora should star in her own movie about a beautiful, intelligent, and mysterious woman. A woman who also happens to bake edible heaven. If our lives were a movie, it would be easier to uncover her secrets.

I think about the movies I used to watch with my mom on the Lifetime channel. As much as I hate to admit it, some of those movies were pretty dang good. They always had insane plots, like psycho babysitters who try to steal husbands, or husbands who turn out to be con artists, sometimes even murderers. If Nora was the star of a Lifetime movie, she could be a spy or even an assassin. In my head, I piece together what I know.

With her shady trips to Scarsdale, she could be either. From what Google knows about Scarsdale, it's a pretty wealthy area with an older population. Her family lives in Washington, so it has to be someone else. My phone buzzes across the table and I grab it, reading the name on the screen.

Dakota.

Why is she calling me?

And more important, why don't I want to answer it?

Guilt washes over me. I shouldn't be avoiding her. She doesn't deserve that. But I can't keep balancing on this rope between them; eventually I'll slip.

Nora's voice saying *"I'll come back to you"* plays and plays in my head. I think about the way her eyes flash with mischief when she challenges me, and the way my name sounds when it comes out of her mouth. I lay my phone on my chest and let the call go to voicemail and continue to make up plotlines for Nora's Lifetime movie.

The night I followed her, she changed her clothes before she got off the train. We can refer to that night as the Scarsdale Night. She changed her shirt and took her hair down from its braid. She even ran her fingers through the messy strands, and they bounced on her shoulders. She shook her head, and I remember thinking she should star in a shampoo commercial.

But enough about her bouncy things . . . I need to focus on my conspiracy theory surrounding this girl. I raise my hand and hold it up over my face and make a fist. I lift one finger for random subway rides an hour away. What else? Hmmm . . .

She's had shady phone calls come in while with me and then left my apartment. I raise another finger. As for disappearing, she's done that more than once, and I would have to be an idiot to ignore the warning signs as I raise another finger. If I get to five, I need to enter witness protection and escape her.

Speaking of witness protection, is she in it? She does have two names . . .

Was her ex-boyfriend in the mob or something?

Does she have a boyfriend now, and if so, is *he* in the mob?

I'm not sure why my brain goes straight to everyone's being in the mob; I've definitely watched too many movies. I did watch *The Godfather* when I was a teenager. More than once.

It's amusing to think about, but I'm not one of those people who blame their inability to function in society on a movie they watched at some pivotal age. Tessa made me watch this movie the other night that had a scene where a woman was sitting with her mom, telling her that she failed her by letting her watch *Cinderella* as a child. That's what happened to me: I watched *The Godfather* and soapy Lifetime movies with my mom, and now I'm convincing myself that my girlfriend is an assassin or an ex–mob member.

Maybe Nora has a secret child? She *is* older than me, and she *does* have that soothing voice. I could totally see her as a mom.

Maybe she's hiding something bigger, like that she actually *does* like Gatorade after all?

I would rather find out she's an assassin than discover she's been falsely throwing shade at my favorite drink.

I'm getting way, way too creative here. I need something to do. Pronto.

I lay the remote down on the coffee table and sit up. Should I call her?

She promised she would come back to me. Will she?

She was looking straight at me. Am I a fool to think that I could tell if she was lying? Can I trust her to actually keep a promise?

"I promise to not say things I'll want to erase," she told me.

We made a deal. It was set in stone from that second on, and I fully expect her to keep her side of the agreement.

If she comes back today, I'll make a promise to myself to trust her. If she keeps her promise, I'll keep mine. I'll make sure I give her time to open up to me. Her petals deserve to have time to bloom.

I busy myself by walking into the kitchen and opening the fridge. I should have checked in on Tessa today to see how she's doing. She seemed fine the last time I saw her. Hardin did, too, aside from choking that dude in my living room. My eyes scan the kitchen, remembering the taste of Nora on my tongue. The sweetness of her fills my senses again, and I grab a cupcake from the pan while I daydream. The way her fingers dug into the countertop when I lapped my tongue over her wetness will forever be etched into my mind.

The noises she made when she came set off an animalistic need inside me. All I could think about then, and even now, is her. She's quickly becoming an obsession of mine, and I don't think I could stop now if I wanted to. Nora's clothes were all around my kitchen only hours ago. Two hours and fifteen minutes ago, to be exact. She must have grabbed them and changed on her way out. My clothes did look so, so good on her.

Too good on her.

Everything she wears looks too good on her. She has one of those bodies that make oversized T-shirts and jean shorts look sexier than lingerie.

When I take a bite of the cupcake, my stomach growls, annoyed at how long it's been since I ate. The only thing that's been on my mind is Nora, Nora, Nora. How can I find out more about her? I bite off another piece of the onion cupcake and walk to my room to get my laptop.

When I get back to the couch, I have another missed call from Dakota. I flip my phone over so the notification doesn't distract me and open my laptop. I'm not even sure what I'm looking for, but my first instinct is to go to Facebook. Facebook is definitely the home base of internet sleuthing. I click on the search box and type in her name. Nora . . . wait, what's her last name?

Oh, man. I don't even know her last name.

I run my hand over my hair and grab my phone. I tap on my mom's name and put the phone on speaker.

She answers on the third ring. "I was just talking about you." I can hear her smile through her words.

I laugh. "Good things, I hope."

"Of course. We're here at drinks—well, I'm not drinking, of course—at South Fork, and we ran into Sophia's parents. We were literally just talking about you; how strange." Her voice is soft, and I try to keep my voice the same, despite the nervousness creeping up my spine.

I peer at my laptop and look around the room. Her parents are there, right now, with mine. What are the chances?

Another sign.

"Umm, t-tell them I said hi?" I stammer.

Maybe something will come up related to their last name, since I can't exactly ask my mom while I know she's with them.

"Landon says hi," my mom says, and I hear muffled voices in the background. A few seconds pass. "They told me Sophia moved back to Scarsdale. I didn't know that, honey." I get the feeling that this is something my mom expected me to mention to her.

If it were true, I would have.

Why do Nora's parents think she moved, and what did they mean by "back" to Scarsdale? If I hear *Scarsdale* one more time, I may lose my mind.

Maybe I can get some information from her parents. It would help me solve the mystery of her.

"How long ago did she live there again?" I ask my mom, and I hear her ask them.

"Just recently. A few months before you moved to Brooklyn," she says. "They say they send their best wishes to you and they hope you're enjoying your new city. They're used to their babies being out of the house." Then she teases, "I'm not."

"Tell the . . ." I pause, hoping my mom will fill in the blank.

"I'll tell the Rahals you said thank you, and I'll call you back later today. Is that all right?"

Jackpot.

I type Nora Rahal into the search bar, and a few pages pop up, none of them her.

"Landon?"

"Umm, yeah. Sure. Thanks, Mom, love you guys." I hang up and toss the phone onto the couch next to me.

I type Nora's sister's name, and hope I can spell it correctly. Stausey Rahal doesn't appear, but a profile under the name Stausey Tahan does. When I click on the profile, Stausey's face appears. I know instantly that it's her; I can tell by her features. Dark green-brown eyes and high cheekbones. She's slightly thinner than Nora; her face is more narrow, and her lips aren't as full. I scroll through her profile and quickly discover from the photos and comments that her husband, Ameen Tahan, is a surgeon. He seems to have had quite the career. I scroll through picture after picture of Stausey and her husband holding huge plaques and diplomas with his name on them.

And I work at a coffee shop . . .

I should fit right in with this family.

I manage to navigate through her photos and find an album named "Bandol," dated two years ago, and click on the folder. At least fifty pictures load onto my screen. Nora's sister should update her privacy settings. Any crazy person could find out so much about her in just a few seconds. Especially given the pictures she has here. The photo that catches my eye first is of Stausey in a tiny red bikini, kissing her husband, with his chiseled abs, under the stars.

I keep going to find pictures of Nora. A flash of a yellow bikini catches my attention, and I enlarge the picture. It's Nora, all right, wearing a strappy yellow bikini that barely contains the curve of her hips. A man is standing next to her; his black hair is thick and heavy on his head. She's laughing, and his arm is around her waist, holding her to him. I can see the possessive position of his shoulders, and I can sense his ego in the set of his strong jaw. I mean, seriously, the dude could cut a steak with that thing. I brush my hand over my own jawline. I could maybe cut through warm butter?

I stare at the picture for so long that it hurts.

Who is he?

I scroll over the image, hoping either of them are tagged, but no luck. Nervously, I click to the next picture. Nora with her feet in the ocean, a notebook on her lap. She's wearing the yellow bikini again, but the man from the other picture isn't in this one. Her hair is braided into two strands, and she's even more tan here than she is now.

God, she's beautiful.

Someone knocks at my door, and I jump up. *Nora, please be Nora.*

I wipe my palms on my sweats and open the door.

A little surprisingly, it *is* Nora, dressed in black pants and a red shirt with a plunging neckline. Her lips are painted bright red, and her eyes are lined with dark makeup.

"Hey," she says.

Her lips are so . . . so . . . I can't form a thought except that I feel immense relief to see her standing here, in my doorway.

"Hey." I hold the door open for her and she walks past me, her shoulder brushing mine.

When I join her inside and close the door, she grabs hold of my T-shirt and presses her lips against mine.

chapter

Seventeen

*N*ORA'S LIPS ON MINE are more than welcomed, if not exactly the first thing I thought she would do when I saw her in my doorway. But here she is, pushing my shoulders against the back of the door, her breath hot on my lips. Her hands are wild as her body presses against me and I attempt to catch my breath.

I put my hands on her hips, and her teeth gently pull at my lower lip. I lift one of my hands to cup her breast, and my fingers brush over her hard nipple. She's not wearing a bra.

When she pulls away, I reach for her. My back is tight against the door, and she's stepping away from me. Red stains of lipstick practically illuminate her full lips, instinctively causing me to lick my own to remember her taste.

"I . . ." Nora starts, stops, searches for words. Her eyes circle the room and land back on me. Her mouth falls open, but she doesn't speak.

I don't think I want to hear what she has to say. She's good at making excuses for why we shouldn't be doing what we're doing, and right now I want to ignore what might be right or wrong and just grab her by the waist and pull her to me. Her breasts are full, barely contained by the low cut of her shirt, which is the same bright red as her lipstick.

"What are you wearing?" I'm mesmerized by the shirt.

Nora cocks her head to the side and looks at me. She looks down at her outfit and back to me. "Clothes?"

Thinking before I speak is definitely something that I should work on. To try to wash away that awkward moment, I reach for Nora's arm and pull her back to me. She doesn't stop me from pulling her into my arms and holding her.

"I missed you. When you were gone just now," I say through her lips on mine. She's so warm, her body feels like summer nights in Michigan: languid humidity and fireflies twinkling in the yard. I would catch the fireflies in a jar but let them go soon after. Nora reminds me of a firefly, surprising and bright. Not to be kept in a jar. Never letting herself be kept in a jar.

She makes a sound like a sigh, and her hand touches my stomach and travels down, lifting my T-shirt up. When her fingernails slide down my bare skin, the memory of the first time she touched me flares to life. Her finger slid down my stomach then, too, and I should have just grabbed her by the ponytail and kissed her mouth. I should have tasted her lips and felt her body melt into mine the way that it is right now. But I didn't, and somehow we still got here.

Her hand continues lower, and she brushes over my arousal. She's completely hijacked my body, taking control in the most visceral way. Her tongue teases at mine, and I tug at the top of the fabric of her soft, silky shirt to expose her breasts.

Nora grips my cock, and I feel the familiar aching pull in the bottom of my stomach. I groan for her and she grips harder. The pressure almost hurts, but the pleasure overpowers the pain and I reach down to unbutton my pants. Her hands assist, tugging them down my legs.

"Are we alone?" she asks, her voice low.

I can't help the small laugh that escapes my lips, and look down at my pants around my ankles. "You're asking this now?"

Through a bitten lip, she laughs with me and drops to her knees. Nora's hands are steady when she pulls my boxers down, and I'm envious of how comfortable she seems to be with her sexuality. Her hands don't shake when she undresses me; her lips don't quiver when my tongue glides over them. For my part, I'm all nervous, shaky hands and awkward moans, and I couldn't be sexy if I tried.

Maybe if I pretend to be someone else for a minute I could be sexy. I could be like those guys in romance novels who can make panties drop with the sound of their voice. Nora's hands are stroking me, and it's impossible to focus on being sexy when her hands feel so, so good.

I look down at this beautiful, mysterious girl and try not to come as fast as I did last time—but she's making that very, very difficult with those red lips and hungry eyes. She places a wet kiss on the tip of me, and I groan and grab the doorframe to keep myself up.

"Mhm"—she kisses me again—"you taste so good."

That ache climbs up my stomach to my chest. "Nora . . ." Her name is dissolving cotton candy on my tongue. I moan again, not giving a crap about what does or doesn't sound sexy.

Nora's lips part, and she takes me inside her mouth. She's just so pretty with my cock inside her mouth. Her dark eyes are looking up at me, and it's hard to think about anything but filling her mouth with my come. I need to last longer—*Please let me last longer than last time.*

Watching her taste me, I think about how heavenly *she* tastes, better than any maple square my mom ever made.

Okay, enough about my mom, but I do need to think about nonsexy things to last longer. When Nora's warm tongue gently grazes over the tip of me, I force myself to think about school.

I have an exam next week.

Work—I have to work tomorrow.

When I look away from Nora, she pulls back and looks up at me. "What's wrong?"

"Huh?" I blink at her. "Nothing."

Nora shifts her body and rests her hands on her thighs as she sets her eyes on mine. "Liar." Then she adds gently, "Talk to me."

I take a deep breath. What the heck am I supposed to say? *Sorry, I'm just trying not to come in less than five seconds like last time?*

No freaking way in hell.

"I'm just thinking, I guess."

She tilts her head to the side. "Thinking about what?" A hint of red touches her cheeks and, oh, no, I don't want her to think I'm thinking something bad about this . . . Or even thinking about anything other than the moment we're sharing right now.

"Thinking?" she repeats, dipping her head down slightly. She moves her body a fraction of an inch away from me, and I feel the distance like a big, gaping hole in my chest.

I reach down and cup her cheek, forcing her to look up at me. "Nothing bad," I promise. "I'm just nervous. Honestly, that's what it is. I don't know why." I stop my rambling before I make a bigger fool of myself.

"Nervous? About what?"

"I don't know." I brush my thumb over her cheek, and her eyes flutter closed. "I'm trying to be cool and stuff, but last time I"—I pause—"last time, I was an idiot."

Nora leans up and my hand falls from her cheek. "An idiot? How?"

My face is hot with embarrassment. "I came so fast, and—"

Nora stands up before I can finish my sentence. "Don't call yourself names in front of me again." Her voice is harsh, her eyes even more so. "By calling yourself an idiot, you're contradicting my opinion of you and basically insinuating that I would be with an idiot." She looks around the room and back to me. I get the feeling that she's nowhere near finished. "And, you don't need to be embarrassed about that. I enjoyed it, and it's never a bad thing when someone is so turned on that they can't wait to come."

Relief floods me, and my shoulders relax. "It's not very sexy."

She glares at me. "You don't get to decide what I think is sexy." Her hand is on her hip now.

"I'm sorry."

"And stop saying sorry for things you didn't do, Landon. You did nothing wrong. You do that too much."

I guess I do. When I think about it, I spend about half of my life saying sorry. Even if I haven't done anything wrong. I fuss with the bottom of my shirt, trying to cover at least some of my body.

"If I didn't think you were sexy, I wouldn't be here, on my knees in front of you. You don't have to be whatever version of sexy you think I want. You just have to be here, with me. Do you want to be here with me, right now?"

I nod.

"I need words, Landon."

Of course she does. *"Words aren't real until you say them."*

"Yes, yes, I do. More than anything."

"Okay." Nora lowers herself back to the floor.

As sexy as she is in front of me, it seems wrong that she's kneeling before me.

I should be kneeling before *her*.

I grab her hand and pull her up. The confusion is clear in her eyes as she stands.

"Come to my bed. I want you in my bed."

"Is that so," she says with a wicked smile.

Without thinking, I scoop her into my arms and move toward my room. My pants are at my ankles, so I pull one foot free. It's still difficult to walk, but I would rather spend a year in Azkaban than drop Nora or have to put her down. Nora buries her face in my neck, and I love the way she feels in my arms.

When I reach the hallway, I kick my pants off the rest of the way, and she giggles against my neck. I try to open my bedroom door with one hand, and Nora realizes that I'm struggling and reaches out to open the door for me.

As I walk over the threshold, I hear the sound of her foot smacking into wood.

"Ouch!"

Shit. "Sorry!" I take two quick steps forward and drop her onto the bed as she untangles her arms from around my neck.

"I think my foot is broken." She laughs, holding on to the red mark on the top of her foot.

I don't even remember her taking her shoes off. Then again, I'm not great at focusing on the details when she's around. "See, *this* is why I'm nervous." I move up on the bed and sit down next to her. Nora extends both legs. When I look at her, I'm distracted by that dang shirt again.

Nora leans her head onto my shoulder. "I missed you while I was gone, too," she says, finally responding to my words from a few minutes ago.

I stay quiet for a moment before asking, "Where did you go?"

She turns to me and shakes her head. No response.

"Are you cheating on me?"

I mean it as a joke, but her back goes rigid and the energy between us shifts. Nora smiles, but it's faker than a plastic doll's. "I wasn't aware that I was in a position to be cheating on you."

Now the tables have turned. She's nervous; I can sense it. There's something else, too, and I can suddenly feel a great pain inside her.

I lean up and study her face. "Would you like to be?"

Her lips shake and she opens her mouth, then closes it again.

Guess not.

"Don't look at me like that," she mumbles. "I'm thinking."

"You're always thinking." I ignore the probing ache in my chest at the idea that she could possibly want to be more with me.

After a few moments of silence, her voice breaks the stillness—small, unrecognizably so. "I want nothing more than to be yours—"

I don't give her a chance to add anything more, to take anything back. I turn my face to hers and take her mouth to mine. My hands cup her cheeks, move down to her neck, and I push my tongue through her lips.

She groans into my lips, and I move in front of her. Her thighs spread open for me, and I push my body between them, kissing her hard. I kiss her longer, harder, deeper. My mouth grows hungrier, my hands grow fierce, and my insides feel as if they are turning to liquid. I pull away to admire her face. My eyes take her in—every centimeter of her face deserves to be admired; I could stare at her for one hundred years and it would never be enough. I brush my hand over her hair and rest it at the base of her neck. She's watching me, her arms motionless at her sides. The corners of her mouth are upturned, but she's not quite smiling.

I'm over her now, her face inches from mine. I lean in and brush my nose against hers; her eyes flutter briefly, and a small noise comes from the back of her throat.

"Are you still thinking?"

"Only about one thing."

She keeps a steady gaze, her eyes careful. "And what's that?"

Instead of answering her, I lean into her and press my lips to hers. My hand fists in her long hair, and I move one arm under her back, lifting her to press her body against me. I can't seem to get close enough; the urge to hold her closer and closer still is an overpowering one.

I don't remember ever feeling this way about a person, wanting to be close enough to become one.

With one hand holding her neck still, I move my other hand down to her bottom, gently caressing the soft flesh. Her moans fill my ears, my small bedroom, my apartment, my block, my city, my world.

Her body was made for this. She was made for me.

Her warm hand grabs hold of mine, and she guides it back to her front, between her thighs. Her black pants are tight, the fabric thin. When I touch her, I feel her wetness through the material. My God, this woman's going to kill me.

"Don't stop, Landon. Please."

Her words are a spark of flame to a forest of trees, and I'm no longer here in this room. I'm above it, watching from the sky, wondering how I got lucky enough to be with her, like this.

My fingers move to the waistline of her pants, and I unbutton them quickly. She lifts her back up to help me, and I make the mistake of looking at her—from her low-cut red silky shirt with her breasts swollen and nearly completely out of it, to her red panties. My heart is pounding through my rib cage, threatening to break free.

I recognize the look in her eyes and still can't believe that I'm worthy of her beautiful gaze on me. She's breathing hard, lips parted, and staring. She raises a shaking finger to my face and traces the outline of my lips. I kiss her finger, and she groans, still caressing my wet lips. I wrap my lips around the tip of her finger and gently bite down. Her hips lift off the bed.

"Landon," she breathes, my name as soft as ash.

"Nora."

She guides me to enter her as she slides those damn red panties down her thighs. "Do you have one?"

Have one what? "One . . . ? "

"Condom."

Oh, duh. "Uhm?" I'm sure I have one somewhere around here. Where would it be? *If I were a condom, where would I be . . . ?*

Inside Nora, that's where.

"I'm on birth control . . . " she says, but looks uncertain.

I climb off the bed and hurry to my dresser. Digging through the folded briefs and socks, I feel a plastic wrapper. *Bingo!*

"Bingo?" Nora says with a youthful giggle.

My stupid mouth never waits for my permission to speak. I don't try to defend myself and instead just laugh with her and climb back between her legs. With steady hands she helps me and once again guides me to her. I lean my face to hers and kiss her lips, her cheeks, her chin, even her closed eyes.

She sighs and wraps her arms around my back, pulling me to enter her. Fuck, she feels . . . She feels like nothing I've ever before felt. Maybe she's just perfect for me. Her body, still and soft under me, is all curves and tanned skin. I didn't take her shirt off, but I can see plenty of her breasts. She catches me looking at them and pulls the fabric down, cupping her breasts and pulling them out from her shirt. I bend my neck to pull one of her soft, dark nipples into my mouth. I gently nibble her, eliciting a sharp whimper.

Her arms go behind my back again, urging me to her. "Are you okay, Landon?"

I thrust into her slowly, reveling in the exquisite feel of her body taking mine. I nod and lift my mouth to hers. I keep moving slowly, in and out. In and out. Tenderly touching her, claiming her as mine.

She kisses me until all I can feel is her heart pounding against my chest, her body flush with mine. Her legs grow stiff, and she whispers, begging me not to stop. I don't until my body splits in two and falls onto hers in a fit of sighs and rising and falling chests.

I roll off of her warm body and lie on the bed beside her. "That was—" I try to catch my breath.

"Perfect," Nora says for me.

chapter

Eighteen

*H*ALF OF NORA'S BODY is on top of me, lying across my chest. Her chin is resting just below my breastbone, and her fingers play in my chest hair. She swirls her index finger around, and I watch her in silence. The air conditioner hums in the background, and my mind is replaying the last few minutes over and over and over. Her cheeks are still tinted a blooming pink, and she looks refreshingly, painfully beautiful. She's taken her shirt off and is wearing nothing but those beautiful eyes, those pouty lips, and that dandelion tattoo midway up her back.

"You know, I've never had a lover be so gentle with me," Nora says, her eyes not meeting mine. She stares at my chest, and her fingers continue to caress my skin.

You know, I've never had anyone call me a lover, I want to say, but decide against it. "Is that a good thing?" I cringe, thinking of all the whips and chains and things people seem to be into nowadays. Am I too gentle? Dakota sure thinks so, not that I want to think any more into that . . .

Nora beams. "Yes. A very good thing." Her voice changes to a whisper, even though we're alone. "Though"—she regards me thoughtfully—"sometimes I'll want you to be rough."

I'm surprised by the way her words make me feel and also ecstatic that she wants to do this again. My body, though still recovering, aches to be inside her again. Just how rough is she talking here? I'm intrigued by the wide world of sex that I'm unfamiliar with, but I don't know if my mind can separate being rough from hurting her. I know there's this whole gray space between rough sex and plain old sex, but just where does her arrow rest on the spectrum?

"How rough?" I ask.

One of her hands moves over mine, and she guides it to her hair. Wrapping our fingers around a chunk of dark strands, she yanks on it. My cock throbs.

"Rough enough." She smiles delightfully and mischievously. She rubs herself against me. It's like her body is completely in tune with mine. "Does that sound like something you would like?" Nora's voice is husky. She tilts her head down to my chest and swipes her tongue across my hardened nipple. Her teeth graze it, and she flicks at it with her tongue. The sensation shoots straight to my groin. No one has ever touched me there, let alone used their mouth on me. My heart is racing—more than usual—and I'm both excited and a little afraid. Not because I don't want this, but because it's all so new to me. I heard someone say once that there was a sweet spot between thrill and fear, and it's a spot I think I've jumped right into the middle of.

I nod in delayed response.

She presses her lips against my chest. She makes a humming sound in the back of her throat. "I love your body."

She moves her hands up to my neck. Her fingers skim over my clammy skin, and my cheeks heat under her compliment. Her hands span my shoulders and back down my chest. It takes everything in me not to writhe under her.

"You're one of those people who don't have to work out to have an amazing body, aren't you?" Nora gives me a conspiracy-filled smile. "Actually, don't answer that. I want to imagine that you work out twice a day to look like this." Her fingers leave my chest and travel down my stomach. Her long nails drag down the ridges of muscle.

I move my hand to her bare behind. "I love your body." I grab a handful of her thick ass, and she purrs. Literally purrs from my touch, and I want to hear that sound again. "You have the kind of body that men have bowed to since the history of time." I think back to all the ancient beauties and the spells they cast on men. Despite my love of all things history, in this moment, naked beside her, I can't think of a single one of their names.

"Hardly." She snorts. "I love my body," she says with certainty, "but it took me a long-ass time to get there. My teenage years were awful, with every girl on TV a size zero and airbrushed to death. Even the girls at my school—I went to a private school, and they were all these tiny little blondes with rich daddies. From magazines to movies to the hallways, there were no girls who looked like me."

This part of her, the insecure teenager, tugs at my heartstrings. Having been with Dakota, who is darker skinned than Nora, I remember these problems coming up. If society tells us that all women should look a certain, very specific way, who are the young girls such as Nora, with two races running through their veins, supposed to look up to?

I try to think of Nora as a happy teenager, and it brings a smile to my lips. "How were you as a teenager? I would have liked to know you then."

She laughs, a small sound. "Oh, no, you wouldn't have. I was wild, too wild for you."

Too wild for me? Once again, I'm reminded that I'm not the life of the party. Since when is being tame so bad? Why is it that girls and women alike always want the drama and wild nights? Why are illegal street races and explosive arguments and gut-wrenching angst more fun than lying on the couch in each other's arms and watching Netflix? What's that thing everyone is saying?

Netflix and chill?

Yeah, that's it. Why can't women just be happy with Netflixing and chilling? Netflix has all the good shows and movies now anyway.

"I got in a lot of trouble, with my school, my parents. To say that they were embarrassed by me would be the understatement of the century."

I study her, this wild, fiery woman. I drag my fingers down her bare back. Even her back is sexy—who would have thought a back could be so sexy? The soft line of ridges down her spine curve into her full ass, and I brush my fingers over it, gently squeezing a handful of her flesh. "Everyone has their own way of crying for attention."

Her eyes change; little storms brew in the depths of them. "I don't know if that's what I wanted."

I've offended her now.

Great.

"I didn't mean to upset you." I draw small circles on her skin and hope that she doesn't get up or move away from me. I like her body pressed against mine like this. I like the warmth of her enveloping me.

She sighs. Then licks her lips. "It's fine. I mean"—she stares up at the ceiling with a thoughtful expression—"I guess when I really think about it, I did want attention. My sister, Stausey, she has always been the center of my parents' universe, and I was just a little speck in the abyss, not even bright enough to be a star."

Not even a star? I look at her closely, contemplate the longing in her voice. I memorize her face, the little freckles on her forehead and the small scar near her chin. It's so light that I never noticed it before. I thumb over it, wondering where it came from. My eyes follow up to hers and back down to her mouth.

I think about her bright laughter. Her fiery sass. Her blazing confidence. She's certainly a star. If people were stars, she would be the North.

"And what about you?" Nora snuggles closer. "How were you as a teen? Wild as a boar?" She giggles.

I shake my head. "Hardly. I read a lot and just hung out with my friends."

Nora's fingers feel so good on me. "Did you have a lot of friends?"

"Nope. Like two."

"Well, everyone at your school must have been too stupid to realize how great a friend you are." She says that like it's the surest thing in the world.

I chuckle. "That's one way to look at it."

Nora's fingers climb up my neck to my chin. "It's the only way. If I had a friend like you in high school, my life would have been easier. That reminds me"—she looks up at me while brushing over my facial hair—"you've been such a rock for Tessa these last few months. I'm so glad she has you."

When I look away from her praise, she turns my chin back to her. "Seriously, you're such a rare kind of person. I don't think you realize how special you are. It sounds stupid and weird and corny, but *special* is too light a word for you."

My cheeks are on fire. "I would do just about anything for Tessa."

"I know you would." This time it's Nora who looks away. "Anyway, what kind of books did you read?"

Back to the superficial subjects. I'm okay with this. I can only take so many compliments plus sex within a one-hour period.

"Mostly fantasy. I loved all of the Lord of the Rings books, Harry Potter. I liked some dystopian, too. I mean, I'll read just about anything."

"I *hate* dystopian." Nora groans.

I gently shove at her shoulder and smile. "What? How could you?"

She rolls her eyes and props herself up on her elbows. She tucks her hair behind her ear and licks her lips. "Because, let me tell you why. In nearly every single one of them there's some warrior chick who's like fifteen and who has these amazing friends, and together they're strong enough to save the world, of course. Let me tell you, at fifteen I had no fucking idea who I was, and I sure as hell couldn't have saved the world."

"I disagree. You could totally save the world."

She nods. "Yeah, sure, *now* I could. But as a teen? I felt weak and confused, and sometimes I made shitty decisions. Where are those books?"

Her passion and ferocity make me like her even more. "I don't know. Maybe you should write one."

She smiles at me, and my breath gets caught in my throat. "Yeah. I should. I bet it would be a hit."

I don't doubt that it would. I would love to read anything she wrote. I've thought about writing something myself many, many times, but I'm not sure I've had a dynamic enough life yet.

"Are you hungry?" Nora sits up, taking my eyes with her.

God, she's so fucking hot. I can't believe I just had sex with her. "I'm always hungry."

She grabs my hand and pulls me up. "Let's go. I'll make us some food."

"I would rather do something else," I say, feeling rather brave.

Nora's brows rise in surprise. "The night's not over. We can do both," she says with a mischievous smile, and drags me out of bed.

WE ARE SOMEWHAT DRESSED—her braless and wearing one of my WCU T-shirts with a pair of my boxers, me in thin cotton sweatpants—and when I try to put on a shirt, Nora yanks the gray cotton from my hands and tosses it across the room.

Shaking her head, she grabs my hand and pulls me out of the room. Nora holds me tightly, her hands always so warm. So we walk, hand in hand, into my kitchen, where she goes straight to the fridge. I lean on the counter and she busies herself.

Her head pops out from behind the open fridge door. "Do you like cabbage?"

I recoil. "Does anyone?" My mom's cabbage rolls would smell up the whole house for at least two days. It was horrible.

A smile creeps across her face. "Have you had it recently?"

I shake my head.

She nods and closes the fridge. "Will you try it my way? If you don't like it, I'll make pizza."

I can name about thirty things I would rather do than eat cabbage. Twenty-nine of them have to do with Nora's naked body . . . Unless I get to eat the cabbage off it?

I wonder how hard it would be to get her to agree to that.

Nora walks to me, a whole cabbage head in hand. I back away with a smile, and she advances on me, her smile even bigger than mine.

"How about this?" She moves the head of cabbage behind her back. "If you promise to take two bites, I'll make cookies, too."

As she takes a teasing step back, she licks her lips, and I don't tell her that with a mouth like that, I would do many, many things for her.

"Hmm." I press my fingers to my chin, pretending to be weighing the bargain in my head. I love to tease her and watch her eyes crinkle and sparkle, and the sassy smile that fills her face gives me the instant gratification I was searching for. "And you'll feed the cookies to me?"

She nods, beaming. "And the cabbage."

I walk over to her, lean into her body so that the fridge touches her back, and bring my lips to her ear. "You've got yourself a deal, little lady."

She's breathless when she pulls away from me.

A few minutes later, when the oven is preheating and Nora has already cut and pulled apart the cabbage leaves, I decide to try to connect a few more pieces of the puzzle that is her.

I start with simple questions. "Did you grow up in Washington?"

She shakes her head. "No. I lived in California for a while when I was young. Then we moved to Las Vegas, then to Washington."

"Wow." I remember the move from Michigan to Washington, feeling like my little world was being flipped upside down. For the first two months I missed my house, my school, my girlfriend. Well, I missed Dakota all the time, until now. Guilt rumbles somewhere inside me. I miss her sometimes still.

I've never been to California or to Las Vegas. "How was Vegas? Is that where you were wild?" I tease.

As if in reply, she asks me to grab the olive oil for her, and I walk to the cabinet to look for it. I didn't even know we had olive oil.

When I find it, she reaches for it. I lift it high in the air. "Is Vegas where you were wild?" I ask again, lifting the bottle too high for her to grab.

She looks up at me and then to the bottle and back to my eyes. She's humored and surprised by my game. "Yes and no. I was sixteen." She moves closer to me, brushing her body against mine as she tries for the bottle again.

"Tell me about the *yes* part of that."

She presses against me farther. Her breasts push against the top of my stomach, and it starts to require effort to keep my hand in the air. I feel her fingers gently stroke over my sweats, and when she wraps her fingers around my growing cock, I can't control the groan from my lips.

She moves her hand, up and down, up and down, over the fabric. My vision is foggy, and my head is swimming when she leans her face into my neck and her hot breath caresses me.

"Got it," she says, and it takes me a moment to realize what she means.

I stare at the olive-oil bottle in her hand. "You cheated!" I reach for her arms and pull her back to me. "So, so unfair."

Her hair smells like coconut, and it's soft against my lips. I kiss her head again, and she melts into me. Holding her closer, I press my thumb and forefinger under her chin to lift her eyes to me.

"No one said I played fair," she says with a perilous smile.

I lean into her to press my lips to hers, but she ducks out of the way and untangles herself from my grasp. When she gets back to the stove, the devilish woman turns and winks at me. Winks! I love how wicked she is.

I try to keep my hands off her while she talks. She tells me about her parents, their big house in Las Vegas, her summer spent learning to play the piano. Piano lessons, a big pool, and the hot Nevada sun—sounds like heaven.

She brushes the cabbage leaves with olive oil and tells me

stories about her sister pranking her and the winter in Southern California, where there's really no winter at all. She talks about palm-tree leaves and horrendous traffic. She made a friend, named Pedra, and Nora's sister, Stausey, met her husband, Pedra's brother, that winter. The doctor husband I saw online, I realize. His big white smile and gazillion certificates fill my mind. Nora remembers that winter with a pained expression, and I remember the Ken doll from the Facebook picture.

"Did you have a boyfriend there?" I ask, prying.

Nora doesn't turn to me when she answers, "Something like that."

Why is she so secretive? It drives me crazy. Crazier than crazy.

"How was he?" I know she doesn't want to talk about him. But I do.

Before responding, Nora opens the oven and places the sheet pan full of green leaves on the rack. She sets a timer and finally turns around to face me.

"Are you sure you want to go there?" Nora's questioning eyes lift to mine. "Once we go there, we can't go back. I just want you to know that before we do."

Do I want to go there? Where exactly are we *going*?

I want to know as much as I possibly can about her, but what if I don't really want to know once it's all laid bare? What if the reality is worse than this fantasyland we're playing in?

Can't I just stay here a little longer? What's the harm in being ignorant? I decide that the saying "Ignorance is bliss" was made for moments like this.

I look at her, her hands clasped in front of her body and her eyes staring into mine, and decide to live in ignorant bliss just a little while longer.

"What's your favorite food?" I ignore the chill that runs down my spine when she looks a little more relieved than anyone should.

chapter

Twenty

*N*ORA WAS RIGHT. Her cabbage was delicious. It didn't taste anything like the smelly rolls my mom would make. She pulled the leaves off and sliced them up, then threw them onto a plate for us to munch on. That's it. And it was much, much better than I thought it would be. Nora sat perched up on the counter and fed me bite after bite. It tasted like garlic and salt, and, given that she kissed my lips after each bite I took, I ate the entire pan.

"I told you it was good." She squirts soap onto the pan she cooked it on. I watch her clean the dishes and wonder if I should offer to help.

I probably should. "Can I help you?"

Nora turns, half-surprised, half-smiling, like I just offered a fluffy white puppy. "Let me get this straight." She licks her lips, and I walk closer. "You not only have the tongue of a saint, the body of a god, and the brain of a philosopher, you also help wash dishes?"

Something pulls at my chest with each word of praise.

Her expression is amused, and I love the way her unguarded smile hangs from her lips. Just as I love the way my boxers hang low on her hips. My shirt doesn't swallow her; the fabric is somewhat tight against her chest and hips, but loose on the arms. Now my shirt will smell like her. I'll never have to wash it again. Okay, maybe not never again, but not anytime soon. I barely do laundry anyhow.

I stand behind her as she pretends to wash the same pan that has been in her hands for two minutes now. What is she daydreaming about? Me helping her with dishes? Is it that simple to climb into her heart?

Finally I say, "That I do, little lady."

Her long fingers hold on to the sponge, and she dips it back into the soapy water. "Again with the *little lady*?"

She tilts her head slightly, exposing her neck. I can't tell if she's purposely encouraging my need for her, or if her body is calling to me without intention. Either way, I'm a lucky SOB.

"I'm older than you," she notes.

I laugh under my breath and watch small bumps grow on her neck. Did I cause that? Holy shit! I think I did. I wrap my arms around her waist, and she leans back into me, her bare neck calling my name. I kiss her there, just above the curve of her throat.

"I'm bigger than you." I kiss her neck again. My tongue swipes over her warm skin, and she groans, breathless. My hands move to her hips, and I give her a light squeeze.

"Bigger, are you?" Her voice is small and gruff. Nora pushes back, her ass pressing against me.

"I am." My hands travel to her breasts, and I rub them softly, gently caressing her flesh. When my fingers find her nipples, covered only by the thin fabric of my cotton T-shirt, my fingers tug at them and they harden under my thumb. I tweak them; with each pinch my touch grows stronger, her moans transform into mewls, her whining gasps make me throb for her.

Her unmoving hands are still in the water, and I move one of my hands down to her stomach. I stop there, unsure how far to take it. As if she can hear my thoughts, she looks over her shoulder at me. "You can be whoever you want with me, remember?"

I can be who I want to be with her. No pressure, no worrying about whether I sound cool or lame, or strong or weak. I don't have to push through the fields of doubt in my mind; I don't have to question every single thing I say or do. I can sidestep all that. With her, there's a calm silence like I've never known.

She turns the faucet off, and I watch her rinse the soap from her hands. "What do you want, Landon? Tell me." Nora moves her hips, rubbing her ass against me. "Don't be afraid. I want you." Her hand wraps around me through my thin pants. "I need you."

"Turn around," I growl, barely recognizing my own voice.

Nora doesn't hesitate; she turns around to face me. The sheepish gaze isn't one that I'm used to from her. Her expression is timid, she's panting, her shyness is new but so, so hot.

"Do you want me to tell you what I want?" My voice comes out much clearer than in my head. In my head, I'm nervous, excited. I'm jumping up and down with the anticipation of touching her. But here in reality, I'm standing tall, my unwavering gaze swallows her, and I can't believe I'm this damn lucky.

She nods, her eyes staring right through me.

"I want you to sit in this chair." I reach for the chair closest to me and pull her away from the sink. Her hands are still dripping with water, and the front of my pants are wet. She sits down in the chair, hands folded on her lap.

"Stand back up," I instruct.

When she obeys, I tug at my boxers to pull them down her thighs. I lift the shirt up over her head and watch, enthralled with the way her tanned breasts hang heavy and full, how her nipples are hard and ready. Her body is something to behold, and I drop to my knees to worship her.

"Sit down," I say when my knees hit the floor.

She sits, and I run my fingers up her legs to the tops of her thighs. A shiver runs through her, and she watches me, her breath hitching each time my eyes meet hers. I gently spread her thighs and bend my head down to kiss the tops of them. Nora's fingers thread through my hair, and she caresses my head as I give her body my full devotion. My fingers tease her, running over her pussy, and I push one inside her. I watch her face as her eyes roll back and her mouth parts in ecstasy.

I pump my fingers slowly and tease her with my lips, softly brushing them over her sex. She groans and groans with every stroke of my fingers. I love how vocal she is; it does amazing things for my ego.

After a few seconds of torment, I end her suffering by swiping my tongue over her wetness.

"Oh, God," she says, and I repeat the motion. She tastes like sugarcoated honey, and I've always had a sweet tooth.

When her legs stiffen in the chair, I wrap my arms around her thighs and lift them just enough to support her as she comes. I press my mouth against her hard.

She says my name.

She says how sweet I am.

You're so good, Landon. So, so good.

I taste her as she climaxes, and I hold her legs still as she recovers. She's completely naked, sitting on the chair, breathing hard, and I don't want to stop. I can feel her throbbing through my tongue, pulsing from the orgasm she just had.

I'm not done. She told me to do what I wanted, be who I want to be. This is who I want to be. Someone who worships her body and finds pleasure in her pleasure.

By the third time she comes, her body has turned to jelly. When she falls back, done and finished and sated, I pull her down to the floor and into my arms. She melts into me and I stroke her back with soft touches, and after a few minutes I think she may have fallen asleep.

"I tell you to do what you want with me, and you make me come three times," she whispers, burying her head farther into my chest. Her arms tighten around me, and I find an immense satisfaction in cradling her on my kitchen floor.

I touch her cheek and brush her hair off her face. "That's what I wanted to do."

Nora sits up just enough to look at me and repositions her body so her thighs are on either side of my hips and her breasts are in my face. Bare breasts, I might add. It takes every ounce of self-control not to lick them.

"Can I keep you?" She smiles playfully.

I decide to lick her breasts, and when I do, she wraps her hand around my neck and pushes my face into them. *I could live in here, buried in her beauty,* I lamely think to myself. *I could definitely just sit here all day and night with my face buried in her bosom.* Do people still use the word *bosom*? Probably not.

She giggles when I bite at her. "Is that a yes?"

I nod, rubbing my face in her chest.

After humoring me for a few minutes, she drags me off the floor, and I finish washing the dishes while she makes the cookie dough that I earned for eating the cabbage. If Nora promised to feed me my vegetables each day, I would become a herbivore in no time. We could eat kale smoothies and grainy cereal things all day if she made them.

When I finish drying the dishes, I join her at the counter and watch her roll the dough into balls. White chips are in them and something that looks like a berry.

"What kind of cookies are those?"

"White-chocolate raspberry."

While the cookies bake, my small apartment fills with that familiar sweet smell, and I decide that Nora should come over every day. I would be very, very happy with that.

Where does she live now? I had nearly forgotten that she came to my house with her hands full of her belongings.

"Are you back in your apartment?" I ask when she sits up on the counter and I stand between her legs.

"No."

And that's it. Just a "No."

"Where are you staying? Do you need to stay here?"

"No." She smiles this time, and I brush my nose over hers. "My sister is coming tomorrow, and she's going to let me stay in her condo across the bridge."

"In Manhattan? That's far from your work."

"It's not too far."

"You can stay here."

She wraps her arms behind my neck and pulls me closer. "No, I can't."

"Why?"

But Nora shakes her head.

"So if your sister is coming tomorrow, does that mean I won't see you?"

She nods.

"I would like to meet her."

Nora's back stiffens slightly, and she shakes her head. "Meet my sister? Oh, that's a horrible idea." She smiles at me, but I'm not smiling. She's using that beautiful face as a shield against my intrusions again.

A horrible idea? Why would that be a horrible idea? If we are trying to get to know each other better, why would I not meet her sister? It's not like I asked her to marry me; I just want to meet some of her family.

"And why is that?" I hope she can't hear the uncertainty in my voice.

Nora pulls away from me and leans back against the cabinets. "My sister . . . My sister is not someone you just *meet*—it's a whole production. We would have to plan this much, much better. I don't think it's a good idea. I mean, she and Ameen are not people who just *meet* people."

As Nora spoke, her voice became increasingly frantic, so very different from what it was moments ago. What is she so afraid of? Why would it be such a big deal for me to meet her sister?

I look around my small kitchen, down my narrow hallway. I recall the size of my bank account and take note of my sweat-pants. I remember how well her sister was dressed in all those Facebook pictures. Sleek hair and heavy makeup, perfect white teeth and a pristine white dress. In one pic, her wrists were covered in diamonds as sparkly as her teeth as she held one side of her husband's award. Well, awards. As in award after award after award . . .

This time it's me who pulls away. "Okay, so I won't meet them."

I don't explain my sudden change of thought, and Nora doesn't ask me to.

chapter

Twenty-one

IT'S A HAPPY DISCOVERY that my bed is the perfect size for two bodies. It's the exact size for Nora to have to cuddle up next to me. Her body is warm, as it always is, and she's lying in the crook of my arm, staring up at me with those seductive eyes of hers. The shine in them is downright provocative, and happiness looks so damn good on her.

The loud knocking of something against the wall is just too intrusive to ignore. Muffled sounds come from Tessa's bedroom, and we try to ignore them, but they are just so extreme.

Suddenly I'm back in my mom's house in Washington, hearing Hardin and Tessa having sex in the room down the hall. I don't even think those two try to be quiet.

"They're awfully loud," Nora laughs.

I do, too. "Oh, this is nothing. Wait until you hear them fight. The people in Jersey will hear them." I've experienced this plenty of times. They don't make walls thick enough to block out those two.

"Are they always this loud?" she whispers.

"Yes. But still not anything close to when they fight."

"He's met his match, though. Tessa isn't someone to trample on." Nora's voice drips in admiration.

"Yeah, he has." I don't say how many tears it took to get to that point. I thought I would have to kill them both on a few occasions. They are both stubborn as all get out.

My phone rings from the nightstand, and I reach for it. Dakota's number pops up, flashing and practically screaming in my dark bedroom.

Nora leans over me and reads the screen. "Dakota."

My chest aches. I hate this part of dating, or whatever this is that I'm doing.

"Answer it."

I shake my head and ignore the call.

Nora leans up on her elbow. "Why didn't you answer it?"

Why? Uh, perhaps because it would be incredibly awkward to talk to her in front of you? Because she's my ex and it's weird between us, and even weirder between you two?

"Wouldn't that bother you?" I ask, unsure how to handle this.

Nora scoots up into a sitting position. "If there's something going on between you still, then yes. But if you don't have a reason for me not to hear what you're talking about, then, no, it wouldn't bother me. Lies bother me. Not truths."

Funny coming from you, I want to say. She doesn't lie, but she's the queen of omission and keeping truths to herself.

"I don't think I have anything to hide, really. I just don't want it to be weird. I know you guys were friends—"

Nora snorts. "We were *never* friends!"

"Well, roommates. That still qualifies as murky water. I don't know what happened between you two that made things turn sour, except me. Was I the only reason?"

"Yes."

A yes—that's all I get. This frustrating woman . . .

"Why won't you let me meet your sister?" I ask suddenly. If she wants to evade questions about her and Dakota, I will just shine the spotlight on something else.

I look directly at her, and she tucks her messy hair behind her ear.

"Is it because I'm a broke college student?"

She jerks, offended. "No. What the hell kind of question is that?"

A reasonable question, Miss Travels the World with a Family of Surgeons. "A fair one," I respond to her angry glare.

"Not fair at all," she retorts.

How do I tell her that I was a grade-A stalker and found her sister's Facebook profile? Should I even tell her? Yes, I should, because I demand honesty from her. It's only fair, and she's all about being fair, right? So I should say something . . . But she'll be mad.

How important is being fair, really? Sometimes it's better to omit things, right? I mean, if I were wearing an ugly shirt and asked Nora if it was ugly, should she lie? Yes. Images of me wearing one of those vacation-dad shirts, the ones with the flowers on them, pop into my head. Yikes. I make a promise to myself to never be that kind of dad. I want to be a cool dad, and if Nora goes around lying about my shirts, I can't be one.

So, no, maybe omitting is just as bad as lying.

"I found your sister's Facebook page and I looked through it. I saw her husband and his gazillion certificates and awards. I saw your beach vacations, and your yellow bathing suit."

Nora's face pales, and she sits in silence.

"I saw her big house and the brand-new car he bought her, and I saw the guy who had his arms wrapped around you."

Nora's breath catches in her throat. I've truly shocked her, and after a few seconds of her blankly staring at me, she manages, "Why—why did you do that?"

"Do what? It's Facebook, it's public property." I defend my stalking with the lamest excuse I could have mustered. That's a horrible answer. And a poor excuse for being a creep.

Nora shakes her head and moves farther from me. "How long ago was this?"

"Just today, when I was waiting for you to come back." Was it just today? Time doesn't seem to make any sense since I met this woman.

"What else did you find?" Her hands are shaking slightly.

I look down at them, and she immediately stills them by folding them together.

"Nothing. You don't seem to really have a Facebook of your own."

She nods, not meeting my eyes.

And I realize something: she totally has a Facebook.

"What exactly were you hoping to find?" Her eyes are on her hands clasped in her lap.

Not so fast . . . I grab her arms and pull her back to me. She doesn't stop me, but she does move her thighs to frame my waist.

Is dating always like this—this squeezing feeling that no matter what's happening, there's always something hidden around the corner waiting for your happiest moments to occur so it can crush you and take them away?

"What are you hiding?" My voice is level, unlike my head right now.

Nora shakes her head. "Why do you assume I'm hiding something?"

I roll my eyes at her and put one arm behind my head so I can get a better look of her on my lap. My other hand is resting on her leg. It feels like the only connection between us right now, like a fraying thread keeping us together. "Maybe because you are. You don't want me to meet your sister. You have some secret Facebook page. You won't talk about your ex-boyfriend—or any other relationships, for that matter—and you've shut me down when I've tried to understand why you hide so many things from me."

I sigh and lift my upper body to rest my back against the headboard for more support.

Nora breathes, gives me that fake smile. "You know what? You wanna meet my sister? Let's go, then. You can meet her after I get off work tomorrow. What time is your shift tomorrow?"

I nod. "I'm off at two."

She nods. "Good. It's settled, then. Now stop snooping around my shit unless you want me to expose yours, too."

I furrow my brows and look up at her. "My shit? I don't have any shit to expose."

Nora laughs. "Oh, yes. You do."

I grip her hips and pull her forward on my body so her butt sits right at the bottom of my stomach. Wrapping my arms around her back, I pull her to lie on my chest. "Explain." I kiss at her, right beneath her ear.

"You and Dakota. I would say that's sure something to talk about. You hide your relationship—whatever's left of it—from me. You don't answer her calls when I'm around. That's pretty shady for someone pretending to be a saint over there."

This woman is absolutely insane. I turn her cheek so she has no choice but to kiss me. "I don't have anything to hide from you, aside from the fact that Dakota and I are friends. She wants more, I think, but I can't give her more." I take Nora's face into my nervous hands. "You've taken it all from me. There's nothing left to give her. You have it all."

Nora softly kisses me against the corner of my mouth. Then her mouth grows fierce. Her tongue makes smooth circles on mine.

"Hm, that sounds good," she says into my mouth.

"You sound good," I mutter, and I'm glad she doesn't seem to notice or care. Her mouth is hot on mine.

chapter

Twenty-two

Nora

*M*AN, IS HE GOOD at distracting me. I pull back a little, to be able to focus again. A few inches separate our bodies, but I keep my mouth on his. His lips are so soft. Too soft for me to be able to pay attention to anything else.

I need to regain my composure.

I open my eyes while he kisses me. His hand moves from my thigh, so I have a tiny bit of control over my body for now.

I look around the room, trying to find a focal point. I spot a hockey poster on the wall; two rows of beady eyes on bulky men gawk back at me. Each of them, hockey stick in hand, is staring down at me like I've done something that deserves their judgmental yet surprisingly hunky stares.

Why the hell does Landon have this hanging over his bed? Sometimes his age is *so there*, like it's a massive neon sign over his head, screaming at me. Like now, when I'm lying here in his bed reading the calendar schedule for a hockey team. He clearly doesn't have women in here often, which kind of makes me love the poster a little more.

But other times, he is nothing but pure *man*. He has an old soul. A wise-beyond-his-years smile and a heart of dripping gold. He's careful, and each of his touches means something. He puts thought behind his glances, his kisses. He doesn't just put his mouth on me, he puts his entire soul into me, taking a piece of me with every drawn breath.

And his body. He has the body of a man; threaded ropes of muscle make up his arms. His cheeks are covered in hair, and his broad shoulders carry the weight of so many others. He's the most thoughtful person—man or woman—I've ever come across. But no matter how I try to justify it, he's still five years younger than me. When our ages are pointed out, when they're focused on, the numbers change things. He feels young; I often feel old.

The air shifts; the energy between us thrums a little louder. He's only in his second year of college—what do I have in common with him?

His mouth moves down to my neck, and his tongue makes sweet swirls against my skin.

Maybe I can name a few things we have in common . . .

But then there's Dakota. She called him again. What am I going to do about this girl? I don't have the energy for this high-school love-triangle bullshit. I'm too old for that. I've done that. I've fought with friends over boys and cried my fair share into bottles of cheap wine. Landon didn't even have time to get her out of his system before I came around, pulling him in the other direction.

Part of me can't possibly understand what he sees in her, besides her appearance. She's beautiful, and works hard for the body she has. But inside, she's rude and dramatic and childish and—

Am I really doing this? Am I lying here, in his bed, with his mouth on me, curating a list of reasons why his ex is awful? Is that the level I've stooped to?

I drag my fingers down Landon's back as he continues to lick at my neck. I've never before felt this content with a man, and I sure as hell haven't ever met a man who, given complete control over my body, would choose only to use his mouth on me until I'm a blissful puddle cradled in his lap on the floor.

Still, he hasn't had time to properly date anyone. He's never even gone out on a date with anyone *other than her*. He's living in his first apartment; I paid a mortgage on a condo. He hasn't had his college experience yet; I had my share of waking up on someone's lawn with a hangover. He's never been to a college party. He's never had a one-night stand. Dakota is all he knows about women.

He has roots with her. She owns a part of him that I'm never going to be able to take away. That part of him, all his first memories, will never be mine. But do I need them? He doesn't have my first, either. I shared them with another man. Why does it bother me so much, then? Is it because my ex isn't hanging over us, still calling my phone while we lie in bed together?

My mind pushes a memory forward: the look on Cliff's face when Hardin had him in a headlock. The way his bones crunched when Hardin's boot pressed them into the floor. Cliff was sent here to check on me. I know it, though I haven't had the courage to ask. I would rather not confirm my worst suspicions.

Dakota begged me right outside this very apartment to stay away from Landon. She wants another chance to make things right between them. I wish I knew what it was that tied them together so tightly. What is it that's hanging between them, left untouched and unhealed, open and bleeding out?

Am I going to be strong enough to put pressure on that wound and find the stomach to stitch it up?

That depends on what it is that they share. I know there's a reason he isn't ready to let her stand on her own; I just don't have a clue what it could be. It's not just her taking his virginity; it's something more.

Still, it's not fair for me to demand to hear it when I'm not ready to share my past with him.

Why would the universe allow this to happen? Why would it allow two people who are clearly still stuck in the limbo of our last relationships to become so attached to each other?

I don't know why I let this mess continue, anyway. I should have left it as a flirty friend-of-a-friend relationship, but I didn't. Mostly because he became an itch I couldn't scratch, and partly because I just couldn't keep my distance. My thoughts of him quickly became unmanageable and uncontrollable, much like his mouth on my breasts right now.

I hold the back of his neck, guiding his mouth to be greedy.

This probably isn't the best time to think about all this, but this is the only time I have. I made a promise to Dakota that I had every intention of breaking, but the pinch of guilt is still there. She isn't that bad when she's not threatening to run her mouth about my life or kicking me out of an apartment that was just as much mine as hers. She can be funny, and even fun to be around. The first time I met her, she asked me to go dancing with her. I had just unpacked my boxes and wanted to get to know my new roommates, her and Maggy.

Dakota got dolled up, in a tight red dress and sparkly black shoes. She had her curly hair straightened out down her shoulders. She looked smoking hot and ready to take on the world, told me she had just gone through a breakup and needed to clear her head. I suggested she dance with Aiden, the tall blonde from her dance academy. If I had known what kind of breakup she had "suffered" through, I would've never suggested that.

I was used to the typical breakups: my friends' boyfriends cheating on them, or one person or the other deciding to focus on a career. Those are the kind of breakups I'm used to being soothed by a night out with the girls.

If I had known that half of her breakup was made up of Landon, I wouldn't have pushed her toward that guy. Back then, Landon was nothing more than a tiny picture cut out from a high school prom picture. He was this college freshman living across the country. Not until I hung out with Tessa the first time in New York did I put it all together.

I had already started paying attention to Landon; we had already had our little moment in his bathroom. Dakota acts as if I purposely sought him out to prey on him just to hurt her. I'm not that evil. I could have pulled back from him when I realized that Tessa's perfect roommate—the epitome of everything I've wanted in a man wrapped into one—was also my roommate's ex-boyfriend.

Landon was the nerdy, devoted boy from Michigan, the one who was afraid of hurting a fly when fucking. Dakota told us so many stories about Landon and his fear of trying new things. She told us that she once tried to get him to take her doggy-style, and he finished before they even started. Which, well, isn't good.

I look up at Landon, the Landon who's mine and mine to keep, at least while his body is under mine. His hands are digging into my hips. His mouth is so possessive. He's saying the things his lips are normally too timid to reveal. I love how full I feel with him. It's hard to explain. He just makes me feel taken care of, satisfied, important, and just *full*—of life, of happiness, I don't know. But I feel a sense of peace with him.

I drag my nails down his stomach, just hard enough to leave thin red marks. They're lines drawn on a battlefield. *He's mine!*, I want to scream to Dakota—but maybe he isn't? Maybe he's too good for both of us, and we would be doing him a huge favor leaving him the hell alone.

She would never, though. She wouldn't stay away from her crutch long enough for him to breathe, and I would like to think I open his lungs. I want him to be free around me, able to be himself and put his own needs first for once in his life. Dakota seems to want to keep him locked away in a childhood romance that she's too afraid to leave behind. If I knew what it was between them, I would have a better footing while trying to navigate.

When she confronted me about him time after time, I should have learned my lesson. She isn't going away without a fight, and I'm too exhausted to give her one. Something has happened between them that made Landon her knight in shining armor and she the perfect damsel in distress.

But what about me?

Where the hell does that leave me?

I don't need Landon for the same reasons she does, but does that make me less worthy of him because I want to bring him up and hold him there, like he deserves?

I don't have the past that she shares with him, but I can make a good future for him if given the chance.

Landon groans as I grind my hips over him. He's hard. He's hard for *me*. His hands are on my body, pulling and tearing at every inch of me. It's a desperate fury that I'm enjoying getting to know. I pull at his hair and drop my mouth to his ear.

"You're so good, Landon. You're too good," I encourage, and he pants beneath me. He makes me feel like a queen—he isn't some peasant to me; he's the adored king. My king, and with him we would rule equally. I wouldn't be stuffed into a dress and heels and forced to be a trophy wife for anyone. Not like Stausey.

That was unfair. Ameen loves her. I know he loves her, and a part of me is envious that their life is what it is. It's not that I want her life; I just want a partner. I don't need a big house with matching towels and china sets, I just want someone to want to spend time with me. I would rather have someone listen to me talk through a movie than wake up to a Mercedes wrapped in a big red bow.

Landon's hands lift to my breasts and he fondles them, claiming the flesh in his strong palms. I would take this over any material thing. I could spend hours and days and weeks with him like this. But my time is running out; I don't have the luxury of time here.

Dakota does. She has years on me. That makes her relationship with Landon more than some child love. That I could handle—if it was over. That same old parable about two childhood neighbors who grow up together and share lemonade on the steps of their childhood homes. Their friendship grows into love, and the rest is history. I had that, too. Even though I find that predictable and a little cliché, there is something to be said about the convenience of it.

I'm talking about something deeper; something happens when you share a tragedy. I know this firsthand. I remember when the worst thing in my relationship with Ameen's little brother was when he told me that my sister was pretty. I was jealous, and only fourteen. I grew out of my jealousy and went on to be friends with him after our breakup. Well, the first breakup.

Since then, we've created our share of adult problems, and now that our siblings are married, the mess has become too big to clean up. Our relationship has been over for a while, regardless of the fine print.

Our siblings remind us how perfect we are and how we spent years eating their fancy cheeses and drinking their sour wine, which was twice my age at least. And now we're going to share a baby, our little niece. The darling angel child that my parents are expecting to mend the crumbled bridge between the two families. I'll be an aunt. He'll be an uncle. But we won't be together. I wouldn't hold my breath if I were my parents.

I know that my sister, and my parents, blame me for the hostile relationship with his parents, but they only blame me because it's easier than admitting the truth.

What was I thinking telling Landon that he can meet my sister?

"What are you thinking about?" Landon kisses his way down the column of my neck and between my breasts. This sweet, sweet man. I can't tell him that I'm analyzing every bit of our relationship and deciding our future while he kisses every inch of my neck and chest.

"That I want you." My lips are on his chin, peppering his jaw, before moving up to his lips. I lift my hips to him, letting him know what I want, and how I want it.

chapter

Twenty-three

Landon

THE UBER TO HER SISTER'S APARTMENT feels longer than the thirty-seven minutes it was supposed to take. On my app it says we have six more minutes until we arrive at the building on West Thirty-fourth Street. I was going to take the subway, but this felt less chaotic. When I got home from my shift, I had a text from Nora with her sister's address, telling me to meet her there at eight. She didn't go into any further details. Just address, time, and a smiley face.

Nora was shy this morning when she left. She kissed me and whispered how much fun she had with me, but Hardin and Tessa were there, so she didn't say much else.

I have a feeling she wanted to get there before me for a reason. Maybe she wanted to talk to her sister privately first. I won't know what exactly I'm walking into until I cross the threshold of the Manhattan apartment. During the ride, I text Tessa twice, but she doesn't reply. I'm sure Hardin has her otherwise occupied.

I glance down at my phone again and do a text check-in with my mom and Ken. I don't mention my plans for the night. I don't need to stir the pot any more than I already have, and I don't want to give our parents any more table gossip than they've already got. I'm meeting Nora's sister, so I'm sure word will get back to my mom sooner or later anyway.

"Is this it?" my shaggy-haired driver asks. His turn signal is on again, and I hope the street isn't a one-way this time. I think he's used to driving in Brooklyn, not Manhattan. This intersection is busy; we're between Ninth and Tenth Avenues somewhere. I haven't spent much time in Manhattan since I moved here. Now I get why locals don't spend a lot of time near all the tourist attractions.

My driver repeats himself and finally turns down his radio. Apparently he really, really loves listening to Linkin Park. I wasn't sure anyone was left in the world who still played their *Hybrid Theory* album, but this fateful Uber ride proved me wrong. That album came out when I was in elementary school, but liking Linkin Park was a staple of being cool during my youth. Something I wasn't, but when wide-leg JNCO pants were a thing, I tried my best. I even wore a wallet chain.

Oh, man, I'm glad there was no social media in those days. If I had a Facebook or Twitter back then, there would be too many leftovers of my wannabe-grunge days. To this day, I can't stand the smell of lemons because I spent the summer spraying the ends of my hair with my mom's Sun In. I have a feeling that my driver had his own relationship with Sun In.

I glance out the window and read the all-capital white letters on the black awning in front of the building on our left: 408 WEST THIRTY-FOURTH STREET. "Yeah. I guess so." Here we go . . .

I climb out of the car and straighten my shirt. I went for a simple, nonthreatening look today. All-black. The shirt is a little tighter than I would have liked, but that's what I get for shopping online and guessing at my size. It's not too snug, though; I think it looks fine.

Well, I hope it does.

As I get closer to the doorman, he waves at me. He's waiting by the entrance, sitting perched on a stool. He looks familiar, like a cartoon character or someone from a movie. When I approach him, I notice just how short he is. His little body is round, and his nose is a tiny bulb covered in broken capillaries.

I brush my fingers over the manicured bushes lining the front of the brick building. Even the outside of this place looks expensive. I pick a small pink flower and toss it back. Why did I do that? Is it a weird impulse to pull a flower from its soil and rip it off? I can't even count the number of times I've done that without thinking. Am I like some secret sociopath who loves to rip flowers out by their roots and toss them back into the dirt?

Am I overthinking this?

Probably.

The doorman and I exchange simple pleasantries, and then he asks who I'm here to see. As he calls up to Nora's sister, I look around the inside of the building, which reminds me of a hospital. White walls, shiny surfaces, and that clean like Pine-Sol and artificial aromas. It's nice, but the only decorations, fake flowers, just add to the hospital feel.

The doorman indicates I can go up to the something-or-other floor and points at the elevators. I was too distracted to hear him right, and I'm a little shy about asking him to repeat himself, so I peer down the long hallway and wander over to where he pointed. All the while I'm hoping Nora will pop out of nowhere and take me to the right place. This is the kind of building that I can't just roam in aimlessly without the cops being called.

Like a miracle, the elevator opens in front of me and Nora is standing inside. Her long, dark hair is sleek and shiny, running down her shoulders in two glossy lines. It's beautiful; she's beautiful. Her eyes are made-up, lined with black wings, and her eyebrows are darker, more defined. She looks so different—not in a bad way, just in a way that I haven't before seen her.

I'm used to her wearing makeup—the red lipstick from yesterday was hot—but today she looks like a woman. Her pristine black shirt and pants are gleaming, like her dark hair and dark eyes. The green is more prominent in her eyes now that the dark lines bring the color to the surface. Her outfit is sexy; the black shirt hangs off her shoulders, and the neckline scoops down like a heart over her cleavage. It's almost inappropriate for her to look this good when I'm supposed to behave myself in front of her family.

"This elevator is too small," I tell her when I step inside.

She smiles at me sheepishly. I take her hand in mine and kiss her palm. When the doors close, she presses a button with her free hand and I gently pull her to me.

"How was work?" I kiss her forehead, then her nose, then the corner of her mouth. I give one last kiss to her hair.

Nora's lips part, and she moves her body into mine, letting me lean her against the wall. "Good." Her lips taste like syrupy gloss. "Did you miss me?" she asks in a hushed voice.

The elevator opens, and I look down at her as she pulls away. "Is the sky blue?" I ask, even tilting my head and smiling my best puppy smile.

Her face lights up, and she shakes her head at me. She touches her long nails to her chin and grins back at me. "Actually, I think the sky is a little gray today." I reach for her waist, but she moves away just in time. "Patience, little one."

I look past her down the hallway, and when she falls for my trick and turns her body, I catch her off guard and wrap my arms around her, pinning her arms to her chest. I use my left hand to move her hair away from her neck and press my lips to her perfumed skin.

"I think you should look again." I pin her gently against the wall of the hallway. No one is out here. Good. "The sky was pretty clear."

My fingertips follow the curve of her full breasts. This is

the best shirt I've ever seen, Nora's chest heaving up and down, up and down in it. She's wearing a black choker, and it makes me want to take her back into the elevator and press the hold button.

Nora licks her lips, and I feel her hands dig into the back pockets of my black jeans. "I guess you're right; it's pretty clear."

She nips at my lips with her teeth, and I groan, pressing her farther into the wall. A door clicks open, and I withdraw from Nora when I hear the clack of high heels on the floor. A woman, whom I immediately recognize as her sister, Stausey, is standing with her hand over her mouth and her eyes wide. She drops her hand the moment our eyes meet, but she can't seem to blink.

"Stausey . . ." Nora says, and I back away from her, tugging at my shirt. "This is Landon."

I rush over and reach for Stausey's hand. She lifts it to me, and I kiss the top of it. She leans in to kiss my cheeks. I don't know which way to turn, and—bam!—her lips touch mine and she pulls back, horrified. Nora's eyes are wide but amused. Her sister, her very pregnant sister, is half-smiling, too, seeming to understand how that European kissing greeting could be confusing to most Americans and people new to New York.

"Nice to meet you." Stausey regards me, her eyes resting on each piece of my clothing, my hair, my hands, and back down to my shoes. She brushes her hand against her dress, and her fingers fuss with the bow around her waist. Her body looks so tiny to be holding such a big . . . a big ball of baby inside. "How was the drive? Long, right?" Stausey guides us to the door she just stepped out of.

"It wasn't bad." I spot a man inside in the center of the room beyond, behind a bar area. The living room is huge, the size of my apartment, and Stausey's perfect specimen of a husband is pouring red wine into a row of stemmed wineglasses.

"I try to stay on this side of the bridge when we're in town.

Brooklyn is just so far," Stausey huffs. Her heels click against the floor as we walk inside. Nora mumbles something about Miranda and *Sex and the City*, and offers me a drink.

I don't know what to say, and I could use a glass of courage. Taking her up on her offer, I follow Stausey to the bar.

*T*HIS IS A QUITE AGED BOTTLE of Château Moulin de Roquette, Landon. It's from Bordeaux," Stausey explains with a touch of a French accent.

I have no idea what she's talking about. I'm assuming she's telling me the type of wine it is? But I wouldn't know the difference, anyway.

I nod and tell her that sounds great; it could be a bottle of $6 wine, for all I care.

Stausey's husband comes around the bar and reaches for my hand. His outfit is much more casual than his wife's. His dark jeans are worn, and he's barefoot. His plain white T-shirt gives me the impression that he's much more laid-back than I expected.

"Hey, man, nice to meet you." He smiles—his teeth are amazingly white. "I'm Ameen, but you can call me Todd." He shrugs and looks at his wife. "Or Ameen."

"Sophia told us a lot about you. I hear your parents live right by ours. What a small world," Stausey says, looking right at her sister.

So she calls her Sophia? Noted. "It really is." I'm unsure what else to say. It's a small world, Stausey, but you appear to live on the top of it.

I look around the room, taking in the grand piano and the

modern furniture. Everything matches perfectly, from the decorative pillows piled on the couch to the painting hanging over the entrance to the hallway.

"Come"—Stausey grabs my hand—"dinner is almost ready." She leads me to the dining room and sits me at the head of the table.

"Landon, come sit by me." Nora pats the chair next to her as she sits.

I nod and go over to her. Stausey ends up sitting down across from me, and Todd sits next to her, across from Nora.

"Todd is the best cook," Stausey announces to us as Nora fills up my wineglass. The food looks great: a roasted chicken with rice and every other starch known to man. Stausey kisses her husband's cheek, and he gives her a smile of pure admiration. "Isn't that right?"

I look at Nora, who's staring down at her plate. When her eyes raise to mine, she smiles and bites down on her lip to keep her smile small. She grabs a pair of tongs from the center of the table and digs into the second platter, stacked high with vegetables.

"So, Landon . . ." Todd begins, being nice enough to initiate conversation since the rest of us don't seem able to, though I do wish he wouldn't have chosen the exact moment I stuffed a forkful of chicken in my mouth to do so. "Sophia says you're studying at NYU? How are you liking it? I had a lot of buddies graduate from there."

Nora takes another bite of her food, and I chew quickly so I can answer him. "I love it. I'm taking Early Childhood Education, so sophomore year is when it gets fun."

Stausey chokes on her bread, and I reach for my water to calm my itchy throat. "Sophomore? I thought you were a senior at New York University?" Apparently, acronyms like NYU are below Stausey's pay grade.

"No, I'm second year. I'm ahead by a few credit hours, but I just transferred from Washington Central after my freshman year."

Nora stares at me with an unreadable expression, and Stausey turns to her, obviously confused. "Hmm," Stausey lets out, and I catch her looking at my wineglass. It must be occurring to her that I'm not old enough to legally drink in their house. And now they have not only let in a random college kid living in Brooklyn, they've broken the law for him.

"I must have misunderstood." Stausey looks pointedly at her younger sister. "Anyway, what do you think of New York? It's a beautiful city, always something to do. Though sometimes I hate the crowds. We live back and forth between here and Washington State, and I love it there more."

Nora tells me that her sister always moves, and Stausey says they're lucky that her husband is such a good surgeon and real-estate investor. How nice. Is this the part where I mention that I can recite almost every line of the first Lord of the Rings movie? My qualifications and his are polar opposite. I don't have much to add to the conversation.

"I can see why you would like Washington," I say, deciding to agree with everything she says to make it easier.

Nora's sister talks of vineyards and benefits and a symphony that they had to wait a month to see. I nod along, and Nora adds a few words here and there. This Stausey, she's quite the talker. I clear my plate and fill it up again, finishing it all. When I'm done, Nora asks if I'm full, and the second that I nod yes, Stausey stands up from the table and brings back a cake. It's good: marshmallow icing and marbled chocolate cake.

I ask Nora if she made it, and she nods. "This is the best cake I've ever had," I say not once, but twice.

"Sophia is the best baker, isn't she? I used to think she was crazy for turning down medical school. It's such a difficult program to get into, and she had a way in. I thought she was crazy, saying she wanted to go to cupcake school." Stausey's tone could pass for passive-aggressive at best. She delivers the blows with such a sweet smile, you would never know what hit you.

But Nora knows, rolling her eyes at her sister. "Looks like the family is doing just fine with one less surgeon." Her plate is empty in front of her, and she's on her third glass of wine. Or was it her fourth?

I don't want this evening to turn sour so fast. I want everyone to be as comfortable as possible, and of course I want her sister and her husband to get the best impression of me possible. The energy in the room is growing tense, and I can feel the four of us walking on a tightrope. One slipup, and we all fall.

"She's a good chef, yes." I take a page from Leo as Gatsby and raise my glass to my lady. Nora's gaze turns to me, and she pulls her lower lip between her teeth. "It's pretty impressive what she can do. My roommate, Tessa, works with her and told me she's the first pastry chef that's been promoted so fast."

I continue to talk Nora up. I remember her annoyed reaction when I referred to her as a *baker* before.

Todd speaks first. "That's awesome, Soph. I knew since you were a girl you were a hell of a cook. Remember when you had that little oven and would make cakes all day?" He takes a gulp of red wine and looks between Nora and me. "One time she got me to give her twenty bucks! For one cake!" Nora's brother-in-law looks at her with pride. This is good. He must be a decent guy if he's willing to admit that he's impressed with her, as he should be.

"Always sneaky," I tease, poking at her thigh. She reaches for my hand under the table, and I weave my fingers through hers.

"Her and my brother used to get in all kinds of scamming business ventures," Todd continues. "They once asked me to buy them a little cart to sell their stuff out of." Todd's gifted with being able to remember parts of Nora that I would love to be a part of.

I take another drink of wine, knowing I wouldn't dare to ask for another glass when I finish this one. "How long have you known Nora?" I ask, but Stausey answers.

"Since she was ten. He met her about when we started dating. We were high school sweethearts." Stausey holds her husband's hands and he looks at me. I remember Nora telling me about his little sister who she made friends with—Pedra was her name? But she didn't mention his brother. Did I mishear her?

"Yes, but it took us a while to figure that out," Todd adds, reminding Stausey that they aren't perfect, despite her seeming need to be perceived that way. I don't know her well. I don't know why I'm judging her at every turn. If I hadn't looked at her Facebook, how I would think of her?

"Stausey and my brother were very close," he says, eyeing me.

Stausey kisses her husband's cheek. "So were we. Ameen and I were inseparable since the day we met."

Nora's thumb rubs circles into my hand, and I wish I could have a few minutes alone with her. I want to ask her how I'm doing, how she's doing.

"When do you go back to Washington?" I ask whichever of them wants to answer.

To my surprise it's not Stausey. She has been quieter in the last few minutes than she had been the entire night. "Tuesday," Todd says. "Stausey is staying here while I go to DC for a conference. I'll swing back by and get her Tuesday and we will take a late flight back to Washington. We have a benefit that next evening; it's going to be a busy-ass week." He smiles, looking a little worried, and it makes me like him more. The idea that "swinging" back by to get his wife from another city is as casual as taking the subway makes me laugh to myself.

Nora looks over at me, but I pinch my lips closed.

"Do you have time to do some baby shopping with me, Soph?" Stausey asks.

It's weird hearing them call her Sophia, let alone a pet name. What would happen if I called her that? And what is with everyone having double names around here? Nora-Sophia and Todd-Ameen. Should I ask them all to start calling me Matthew? That's my middle name, and I could easily start asking my close friends to call me only that. I wonder if it would confuse Nora the way her name switch confused me?

Nora nods at her sister and looks genuinely interested in baby shopping. Whatever type of relationship Nora has with her sister, it clearly doesn't affect Nora's admiration for the coming baby.

chapter

Twenty-five

*a*NOTHER HALF HOUR OF SMALL TALK passes and the table is cleared. The sisters have disappeared into the kitchen, and I'm sitting on the couch with Todd and an army of decorative pillows. One has small foxes on it, spread out like polka dots. The rest are solid colors. Why are there so many? Does anyone actually use them? I push my elbow into the fox pillow to test how soft it is. My elbow sinks into it, so maybe they are comfortable . . .

"Having fun?" Todd's Disney-prince smile makes me slightly jealous of this guy. I mean, he has known Nora since she was a girl, and he's a surgeon and a husband who has a spare apartment in New York City just in case they decide to visit. I share a tiny apartment with my friend and just started to understand how to separate my laundry. Nora is used to being around these kinds of people. People who have their shit together and are old enough to have mortgages and airline miles.

I situate my body and put the fox pillow on my lap and nod.

"She loves her pillows." Todd points to the one sitting on my lap.

"I think it's a woman thing. My mom is the same way." My mom? Really? I'm sitting in an apartment overlooking downtown Manhattan and talking about my mom.

This whole night is totally out of my league. I think about my family's old house and the way the carpet never looked clean. My mom would rent one of those Rug Doctors from Odd Lots and spend two hours cleaning the carpets, but the years of stains just wouldn't relent.

How would it be having Nora in my hometown? Would she shine too brightly for the cloudy Midwestern town? I look around the spacious living room and count the number of chandeliers suspended from the high ceiling. Three are in my peripheral vision alone. I look at the decorations lined perfectly on the mantel above the electronic fireplace. A little metal statue, a piece of wood cut into a triangle . . .

"They will probably be in there awhile." Nora's brother-in-law rubs his hand over his neck. "I'm just glad they're talking again." He sighs and grabs a bottle of liquor from a cart next to the couch. It's full of different types of alcohol and different mixers. There's a lime, a lemon, and even little straws. I guess that's what it's like to be an adult, you get to have a minibar in your house and your wife gets to buy all the weird pillows she wants.

Should I ask him why they weren't talking? Or would that look like she doesn't tell me anything—oh, wait, she doesn't.

I choose to play it cool. "Yeah, me, too."

Todd pours himself a drink. He calls it a gimlet; I don't really understand the language of wealthy people, but I nod along while he tells me the elaborate origin of the gin used in his drink. He offers me one, but I decline.

"Stausey really does love her. I know she can go about it the wrong way and come off a little too strong." He takes a bigger swig. "But she's just worried about her little sister. She barely sleeps anymore, and not just because the baby is the size of a fucking watermelon."

Todd smiles and I find this comparison funny. His wife does look like she's smuggling a watermelon under her dress.

I continue to bullshit my way through the conversation. The

only other option is to tell Todd that I don't have any freaking idea what's going on between the sisters.

"I'm sure Nora appreciates her worry. She's just not that great at taking sympathy from people. You know how she is," I say, even though I clearly have no clue how she is.

"Yeah, you're right." He rests his back against the couch. He looks around the living room like he's searching for something. I look around, too, staring at a huge print of one of his and Stausey's wedding photos. Nora is there, in a beautiful pink gown, her hair curled and lying across her shoulders. The guy next to her looks somewhat familiar, and so does the guy next to him. My discomfort is clearly making me imagine things.

"Look, I know we just met and I'm completely overstepping here, but we are all hoping you being around will be good for Nora. You know, she hasn't brought anyone around us since the accident, and we were starting to think she would never date. It was starting to look like she would never sign those papers."

Papers? Accident? What the hell is he talking about?

"Um . . ." I clear my throat. Why did I turn that drink down?

"I'm glad to hear it." My throat is on fire. I lean up and look down the hallway. Where is Nora?

"We are on her side. That's why we want her to sign them. My family is up in arms over this." He runs his hands over his facial hair and his eyes are strained.

I'm out of resources here. I can only play pretend for so long. He's getting too specific now, and I'm as clueless as ever. I can't believe Nora would bring me into this place without a warning. She did tell me it was a bad idea to meet her sister, but I didn't think it was anything like this, where there would be family drama and talk of papers and some mysterious accident.

"I can talk to her," I offer, not knowing what else to say.

"Really?" His face lights up. "Anything will help. We just

don't understand why she won't sign the papers. They were already separated before any of this. It doesn't have to be this messy, and honestly"—he takes a deep breath—"I would love to have this all resolved before the baby comes."

Yeah. So would I. I would love to have just a hint as to what the hell is happening around me.

"Yeah, I get it. I'll see what I can do." I stand up. I need to find Nora before my head explodes. "Do you have a bathroom I could use?"

He points. "Yeah, straight down and to your left,"

I thank him and the words burn in my throat. He doesn't move from the couch when I leave the room.

I go to the bathroom and splash cold water on my face. It always works in movies when people do that. However, then I dry my face off on a monogrammed towel and feel even more out of my element.

There's too much going on. Nora, this fancy apartment, and the fancy secrets it holds.

I pee and wash my hands. When I stare at myself in the mirror, I look different. Is it the lighting or do the missing patches of facial hair make me look younger?

I don't belong in this place, with these people.

chapter

Twenty-six

*W*HEN I FIND NORA IN THE KITCHEN, she's scooping diced potatoes into a plastic bag. Stausey is sitting at a small round table in the corner of the room. I can practically hear her feet screaming to be let free of their strappy heels. No way they aren't swollen.

"Nora, can I talk to you for a minute?" I stand straight and stare at her, ignoring Stausey. I don't need either of these two to try to get me off track here. I need to talk to Nora, and she needs to explain what the hell I just walked into.

She briefly looks at me and continues to put the dinner away. "Yeah, just give me a few minutes."

I should nod and walk away. I should be polite and not cause a scene. The words repeat in my head: *"papers," "accident," "before the baby comes."*

I stand still in the entryway of the kitchen. My cheeks are hot and my legs want to run away, but I can't back away now. I need to know what the hell is going on. "It's important," I press.

Nora's eyes rise to mine, and I can see her assessing the situation. A flash of understanding makes its way over her face, and she nods, dropping the bag onto the counter. She tells Stausey that she'll be back, then leads us to the roof to talk. There's privacy out there, she says.

"What's going on?" Nora asks as soon as we get outside. It's a shared rooftop, but we're the only ones using it. Good. Nora saunters over to a couch next to the largest table, and I follow. She sits down, and I take the chair across from her. I don't want to get too close to her or I know how this will go. I'm sure that she'll be pulling out all the stops the moment I begin pressing for an explanation.

"You tell me what's going on." My demand sent, I look at her and wait.

The view up here is incredible. I can see the Empire State Building, and if I weren't so mad at Nora, I would be able to enjoy this New York moment. I haven't had many such moments since I got here. I spend most of my time working and walking around campus between classes. The lights are bright, the city is loud and alive, and this would be so much more enjoyable under different circumstances.

Nora leans against the back of the couch. "Do you want to explain to me what happened, or should I guess?" Her voice is steady—cold, even.

"That's a good question. That's a really good question, Nora. Todd seems to think that I can get you to sign some sort of paper, and informed me that you and your sister weren't speaking recently, and mentioned some sort of 'accident' that is apparently pivotal to something or other."

Nora's face is hidden under the shadow of the night, so I can't see her expression. She doesn't move her body, not one centimeter. "He what?"

If I didn't know her better, I would think she was genuinely surprised. "Don't play coy about it. Just tell me, Nora. You brought me into this apartment knowing that I didn't know a thing about your relationship with your sister. So either tell me or don't. But I can't play these games with you. You either want me to be a part of your life or you don't."

Nora shifts and gapes at me. She looks genuinely shocked,

and I can't believe her nerve, or mine. I scoot to the end of my chair and don't look away from her hard stare.

"Obviously I want you to be a part of my life."

That's it. She doesn't say anything else.

Is she kidding? I don't remember the last time I was this angry. I feel like a puppet on strings, and I'm tired of playing this back-and-forth with her. If she doesn't want to open up to me, I'm done trying.

"If that's true, then act like it. Because so far, all I've gotten from you is mixed signal after mixed signal, and I'm sick of trying to figure out what's true and what's not."

Nora leans up and reaches for my hands.

I pull them away. "Talk to me. If you want to touch me, *talk* to me."

"What did Todd tell you? What is it that you want to know?" This is just her way of still not giving me anything.

Frustration propels me to my feet. "Seriously? Even now you're trying to evade my questions."

"You haven't *asked* any questions."

I throw my hands into the air. "Don't play semantics with me. Just tell me what the fuck is going on. Why weren't you and Stausey talking? I was more than willing to give you time to trust me, to open up to me. But this is too much. Todd's in there acting like you're hiding a freaking atomic bomb under your shirt, something I'm apparently supposed to know about but don't."

Nora sighs but stays seated on the couch. "I wouldn't go that far. Look, I don't want to drag you into the middle of my family drama. It's a mess and has been for a while. My parents will barely speak to me, and my sister chose their side. She didn't want anyone to think that she could think for herself, so she chose them, and that's her fucking choice. She's wrong, and that's the end of it. Todd shouldn't be in there feeding his bullshit to you. He's the better one, for sure, but don't trust him. He mastered the art of walking the line between his parents and mine."

Her explanation only makes things more cloudy. My phone rings in my pocket, for the third time in the last hour. I pull it out, notice Dakota's name on the screen, and, once again, ignore the call.

"Would you just answer it, *for fuck's sake*?" Nora snaps at me.

"No. Now, tell me about this accident. Who was in an accident? You?"

I take a few steps away from her so I can get some fresh air. I put my hands on the rail and look down to the street below. These streets are way busier than those in my neighborhood. The taxi honks are louder, and more snippets of music come from every direction.

Nora points to the circular building with lights shooting from the top. "Madison Square Garden is right there. Halsey is playing there tonight."

The talk of music distracts me from my anger. It's a nice—if temporary—relief.

"Why didn't you go?" I know Nora's a fan.

"Because I'm here." Nora stands up and walks over to me. "Now, stop fighting with me and let me touch you." She reaches for me and her fingertips run down my covered arm. "Landon."

She says my name so softly, I can't help but let her wrap her arms around my waist and bury her head in my chest.

chapter

Twenty-seven

"CAN WE STAY OUT HERE AWHILE?" Nora's lips are against my neck. "I'm not ready to go inside and face either of them."

"Yeah, we can. Let's play a game," I tell her, less spirited than the last time we played this game. "I'll ask my questions first."

I don't give her a chance to opt out of participating. I lead her to the couch and look around again, to make sure we're still alone. The wind has picked up on the roof, and her hair is blowing in front of her face. I sit on the opposite side of the couch and prepare my questions. I don't need much time this time.

"Why did you and your sister get in a fight? What are the papers they all want you to sign, and why did you bring me here knowing that I was clueless? And how long had you known I was dating Dakota?"

Nora lets out a dramatic sigh and lifts her legs and props her feet up on the table in front of us. "That's four. But I'll let it pass, given the circumstances." She eyes me. "I was fighting with my sister because she hasn't had my back for the last three years, and I needed to pull away from my family for a while. I'm skipping the next one, and I brought you here because I wanted to make you happy. I was hoping that for one night my sister wouldn't be a cunt, and that they would love you as much as I do. I knew for a little while."

Nora shrugs and leans up to take her shoes off. She drops

the sandals on the dark-stained wood, and I watch her fingers brush over the neckline of her shirt. We are still the only people up here, and for a moment I can imagine the two of us on a roof-top patio drinking sparkling red wine. We are older and without so much weight on our shoulders.

That moment ends with the obnoxious blaring of a taxi horn. I will never understand why the drivers honk, as if it's going to get them anywhere. I miss the luxury of having a car and the freedom that comes with it.

"My turn." Nora lays her feet back on the table. I wish I would have asked for another glass of wine. Not for me, but for her.

"Why did you come here tonight? What did you and Dakota do that binds you so tightly to her? And . . ." She taps her almond-shaped fingernails against her chin. "And if I met your family"—another pause—"and they didn't already know me, what would you introduce me as?"

With that, it's Nora's turn to stare out into the skyline. It really is beautiful up here.

"I came here to get to know you a little more. I had planned to do that by meeting your sister and her husband. That didn't go as planned . . ."

I hesitate, but realize I need to answer the questions Nora listed for me. If we are going to move toward any sort of relationship, I shouldn't be skipping questions. We are past that, right?

Dakota . . . Dakota, Dakota. Where should I start?

"Well, for starters, she is all alone in the world. Except me. I'm it. So regardless of what happens between us or how irrational she's being, I'm always going to look out for her. I know it probably doesn't make a lot of sense to you." I move closer to Nora and stretch my legs out onto the table a foot or so away from hers. "But she's like my family. I can't just completely quit her."

"Quit her?" Nora's brows curve together, but she moves closer.

"I mean quit on her. And for my third answer . . ." I look up at Nora to show her that I'm not skipping. I crack my biggest grin for her. "If you didn't know my family, I would say, 'Mom, Ken, Hardin, this is my lady friend, Nora.'" I dramatically wave my hands through the air, presenting her to the imaginary crowd of the Scotts.

Nora laughs and puts her finger into her mouth. She sucks at it, and I don't know if she's doing it on purpose, but it sure as hell seems like she wants to disarm me.

Not on my watch.

Well, not if I can help it.

I look away from her tempting mouth and pretend she wasn't making vulgar, and sexy, suggestions at me.

"Your 'lady friend'?" Her voice is high and light through the fall air. The wind has died down a little, and her hair sits calmly over her shoulders. The ends, no longer pin straight, have started to curl up. I lean over and touch the strands. I rub my thumb over them, and Nora studies my face. Her hair is so soft. She is just so soft.

"Yes. I think that's a suitable reference for such a qualified woman." I tuck a section of her hair behind her shoulder. I smooth my fingertips over her shoulder blade.

Her chest rises and falls between each word as she says, "And what qualifications are those?"

I hum and continue petting her skin. She's like a kitten who wants to be rubbed and fussed over all day. Suddenly, I'm a cat person. I don't know if I could handle the hair-ball thing, or the pooping-inside-the-house thing. So never mind: I only like kittens in Nora-form.

"Well, you have these." I drag my finger over her lips and up to her eyes. "And these." I touch her lips. My fingers lead down to her breasts, and I stop over her nipple, gently circling. "And this." I touch over her heart and feel it drumming beneath my palm. "This is my favorite part." I flatten my hand out over her, and the moment I do, she's all over me.

She uses her palms to push my shoulders against the back of the couch. My "Whoa" is lost in the cloud of her. She's on my lap, kissing my cheeks, my jaw, my lips, my eyes. She's so soft in my arms, so warm. She's frenzied in a way that I haven't seen her before.

I keep my little antic going, reminding her why she's so special to this world. "Also, you went to college."

Her lips touch against my forehead, and she laughs. When she cups my cheeks and kisses me, I have to open my eyes to make sure this is all real. I have this piercing feeling inside my ribs, poking at my already fragile heart, that the worst is yet to come with us. I can see images of us inside my head, and they come as clear as day. But when I focus on one, it fades quickly, and one by one everything disappears. Nothing feels permanent with her. Why is that?

"Anything else?" She grinds her hips down on me.

When I stop her body from moving, she scowls at me. I lift her hips higher so she's barely touching me. "Not so fast. We were in the middle of a game." I lean forward and touch my face to her chest. "You almost had me."

I bite at her breasts, and she yelps, climbing off my lap.

"Fine, fine," she says, catching her breath. Her skin is lovely under the glittering city lights. The moon is more visible than I imagined it would be from Manhattan. It's still so crazy to me how vast the difference between Brooklyn and the city is.

"Whose turn is it?" She scoots her butt all the way to the other end of the couch and turns to face me, her legs crossed under her body.

Well, if she doesn't remember . . . "Mine."

"Liar!" she cries out with a smile. I shrug, playing innocent. "Do you think you could be with me? Do you think we are crazy for this?" She points her finger back and forth between us. "And what's your biggest flaw?"

My biggest flaw? Could I be with her? Are we crazy?

Are we crazy?

I don't even give my doubt the chance to creep into this moment with Nora. This is between us, no other voices, just hers.

"I am here, with you," I tell her.

She looks away from me, but she's fighting a smile.

"My biggest flaw is that I take on too much from everyone around me. It gets heavy sometimes." I feel guilty admitting it, but I want to be honest with her. She lifts her eyes to mine for a brief second, then looks out to the view again. "And, yeah. I think we are crazy."

"Good crazy or bad?"

We both have reasons to believe the other one is a little . . . I won't say *crazy*.

Interested?

Obsessive?

I'm not sure what to categorize our behavior as, but maybe it's as simple as the two of us wanting to learn more about the other? I followed her all the way from her job to a city over an hour away. I stalked her family on Facebook, and she knew who I was before she led me to believe. We've both had our share of "nosy," and maybe that's why we understand each other?

"Is there a difference? It usually ends the same, doesn't it?"

She inhales a deep breath, thinking this over. "Yeah. It does."

Neither of us looks at the other, and we continue the game. The questions stay neutral and impersonal. Questions that you could ask your friend. *What's your favorite season?* Hers was summer, mine was winter.

Snow or rain? I took snow; she chose rain and told me about her thirteenth birthday party, when no one came, but her sister took her up to the roof of their villa to dance in the downpour. Her parents were furious when the girls came inside soaking wet, ruining the freshly scrubbed floors. Stausey took the full blame, saying she thought the cat had run outside.

Her mention of the cat led her to tell me about Tali, her family cat, who once jumped onto her mom's back when she was walking down the stairs. Nora swears that the cat did it as a favor to Nora, who had just been grounded for two weeks. She can't finish the story because she's laughing so hard, and I decide that my favorite thing in the world is this: I love the way she tells a story, with every single detail intact. She gives a full backstory and supporting details, too. Maybe she should be a writer. She tells me about her sister braiding her hair and teaching her how to apply lipstick. I learn how her mom started to change over the years. She went from a broke cafeteria worker in Bogotá to the socialite wife of one of the country's most prestigious surgeons.

Nora doesn't sound impressed by her mom's lifestyle. I can't tell why.

"What else? I want to know the important things, not what she does for a living. I want to know your favorite things about her. Memories, things like that."

Nora comes closer, and her fingers caress my chest. She runs an index finger through a patch of hair. "Why do you always ask the most intrusive questions?"

"They're only intrusive if you don't want me to actually know." My voice sounds much sadder than I meant it to.

"Fine. My mother is . . . well, she is . . ." Nora struggles for words. "She used to make the best *arroz con leche*."

"Is that your favorite dessert?"

"It's the only one I like."

My jaw drops. The only one? I must have heard her wrong. "The only?"

"Yep. The only." Her voice lowers to a whisper. "Confession: Sweets aren't my favorite; I'm more of a salty kind of gal."

"What? What kind of fraud—!" I'm only half pretending my horror. "But you're a baker—I mean a pastry chef!"

"And?" Nora's smile grows, and I like the way her eyes twinkle under the city lights.

"And? This is such . . . I don't even know who you are anymore." I laugh.

She nuzzles farther into my chest. "So now you question me when I admit that I don't like sweets, but not when I tell you about my mess of a life?" I hear the pain in her voice, the shame dripping from each word.

"Well, everyone makes a mess now and then." I want to soothe the ache inside her ribs. "But I don't think I can come to terms with this."

I start to pull away from her. She latches her arm around mine, but I keep pulling.

"This is too much." I pretend to cry. For a moment, I consider that I'm a total freaking geek on the roof of this fancy apartment building where I don't belong, but the moment passes and I decide that I don't give a shit. "The betrayal!" I bury my face in my hands.

Nora shrieks with laughter. "Oh, stop," she giggles, trying to pry my hands from my face.

I'm not stopping. She's laughing and I love it. I shake my head in despair, my hands hiding the huge grin on my face. "I thought I knew you!" I mock-cry, and she can't stop laughing as she tries, again, to move my hands from my face.

When she pulls harder, I stop resisting and her arms fly with mine and I grab her waist and lay her down on the couch. Playful surprise fills her face, and her eyes are wide on mine. The neckline of her shirt is ridiculously low now that I've rumpled her perfect outfit and pinned her underneath my body. I run my nose from one side of her chest to the other, following the soft curve of the fabric over her soft breasts.

"What am I going to do with you?" I ask, and she groans under my feverish touch. I lick her skin, then pull away. I keep an arm's length between her body on the couch and myself, and I hold myself up using my arms, like I'm doing a push-up.

"I could think of a few things," she says, inches from my mouth.

If I knew for certain that none of her sister's neighbors would join us up here, I would have dropped my mouth between her thighs.

chapter

Twenty-eight

Nora

*D*O YOU THINK WE SHOULD GO INSIDE?" he asks me after another two rounds of our game. I have come to love this game, and he still hasn't skipped a question. He thinks I don't notice.

I notice everything about him. My head is now in his lap, and his fingers are on my scalp, softly rubbing. I could fall asleep like this. When you go so long without being touched by another person, you forget how important that is. It's ingrained into our brains, that we need the touch of another from our first day of life to our last.

"One more round," I suggest. I've saved my planned questions for the last round.

Landon gently pats the top of my head. "One more."

I close my eyes and brace myself for the turn in the conversation. "Did you believe me when I told you that Dakota cheated on you? Did her brother disappearing make you feel like you had to protect her?" Landon's fingers freeze on my scalp. I force myself to continue. "And—"

"Her brother didn't disappear." Landon puts his hands under my shoulders and lifts me off his lap.

This is it. This is the trigger on their loaded gun.

"That's what I know," I carefully explain. That's the story she told me the night that I found her screaming his name in her sleep. I can't imagine—what could be worse than that?

Landon's face is turned away from me when I look at him. I sit up, facing the door to the staircase behind us.

"You don't know anything, then." His voice is flat.

"Well, then tell me. Because this is a wall between us. You want answers to all of your questions, but you don't want to give me anything in return. That's convenient. This is what links you to her so fiercely."

He shakes his head, still not looking at me. "It's not my story to tell."

"Yes, it is. You were a part of the story—it's yours, too." I'm starting to get frustrated; I could be more understanding if I knew what happened. "Landon, you can trust me. I just want you to open up to me."

The irony of this statement is not lost on me.

Landon seems to take this in. He looks uncomfortable, and I feel like a bitch for pushing him this far. I have my share of secrets around my ex and divert Landon's every effort to get to the bottom of what's up there. I will share them with him one day, one day soon. I just need a little more time to make sense of what's happening. I thought I had my mind made up, but Landon is clouding everything, making me unsure about my future.

His voice starts out quiet, and I keep my mouth closed and my hand close to his, in case he wants to take it. "Carter was having a rough time at school. He was the target of a lot of people in our plat, his dad included. Our plat was the worst of them, all families from Kentucky and West Virginia. Stuck in their old ways and bigotry. It was one of those neighborhoods where you would see a rebel flag hanging from the window where there should be a curtain. Unemployment was incredibly high, and the grown-ups had nothing better to do than gossip about what the young people were up to. It was rumored that Carter and his best friend, Julian . . ." Landon pauses, gazing straight forward. His eyes aren't focused. "It was said that they liked to kiss."

"Did they?" My stomach is tying into knots, and as much as I don't want to hear this, I know I need to. I wish I were magical like Landon and could take some of this pain away, the way he does for me.

"They did. The grown-ups could ignore it for the most part, make their jokes about Carter's clothes being a little too tight and his voice being a little too high for their liking. Those were all jokes, their ignorance shining. Everything was fine until a rumor started that he tried to kiss another boy, and then a little boy down the street said that Carter tried to touch him. Then everyone turned on him."

My mouth and heart fall to the pit of my stomach. My insides echo and rattle, not used to the commotion. It's been a while since I've felt this aware of myself, of how I feel about the things happening around me. I seem to care a whole lot more about what's going on in my world now that Landon is a part of it.

"And did he?" Somehow I already know.

Landon's head shakes furiously. "No. He would never. The people around us were so toxic, so disgustingly vile, and too simple to even understand how simpleminded they were. They were the kind of people who would claim they were"—Landon hooks his fingers into quotes in the air—" 'okay with gay people' as long as they didn't hit on them, yet when asked if they are homophobic, they'd say no."

I know people like that. Most of the Barbies at my school were like that. They would say the most offensive things to me, but in their case, I suspect they knew exactly what they were doing. Because of the color of my skin, I had a girl ask which gas station my family owned, even though my dad had saved her mom's ass from the skin cancer she got from sunbathing for too long.

"So then Carter went from the plat joke to the plat villain. It became like a witch hunt. Just how many of the young boys had been around Carter? Out of all the boys he rode bikes with, how many did he try to touch? Out of all the boys he had helped with their homework over the years, how many had he tried to force himself on? Even though no one else came forward against Carter, and the boy who accused him said he'd just been lying—that his older brother put him up to it because Carter 'creeped him out'—the accusations became a thing. And his dad didn't need another reason to take his anger out on him. When the whispers turned to shouts and the shouts turned to three big black letters painted on the side of the house, his dad had enough. It took me and Dakota to get his dad off of him that night. He missed school the next morning."

Landon's voice crumbles and I move to his lap. He wraps his arms around me, holding me to him like it will somehow comfort him. I wipe at the tears on my cheeks, not sure when they'd begun to fall. Landon's words are painting too vivid of a picture. I remember the night Dakota was hiding under the kitchen table. My stomach lurches. That poor girl.

"We came home and found him. She didn't want to leave." Landon clears his throat and I wrap my arms around him, holding his head to my body. "I had to drag her out of that room, Nora. She snapped, she wasn't even in her body when I pulled her out of his bedroom. She screamed and screamed and even tried to claw her way back in there before the police came and got him down. He'd hung himself in the night, as injured as he was after his father's beating."

A shiver takes over Landon's body and I'm sobbing into his hair. I can't imagine their pain and the trauma that came along with such an event at a young age. No wonder the two of them are the way they are. If Dakota didn't have Landon, where would she be today?

"I'm sorry. I'm so sorry." I rub my hand down his back. I

shouldn't have pressured him to tell me. This was much more than I expected to get when I began this sick little game. "I shouldn't have forced this out of you." I apologize profusely over his head. Images of the unfair treatment of a teenage boy because of who he liked to kiss break my heart. Suicide in any form is awful, but suicide among teens is especially hard to come to terms with. When you're young everything feels so important—every crisis is your whole world and it's impossible to see a light at the end of the tunnel. There's no comfort when thinking of the empty future of an innocent child.

"Shh." His arms hook around my back. "Shh. It's okay."

He's comforting me? I move my hands to his jaw and lift his face to mine. "I could live a thousand lives and never deserve you."

The truth sits heavy with me as he pulls me tight to his chest. I'm falling in love with him and he doesn't even have to do anything. I'm going to fall in love with him, and he doesn't even have to love me back.

chapter

Twenty-nine

Landon

I N THE UBER BACK TO MY PLACE, Nora is quiet and I feel lighter than before. Even after saying an awkward goodbye to Stausey and her husband, I felt better somehow. A sense of relief came to me with each word Nora and I spoke to each other on the roof. There's less for us to climb over now that we've torn down some of the wall between us. It's still there, but relationships aren't simple. The more I get to know Nora, the more I realize Dakota's and my relationship was too much for our age. We fell into a comfortable pattern of dependence, but no matter what happens, I will always be here for her. Nora seems to have a better understanding of this now.

Now that I've shared the worst day of my life with her, I feel closer to her. Why is it that it takes pushing my pain onto her for us to feel closer? Pain shouldn't be something we feel better sharing. Pain is supposed to be dealt with in solitude, isn't it?

Hell, I don't know. Even though I think about that day often, I haven't relived the entire ordeal in a long time. Carter's death had the biggest influence on who I grew up to be. It changed everything I thought I knew about loss and love and pain. I knew nothing about pain or suffering until I held Dakota's thrashing body down on a cold linoleum floor as the paramedics dragged her brother's still body from his bedroom.

They had to give her a shot to get her body to calm. She slept in my bed that night, curled up to my chest, and I could feel her heart breaking every time she woke up and realized it wasn't a nightmare. Her brother was gone. Dakota's dad was nowhere to be found, though I was sure that if we looked hard enough, we would find him at a bar.

Nora keeps shuddering in my arms, and now I'm not sure if telling her was a good idea. I could have told a less detailed version, I suppose. I wish the memories from that day would fade. I keep waiting for that to happen, but it hasn't yet.

The farther we drive from Manhattan, the more distance I feel between Nora and me. Whatever happened on that roof definitely brought us closer, but the darker it gets, and the farther we get from the glimmering city, will we be able to keep this going? Will the darkness make it easier to hide from each other?

"I'm sorry about tonight," Nora finally says when we get to my building. She unwraps her limbs from mine and slowly climbs out of the car. The quiet night of Brooklyn has penetrated our Manhattan bubble.

"It wasn't all bad." I shrug, trying to make her feel a little better.

I can tell by her expression that she isn't buying it. She doesn't say anything as we step onto the sidewalk.

"Do you want to come up?"

She nods and I reach for her hand.

I hear a ragged breath, and then Dakota's voice cuts through the darkness. "You haven't answered my calls all day,"

Nora drops my hand. Dakota stands up from the ledge she was sitting on. She has a leaf in her hand and she's picking at it, dropping pieces to the sidewalk beneath her.

"What are you doing here, Dakota?" My voice is calm. I would love for the three of us to be able to have a civil discussion out here on my sidewalk. A group of young guys walks into the store below my apartment, and my gaze follows them inside and over to the counter. Ellen is working, alone it seems. I watch them, while watching the two women next to me. Nora is standing slightly behind me, not looking at Dakota. Dakota is standing in place, her fingers still picking at the leaf. I wonder if Nora sees Dakota in a different light now—perhaps Nora will understand her a little more?

My eyes take in both women, and I find my memories are mixing with reality. I was just in the past with a broken, sobbing Dakota, and now here she stands, hands on hips, hair and attitude as wild as ever. She doesn't look broken anymore. Does that mean she isn't?

Surely not. Tessa doesn't look broken, but she's falling apart, tearing at the seams.

"I tried to call you all day." Dakota's voice is so quiet, but loud enough for me to hear the edge beneath the words. "This is my second time coming by here. I was just leaving." Dakota stares straight at Nora. "You were supposed to tell me about Michigan."

Michigan—how could it have slipped my mind? "How's he doing?" I ask, trying to gather an answer in my head.

"The same. Since you were ignoring my calls." Dakota's eyes dart to the ground. She looks like the words pain her. "I'm going to assume that's a no. You could have just told me no."

And there's the guilt. Do I deserve it? I can't decide.

Sometimes situations arise where black and white aren't so clear as you grasp for the right answer, wishing the gray didn't exist. This is one of those moments for me. I'm a good person, aren't I? I'm a loyal friend and a stand-up citizen. I help women pick up their groceries, and I once turned in an envelope full of cash—$200, to be exact—to the police in Saginaw. I've never considered myself to be one of those people who find pleasure in causing others pain. I've never had to doubt my intentions or consider that maybe I'm not so perfect.

The thought is weird. This entire time I was judging all the guys around me, all the guys who cheat on their girlfriends and betray their friends, thinking of them as the scum of the earth, and I'm somehow better?

I've lied to Dakota's face about Nora. I slept with Nora and I don't think I ever even thought about telling Dakota. I would normally think this wouldn't be her business—why wouldn't it? She's a big part of my life and she trusts me, yet I was going to keep Nora hidden from her? To make it worse, I have been hiding Nora away like a dirty little secret while making her feel bad for not telling me about *her* past?

I'm not the good guy, the nice friend. I've turned into the manipulative Gamemaker. Not that I'm having innocent children murder each other. Would Nora be the Peeta here in my story, or the Gale? I'm even more manipulative than Katniss—at least she's fighting for her life; I'm just going back and forth between two women who care about me, and I can't seem to figure out what to do. So it's like I'm toying with both of them. Whether it was my intention or not doesn't change the reality. I could have just told Dakota no or yes, instead of ignoring her calls all day while her dad is dying! What's wrong with me? Is this what dating someone is? Losing touch with reality at the expense of everyone else?

That's doesn't seem fair. Or worth the hassle.

"I'm sorry. I should have answered when you called . . ." I start, not able to keep my eyes from peering at Nora, then back to Dakota. "It's been a long night."

I don't catch on to how insensitive my comment was until the words have had a few seconds to marinate in the stiff air.

"Well, I'm sorry to interrupt your *long night*." Dakota's teeth are bared. "I'm flying out in the morning. Your aunt Reese is picking me up from the airport and dropping me off at the hospital."

At the mention of my aunt Reese, my chest aches. I miss her. She offered a sense of normalcy during my entire childhood. Her and my uncle are two of my favorite people. Well, were. When he was alive.

"I'm sorry, Dakota." I take a step toward her.

Her voice interrupts me. "Go with her."

It's Nora's voice.

I turn around to face her. I must have heard her wrong. Her eyes are sad when she looks at me. "Go with her, Landon."

"What?" I whisper, and put my hands on her arms, now crossed at her chest.

She nods and quietly repeats, "Go with her. It's the right thing to do."

I cock my head to the side, clearly misunderstanding what's going on here.

"I'm serious. Being sad for her doesn't take away what we have. It's the right thing to do."

"Landon can speak for himself." Dakota's voice is pulled tight by a string stretching all the way back to our childhood.

"I was trying to *help* you." Nora pushes forward and Dakota moves toward her. I don't know if I can keep the peace tonight. I have no energy to break up a catfight.

"You two, stop it." I push my arms out to my sides between them.

Dakota keeps her distance, but doesn't keep her mouth shut. "Maggy has been trying to get hold of you, too."

Dakota narrows her eyes at Nora, and Nora shrugs her shoulders. "And? I don't live there anymore—there's nothing to talk about."

Dakota doesn't seem to like that answer. I look back inside the corner store to check on Ellen. I don't see her behind the counter. I start moving toward the store and Nora grabs my sleeve.

"Let go," I snap at her. I rush a "Sorry" from my lips, but she couldn't possibly have heard it.

When I pull the door open, the guys are checking out. They are loud, and the two smallest ones are tossing a candy bar in the air between them. Only one of the boys even notices me approach them. He looks at me, but doesn't seem to care that I'm there.

When I look out the door, I see Dakota and Nora talking at a close distance. Neither of them appears to be shouting; this is a good start.

"How much is this?" one of the boys asks Ellen. His voice is deep for a teenager, and I think they have been in here long enough.

Ellen is bagging a small bag of Doritos, oblivious and moving efficiently. She takes a $10 bill from one of the boys and makes him change.

The kid looks down at the five in his hand. "I gave you a twenty." He bought a Mountain Dew and the bag of chips.

"You gave me a ten," Ellen says flatly. She turns her head like she's trying to make sense of what's happening. I can see her questioning herself.

I speak up from behind the boys. "You gave her a ten. Now take your stuff and get out."

Slowly (good thing this isn't a video game, because I would have had them all on the floor by now) they turn around and look me up and down. I get a good look at these kids, and just as I'm trying to figure out if they're going to get aggressive, I hear Dakota yell behind me, *"Get the fuck out!* Whatever dumb shit you're thinking about doing is going to change the rest of your life. If you want to have one, *walk away."*

The crowd of kids (the oldest can't be a day older than fifteen) clear out quickly, grumbling to themselves as they pass. Dakota doesn't look at them. She's staring at me.

I don't know what to do. It's been so long since we've been able to communicate wordlessly. Once we could have held an entire conversation this way. I think back to how she was before. It's hard to put the young version of her up against the one staring back at me now. It's confusing to recognize someone so deeply, yet feel so disconnected. Dakota's expression is puzzled when I force my eyes away from her. Carter is fresh on my mind tonight and looking at Dakota pains me.

I walk over to the counter and approach a confused Ellen. She's straightening out the plastic bags under the register. "You have to be careful down here working so late alone. Do you have anything to protect yourself with?" I glance around the back of the counter. Boxes of papers are stacked at her feet, along with an open tool case. Well, I guess she could have used one of those hammers if she had to . . .

"I'm fine—and I'm the only one who can work this late," she says a little harshly.

I wish it were as safe for her to work alone at night as it would be for me, but the truth is, that's not the reality. And I don't want to embarrass her further by asking *why* only she can be here at night. I don't doubt her, and it's not something I can press.

"Just be careful, okay?" I say. "And call your dad every time a group of boys comes in like that."

Ellen rolls her eyes, but I believe her when she says that she will. After I suggest that she close up for the night, I go back outside.

Just as I step over the doorway, Dakota is in front of me. "Is she okay?"

I nod, looking over Dakota's head to search for Nora outside.

"Landon, I tried to warn you about Nora. I know you won't

believe me, but she's been lying to you from the beginning." Dakota's voice is rushed and I can feel the anger radiating off her. "She knew we were together. She lied to me and to you. She's—"

"Enough," I say, not a drop of hesitation in my voice.

I look at Nora standing alone on the sidewalk, her lips parted, and her shoulders high. She's working hard to keep the flat expression on her face. I can see her concocting all kinds of theories about me and Dakota in her mind. To make it worse, Dakota takes my hands in hers. Nora flinches, but keeps her face flat.

"I can't believe you would still see her and bring her to your place when I've been trying to get hold of you all day. It would have hurt less if you would have just told me. I've had to guess and be an obsessive ex because I get no real answers from either of you. You both have spun a web so intricate that you can't get out."

Noticing for the first time Dakota's outfit, I try to figure out what her plan was tonight. She's wearing a slim-fitting shirt with a serious V-neck. Her tight black jeans are a far cry from her usual workout pants, and the makeup on her skin is glowing under the street lamp.

What was she thinking when she came here? Was she going to try to seduce me into going to Michigan? Or to stay away from Nora?

Or both?

"Dakota"—my anger peeps out from behind each letter of her name—"I said that's enough. You can't just come here and act like this outside my apartment. This isn't Saginaw—instead of people just listening to our business, they'll call the cops on me."

"Landon"—she squeezes my hands, but I pull away—"ask her about her rich family, about her even richer husband. He . . ."

Dakota's voice is still going, moving through one hole in my head and out the other. But I can't hear a single word she's saying.

Husband?

"When we kicked her out, she acted like she didn't have any-where to go. But she *did*—she has a mansion outside of the city. I've seen it."

Scarsdale. The way she changed her clothes. How come she wouldn't let me follow her.

Something, something, something . . . Dakota goes on. Nora is looking up at me and her brows move together. I can feel my face changing, I can see it in her confused eyes.

She's *married?*

Of course she is.

chapter

Thirty

IKE A ZOMBIE, I push past Dakota and stand in front of Nora. "A husband?" My voice is high, broken at best.

She blinks at me, and I hear Dakota approaching behind me. Nora sighs. "It's a long story."

A long story?

A long story is adding a lot of details to something. A long story is much simpler than a secret freaking husband. This is worse than her being a spy. Much worse. She has a freaking *husband* and yet is acting like I just found out she had a sandwich for lunch. I don't know if she really doesn't see how big a deal—how *grown-up*—this situation is, or if she just doesn't take me seriously. I feel like she's writing off my emotions, and I'm exhausted. I can't keep playing cat-and-mouse with her when she's never going to give in. I need answers.

"A story you didn't share me with me," I quietly say. "A pretty important story."

Nora nods, calm and collected, the exact opposite of me right now. I feel like I'm being stuffed into a closet that's too hard to escape. Is she worth all of this trouble? Why can't she just tell me what's going on? I thought she trusted me.

I look at her and try to see inside her. I explore her, remembering how much progress we made tonight. The memory of her laughter rings through my head. The way her fingers feel massaging my skin and the way her sweet mouth tastes. She's left a pretty hefty mark on me. I don't know if I'll be the same after she's done with me.

Another thing I can't forget is how she has been making me feel so good about myself. So powerful. So normal. So okay being me.

But how much weight does that tiny dot of truth hold when it's swimming in a lake of secrets and lies?

"I'm not going to stand here and fight with her all night," Nora whispers to me, just out of Dakota's earshot.

But Dakota clearly has other plans. "Oh, so you *didn't* tell him?" she exclaims loudly. "Well, don't feel too bad, she didn't tell us either until we got a bill for him." In my daze I don't hear the rest of what she says, but Dakota keeps harping, and I know one of these words is going to cause one of us to snap. It's like the whistling of the wind just before a storm, you can feel it coming.

Nora explodes right back. "It wasn't any of your business, Dakota. And it still isn't. I didn't tell you anything about my life because it doesn't concern you. You're not entitled to know what's happening outside of that apartment. The only thing you should be concerned about is whether or not I paid the rent."

Dakota snaps her mouth shut and opens it again. "You—"

"Both of you—stop it! We aren't going to stand here and bicker all night." I look at both of the women, wearing identical expressions. "*Stop* it." They both look so surprised to be called out.

Dakota talks first: "We aren't bickering. Just tell her lying ass—"

"Stop it!" I raise my voice.

Dakota's eyes widen. Nora is silent, staring at me with calm eyes. I need to talk to her, alone. With Dakota here nothing is going to get resolved. "Dakota. Go home. I'll come get you in the morning. Text me your flight and I'll see if I can get on it. But you need to go, now." I look at her to make sure she knows I'm serious.

"You're choosing her over me?" Dakota asks, and my stomach aches.

I know what she's thinking: after all this time, all of our memories, I'm choosing a stranger over her. It's not that way at all, but it's going to be how she interprets it. This must be strange for her; I wonder if she feels her little world shifting the way I do? I've never done anything in the past that would even be considered close to choosing anyone over her. I've had her back since we were kids, since she caught mean old Mr. Rupert's dog and tried to drop it off at the animal shelter for its protection. Misguided, granted, but she thought he was hurting the dog. But I saw the best in the headstrong little woman then, something that's hard for me to see now. The Dakota I know is hiding under this jealous, immature stranger in front of me.

I refuse to feed the little green monster on her shoulder.

"This isn't a competition. If you don't go, there's no chance I'm going with you tomorrow."

Dakota stares at me, waiting for me say another word. I don't. I have nothing more to say.

I turn to Nora, and she watches Dakota walk away behind me. I can see her from the corner of my eye, and if she says another word, I may lose my temper. I'm fuming, irritated at both of these unpredictable women and at myself for not keeping a better hold on what's happening in my life.

Nora slowly drags her eyes up to mine. "I—"

I hold my hand up, letting her know it's my turn to talk. It's funny how she chooses now to want to talk to me.

I keep my voice down and wait for a man walking his dog to pass by. The dog stops to pee on a trash bag on the sidewalk. Listening to which is a lovely way for us to spend a few tense seconds.

"Before you speak, just know that I'm done playing games here. I'm done with the questions and skipping answers. If you want to be a part of my life, you're going to let me be a part of yours. Think about this before you reply. I'm serious, Nora."

I don't know the extent of what I'm getting myself into, but I know nothing can be worse than being out here, attached to this woman, while remaining utterly unsure of who she is. I would like to think that I know her better than this, that some magical explanation is behind her secrets, but staring back at her now, I'm just not sure. I wish I knew her, and I miss our rooftop in Manhattan. At least that's one thing about Dakota: I always knew her secrets. I was a part of them.

Nora's eyes are glossy when I look down at her. "Can I come up?" She reaches for my hand.

I pull away, but lead her inside my building nonetheless.

chapter

Thirty-one

Nora

*I*S THE ELEVATOR ALWAYS THIS LOUD? The changing air pressure and mechanical noises are making me nauseous. Or maybe it's just the inevitable talk I'm about to have with Landon that's clawing at my insides. When we step out, even the lights in the hallway feel brighter than they usually do. And we are walking abnormally slow. Part of me wants to tell Landon that I have to go and run away and never look back.

I could erase him from my life just as quickly as he came into it.

He pushes his key into the lock and holds the door open for me to pass. I walk under his arm and he clicks the lamp on. Under this light, he looks harsher, all angles, and the softness of his lips is shaded by the darkness.

Like this it's easier to imagine walking away from him. When the light is on and I can see his innate lightness, it won't be so simple.

Tonight has changed the way I look at Landon. Before Dakota showed up, I was getting to know a different side of him. I felt his pain and guilt and I saw him as a protector, a man doing his best in a tough situation.

"Do you want a drink?"

I follow him to the kitchen but think, *Not unless you have a bottle of vodka I can chug down*.

Landon doesn't turn the overhead on, and I listen for Tessa. The apartment is silent. She must be asleep or out. It's late. I don't even know what hour it is.

"A water. Please."

He grabs a water, and a Gatorade for himself, from the fridge, then slams it shut.

Is he mad?

What a stupid question, of course he is.

I follow him to his room and he tells me he's going to take a quick shower. I don't know if the extra delay will make this better, or worse. I nod and he turns his light on, grabs clothes out of his dresser, and leaves me alone in the room. I lie back on the bed and stare at the ceiling.

So Landon is going to Michigan with Dakota. Just the two of them, their memories, and their hometown. I laugh pathetically at my own expense and hastily wipe the tears from my eyes. Her dad is dying; I'm being incredibly selfish by even thinking about myself right now. The sad truth about what happened to Dakota's brother was just one layer of what they have shared. I shouldn't have tried to come between them in the first place. I let myself get distracted, and now everyone around me is suffering because of it.

Landon deserves a quiet life. He deserves to have peace and quiet and a calm love. He's steady, he's the kind of guy that makes sure things are okay. With him I wouldn't have to worry. But he would be getting the short end of the stick. In trade for the comfort he would bring me, he would be thrown into the hectic web that is my life. He has a nice family, not one driven by greed and the desire for notoriety.

The tears burn the back of my eyes and I force myself to sit up and get my shit together. Sobbing on his bed and feeling sorry for myself isn't going to get me anywhere. Tonight is the last night that he's mine, the last time that I will feel his hands on me, if I'm lucky enough for even that.

I climb off of the bed and walk to the bathroom. The door is unlocked and steam billows out into the hall. I close the door quickly and lock it behind me. I drop my clothes to the floor and take a deep breath before I step into the shower. Landon's body is under the shower stream, water coating his naked frame. His eyes are closed and his chin is lifted so his face is directly under the water. He doesn't make any move to let me know he's aware of my presence, but he doesn't flinch when I wrap my arms around him.

I lay my cheek against his wet back and hold him. We stay like this for minutes, hours, who knows, and then he finally turns to face me. His hands wrap around my back and I lean into his chest. His heart beats for me and mine aches for him.

When I put my fingers under his chin and try to kiss him, he turns his head. Pain slices through me. I better get used to this feeling. After I tell him everything and he spends time alone with Dakota, we will be done anyway. I'd known this day would come since the first time I kissed him, but I hadn't expected to care as much as I do. This was all just supposed to be fun, and I was going to be the older woman he could fuck for a few weeks and then we would go our separate ways. But now that he's turned away from me, I don't know how we got here. When did we cross the line from friendship to this?

What is this?

I start to apologize. "I'm sorry about—" I don't even know where to begin.

"Don't. Let's talk when we are . . ." He looks down at me. "Let's get dressed."

I agree with him, not because I want to, but because it's what he wants. Right now I want whatever he wants.

When we step out of the water, he grabs a towel and turns to face me. Landon bends down and rubs the towel over my feet and up my calves, drying my skin. He's dripping wet himself, but here he is kneeling at my feet, worrying himself with drying me.

My throat burns with words for him, but I can't find them. I pull at his arms and make him stand up. With the same towel he used, I dry his body. He doesn't stop me; he closes his eyes, and I take my time collecting the droplets of water on his body. I ask him to sit down on the toilet so I can reach his hair, and he obliges. His eyes and mouth are closed, and I wish I could re-wind to the first day I met him and have a do-over. If this were one of those fantasy books he likes, I could cast a spell and turn back time. I would concoct some type of truth serum to slip my-self so I would be forced to tell him the truth from the start.

I reach for the pile of his clothes on the back of the toilet and take the black briefs in my hands. I bend down, touching his thigh, and he lets me dress him. He balls his fist, then flexes his fingers, and repeats this over and over until I'm finished. His green T-shirt is wrinkly and his wet hair is a mess on his head. It hurts me to look at him.

I dry my body the rest of the way and grab my black pants from the floor. He tugs at them and takes them from me. "I'll give you something to wear." He collects my clothes from the floor.

I wrap the towel around my body and follow him to his room. When the door closes behind us, I drop the towel. Landon's eyes rake over my naked body, and I shiver under his gaze. He pulls his drawer open and hands me a pair of light gray briefs and a sleeveless shirt.

He doesn't look at me as I dress, and my insides feel empty. I know it's a superficial thing, wanting him to crave my body, but his deliberately looking away from me only fuels my insecurity.

When I'm dressed and feeling even more vulnerable than before, I sit on the edge of the bed. He takes a drink of his Gatorade and joins me. He hands me my water.

There's no point in stretching this out any longer.

"I got married when I was nineteen." Landon sucks in a breath and keeps his eyes level on the wall. "I did it for a number of different reasons. To rebel against my parents, to better piss *his* parents off, to be able to go to college for free. I didn't want a dime of my parents' money for college. Marrying Amir was the answer to that. Once married, my income was no longer based on my family's wealth."

Landon seems to take this in and, as always, hits at the heart of the matter. "And where is your husband now?"

If only it were that simple. "My husband is in a field somewhere between here and Scarsdale."

That's where his spirit is, anyway.

Landon's forehead creases and he looks over at me.

"At first, we were just kids who signed a paper and were suddenly married. Both of us felt like we were getting out of the iron grip of our parents. We were in young love, the kind where everything is great until an actual problem comes along."

I pause. *Do you love me like that?* I want to ask Landon.

"And so when real problems came up, like his drinking and failing out of college"—I should have written this down; it would have been much easier than explaining such a complex situation—"his parents blamed me and threatened to cut him off financially. But I couldn't control him, I barely knew him anymore. But I tried, and of course he got angry with me. But he told me that his family wanted him to sign away some land they had purchased in his name. He didn't tell me why, but I did my own research and realized his parents want to make a fortune off the land. Of course they care for their son, but they'd been planning his life for him for years before the accident, and when their plans were ruined, they came up with a Plan B: Get the money from me and sell the land off. With the money, they could build another hospital and plaster their family name on it.

"They wanted him to give away his land to them, like his loyal brother had, but Amir refused. I remember the day I had to drag Amir out of his father's office. He was livid, screaming that his dad was a fraud, a liar. He didn't speak the whole way home, but that was the day I realized I married a friend, not a lover.

"On paper, we had everything right. Our fathers were business partners, our siblings were engaged, we were both well traveled and from wealthy families. The problem was that the small things I loved, he hated, like baking. It would be fine if he had no interest in baking but at least ate the food. But he didn't; he wouldn't even try what I made half the time. His passion was real estate, which I had absolutely no interest in whatsoever. Our families were tied together with money and egos, and the two of us fell into a game we didn't even know we were playing. How perfect would it be if we rebelled and got married without a huge wedding? Our materialistic families would be pissed off, and the thrill was worth it all. We conspired together, but we never had much in the realm of intimacy, physical or emotional."

And after all that, as I'm feeling breathless at having said so much to him—more than I've said to anyone on the subject maybe ever—all Landon says is, "And what does this have to do with you now? Are you separated or not?"

Landon is young. Too young to worry about separations and marriages and legal documents and land deeds. All he knows are his feelings. He doesn't understand the power struggle within a rich family. He's untainted, and here I am staining him.

"Because." I drag a deep breath through my lungs. "Now that he can't sign anything himself, they expect me to just hand over the land. But I won't. Amir doesn't owe his family anything, and I don't either. They would have already unplugged him and let him die if it wasn't for me."

Landon jerks his head toward me. He's struggling to put two and two together.

Why didn't I just tell him? Now that it's out, it doesn't seem so bad. I wish everything were simple. My problems probably sound like rich-girl problems, but that doesn't make them any less relevant in my life.

"We were never happily married. We were childhood friends who made an adult decision we weren't prepared for. It was easier to stay married, but we were seeing other people. Well, he was."

"I'm missing a piece of this." Landon rubs his hand over the back of his neck. "How long has he been . . ."

"In care? He has an in-home system now. His own nurse at his house."

"*Your* house."

"Technically, yes."

"How else is there to be? Technically you're married and have an entire part of your life that you kept from me until someone else forced the truth to come out. Why didn't you just tell me any of this? I would have been able to deal with it, with you. But now everything about you seems fake and dishonest, and I don't really know what to think."

I swallow. "I know. I'm sorry for dragging you into this."

Landon turns his body to me in a swift move. His eyes are harsh. "No. You didn't drag me into anything. You kept me on the outside until you couldn't anymore. God knows how long you would have kept me in the dark."

I shrug. I don't have an answer to that.

"Did you not think you could trust me with this? I really don't get it."

"It's not that I didn't trust you, but this is heavy shit. You're in *college*, Landon." I look down to his shaking hands in his lap and back up to his eyes. "You have exams to worry about and a life to live. You're young, you shouldn't be worrying about this kind of shit."

He stands and his arm swings across, knocking into the wooden headboard. "You don't tell me what I should be worrying about!"

I join him on my feet. "You aren't even supposed to be this involved in my life!" I shout back at him.

"Okay, Nora. You go ahead and try to flip this around and make this my fault. Make up your mind: either you want me and we can figure this out together, or you don't."

I blink at him. "What?"

"What?" he repeats, his hands in the air.

I feel the tear drip down my face before I can stop it. "I can't believe after all this, you're still trying to be accepting . . . and want to give me another chance." I could live a thousand lives and never deserve him.

He shakes his head and stops pacing around the room. "Well, what's it going to be? You decide."

"What about Dakota?"

His eyes spit fire at me. "What about her?"

"You're going to Michigan with her. You two will be alone . . ."

"Are you kidding me? *That* is what you're worried about?" He sits down on the bed and drops his face into his hands.

I had expected this to go a different way. I thought we would go into his room and decide this was just too messy to continue, and he would be sad when I left, but he would be fine tomorrow. My head aches.

Maybe I *can* compete with Dakota? Maybe he *would* choose me?

The story of her brother haunts me, haunts them. The way Dakota went into the convenience store after Landon while I just stood there on the sidewalk. I watched her take his hands in hers, and I watched him not pull away. When she finally walked away, she sobbed into her hands. The reality of it is, my first love is long over, but theirs isn't.

"Touch me," I tell him. I walk over and stand right in front of him and beg him to touch me. I need one last night with him. His hand hovers over my face and I close my eyes as he brushes his thumbs over my cheeks.

"I'm sorry," I say when his finger glides over my lips. I don't tell him what I'm sorry for, but soon enough, he will get it. He will thank me for backing away from him now. Better late than never.

I know how to end this, how to overpower and distract him while I end this.

My hands move to his stomach, to the hard muscles, and I pull at his shirt, to bring him closer to me. His mouth is soft when it touches mine. I could kiss him and kiss him and kiss him and never get my fill. I push him back to the bed. I push at his shoulders and climb on top of his body. I take all of him, circling my hips over his. My hair falls down my back, wet and cold, and Landon's hands move up to fondle my breasts. I take my time with him, slowly scratching my nails down his taut stomach as I move over him. He sighs, he pants, he says my name. I tell him that I can't get enough of him and he agrees, pulling my body to his chest as he comes. I feel him shuddering in pleasure and I try not to cry.

What happened to me? Who is this weak woman crying over the body of a boy she's too complicated to be loved by?

I lay my head on his chest and close my eyes before the tears can fall. I breathe in and out, hoping he doesn't recognize my emotions.

When he falls asleep, I gather my clothes and leave him in the quiet of Brooklyn.

• • •

When I get to the gate of the house, my eyes are swollen and raw. My chest is heavy and my body is weak. It was a long drive here, and it was too late to call a driver. The entire ride on the train, I stared at the seat across from me, remembering the night Landon followed me. The more I try to push the memories back, the heavier they force themselves on me.

I push in the code for the big metal gate, and the cab drives away. The gate creaks open, and I walk slowly up the expansive driveway. Manicured trees and flowers line the way, as if there were life in this estate. I look up to the dark house perched on top of the hill. There's no life here.

The house is silent except for the quiet running of the fish tank and the beeping of the machines as I get closer to the master bedroom. The nurse's car is parked out front, so I know she's here somewhere. Each of my steps echoes from the walls, and I wonder if I would have loved this massive house if things were different.

Would I have learned to love my husband and raised a family in this house? I look up to the chandeliers suspended above me and at the expensive art hanging on the walls. One-of-a-kind paintings and chandeliers for a man who will never see them.

The bedroom door is unlocked, of course it is, and I push it open.

Amir is sitting in his chair.

His eyes are closed.

His face is freshly shaven and his white cotton shirt is unbuttoned at the top.

He was such a beautiful man.

He *is* such a beautiful man.

In the morning, I will yell at his nurse, Jennifer, for leaving him in his wheelchair all night, but for now, I drop my bag and sit at his feet. I lift his heavy arm and lay my head on his lap. The breathing machine hisses, and I move the hose away from my feet and drop his arm over my head.

I don't cry, and for the first time in a long time, I can imagine myself living here, in this room, with my silent husband, for the rest of my life.

chapter

Thirty-two

Landon

THE FLIGHT FEELS SO MUCH LONGER than three hours. I was lucky to even get on the flight on such short notice, but nothing felt charmed this morning. The sun wasn't up when I woke up with a text from Dakota and an empty bed. Nora left in the middle of the night, sending me reeling again.

I feel so much older than twenty, and Dakota seems so much darker than the ballerina I once loved. Her eyes are heavy when we land, still swollen from last night's tears.

I don't look at her long enough to feel guilty. Those tears weren't for me. They were for herself.

While Nora was in my bed, Dakota was sobbing in hers.

When we get to the baggage claim, Dakota stares blankly at the circling luggage belt, so I tell her to go grab a seat, and she nods. I point to the empty row of chairs next to her and she sits down.

Next to me a woman holds her baby, and I think of Nora holding her sister's baby. When I see another woman with long, dark hair, I think of Nora; even a *Game of Thrones* ad on my flight's TV screen made me think of her. Everything reminds me of her, and a small part of me hopes that she can't look at anything around her without thinking of me.

The luggage comes quickly, and I gather it and walk to Dakota, who looks as if she's going to fall asleep any moment.

"You okay?"

She looks up at me with hollow brown eyes and nods. "I'll be fine."

Working toward breaking the habit of pushing for more, I nod instead of telling her that I don't think she's okay after all.

The Kia I rented is nice, but it smells like cigarette smoke despite the NO SMOKING warnings plastered all over the interior. Dakota remains silent most of the drive, and I'm so focused on her state that it takes a few minutes for me to start recognizing my old town when it appears on the other side of my windshield. I drive in silence, my hands clutching the steering wheel, as we pass the old building that housed the Blockbuster my mom used to take me to on Friday nights. Every single Friday we would order from Pizza Hut and rent a movie. Now the building looks as abandoned as the dusty old VCR on my mom's mantel in Washington. I glance over at Dakota, wondering if she remembers the time she stole a Baby Bottle Pop from in front of the counter at Blockbuster. We ran with wild abandon down the street while Carl, the short manager with blond hair, chased us. The rumor around the town was that Carl had just gotten out of prison, and maybe he had, but he never caught us. From then on, I told my mom I was more into watching TV than renting movies, and fortunately she bought it.

The farther I drive into Saginaw, the more the roots of the town take hold of me. I feel like a stranger here, an intruder. At twenty, I've seen more of the country than most of the people in this town.

When we stop at a red light at the intersection between Woodman and Airway, I look at Dakota again. "They tore down the McDonald's." We used to have one of those classic McDonald's right there on the corner, but now there's nothing but a plot of concrete.

Dakota doesn't look at me, but she glances out the window. "There's a new one." She points to a box-shaped building with yellow arches down the road, then drops her hand back down to her lap.

I nod toward another patch of concrete where a locally famous bar used to be. "What happened to Dizzy's?" Memories of dragging Dakota's dad through the doors flood me, but I stay passive, neither a smile nor a frown on my face.

Dakota shrugs. "I heard it burned to the ground. I'm not surprised."

A distant memory pushes through my brain, splaying itself in front of me.

Dakota's dad, Dale, leaning against the wall of the crowded bar. In one hand he held a beer and, in the other, the waist of a short blonde. The woman's body was stubby, compact. Her hair was curled around her face, and she had clearly lived her better years in the eighties, as she still tried to force the style.

When Dakota pushed through the crowd, I followed closely behind her. She found her dad, intoxicated by booze and this woman. Before he noticed Dakota, she snatched the beer from his hand and tossed it into the trash can near his feet.

"What the fuck?" He looked up to see his daughter.

She straightened her back, took a deep breath, and prepared for battle. "Let's go," Dakota said through clenched teeth.

He looked at her and had the nerve to laugh, to actually laugh in the face of his only daughter.

The pouf-haired woman looked from Dakota to her shitty excuse for a dad and then to me. I stared at her, warning her off, but she didn't move. Instead, she took a swig of her drink and squared her shoulders.

Dakota tugged at Dale's shirt. "Let's go."

He furrowed his brows and looked down at his empty hands. "What the hell are you doing herrrrr-e?" he slurred.

My stomach churned.

The strange wannabe Farrah Fawcett stepped forward and wrapped her slimy hand around the back of Dale's neck. Dakota's brown eyes seemed to turn red under the dimly lit bar lights. She hated the idea of her dad with another woman, even though she knew her own mother wasn't coming back from Chicago.

Dakota's eyes set on the woman, and I reached for Dakota's shirt, pulling her back to my side. "Come on, Dale, it's late. You have work in the morning," I said.

"Why are you kids in a bar, anyway? Take your asses home and leave us be." Dale's lips moved to the woman's ear, and Dakota lurched forward. All day she had been surprisingly stoic for a fifteen-year-old girl who had buried her brother that same morning. But not now—now she was feverish and savage, pushing past me to shove at his shoulders, her small hands pounding against his chest.

I lunged for her, grabbing her by the waist, and I pulled her to me. "If he doesn't want to leave, that's his problem. Let's go."

She shook her head furiously, but obliged. "I hate you!" she shouted as I pulled her back—

"I'm glad that fucking place burned to ash. It's more than it deserved." Dakota's voice brings me back to the present.

"Me, too."

We drive on through our hometown. It feels like ages since I left this place, and the gnawing pang of discomfort in my stomach makes me feel guilty as I turn left onto Colonel Glen Highway. When we get to our hotel, a woman is in the parking lot, barely clothed, with sores on her face. She's swaying back and forth on her feet.

"Welcome to Saginaw, Land of Heroin-Addicted Prostitutes." Dakota's voice is meant to be flat, but I can sense the slight tremor of fear at the ends.

I turn off the ignition and stare past her, into the lot. "I doubt she's on heroin." I'm not sure if I really mean the words, though.

When we check in to our room, I ask the woman behind the desk for two beds. Dakota tries to hide the sting, but I saw her flinch when I asked. She knows that we are here as friends, life-long friends—nothing more, nothing less.

The hotel employee, Sharon, hands me two keys, and after a short walk we find our small room, which smells like moth-balls and looks like jaundice in the light of the desk lamp. It's not like there are a ton of hotels to choose from here, and since we waited until the last minute to come, I had to take what I could get. I didn't exactly tell my mom that I was coming, so I couldn't use her member reward points at the only nice hotel in this town.

While I search the walls for another light, Dakota sits her bag on top of the bed closer to the window and tells me she's going to shower. I could definitely use a shower, too. I check my phone and read the messages from Tessa: If you need anything, I'm here and Be careful, in every sense of the word.

I reply that I will indeed be careful, and I remind her not to share my little adventure with my mom and Ken. Not that I'm not old enough to make my own travel decisions, but it's just something I would rather not have them worried about, and worry they will.

It's a little after ten when Dakota comes out of the shower. Her eyes are red and her cheeks are puffy. The idea of her crying alone in the shower makes me lose my breath. Instinct, the evil little thing, makes me twitch to grab her into my arms and hold her until her eyes turn from veiny red to a milky white.

Instead I say, "I'm going to order some food," and turn over the booklet on the desk, searching for room service. There doesn't appear to be any. "No room service," I mutter.

Dakota tells me she's not hungry. I look up at her, her small frame wrapped in a white towel and her curly hair soaked, drip-ping down her exposed shoulders and chest.

"You're going to eat. I'll order Cousin Peppy's," I tell her, and she almost smiles. "Remember how we used to order it and have the driver come to my bedroom window so my mom wouldn't wake up?" I pick up my phone from my bed and search for the number.

Dakota stays quiet as she rummages through her bag. I order a pizza, bread sticks, and a two-liter of pop for us to share. Just like old times, I think. Then I look over at Dakota, who's walking into the bathroom to get dressed away from me, and remember that this is nothing like old times.

When she emerges from the bathroom, she's wearing an oversized T-shirt that hits right at the middle of her thighs. Her brown skin is shiny, and I can smell her cocoa-butter lotion from here. When I tell her that I'm going to shower, she nods and lies down on the bed. She's so distant, almost like a zombie, but worse. I would rather her try to eat my flesh than lie how she is, curled up on her side, staring at the window.

With a sigh, I grab a clean pair of briefs and walk to the bathroom. The water is hot but the pressure sucks. I need it to beat down on me to get rid of this aching kink in my shoulders that doesn't seem to want to go away.

I use Dakota's lotion. It's the same kind she's used since I can remember. I love the smell of it and try to fight my brain's urge to trip down memory lane. I brush my teeth, twice, even though I'm going to eat soon. I brush my hair. I brush my growing beard. I'm stalling, I know I'm stalling, but I don't know what to say to her or how to comfort her from a distance. I only know one way, and that's not the right way for us. Not anymore.

After another few minutes of being a coward, I walk out of the bathroom. Dakota is still lying on the bed, her back turned toward me and her legs curled up to her chest. I move to turn off the light just as a knock sounds at the door.

The pizza! Of course, the pizza. I pay the college kid, who smells like weed, and close the door behind me. I lock it, both locks, and call for Dakota. She immediately rolls over and sits up. Since I didn't remember to ask for plates and Steve the Stoner didn't bring any, I grab two slices and set them on top of the bread-stick box.

When I slide the pizza box toward Dakota, she takes it in silence. I'm going to go insane if she doesn't speak soon. It's hypocritical of me to think that, since I myself haven't said much of anything that doesn't have to do with pizza.

We eat in silence, a silence so deafening that I break it by turning on the TV. I set it to the local news and cringe when they start talking about politics. Enough of that. I flip through the channels until I get to the Food Network. *Diners, Drive-Ins and Dives* is much less likely to give me a headache than a political debate. I can't believe I waited twenty years to be able to vote and these are my choices.

After eating only one slice of pizza, Dakota puts the box back on the desk and begins to walk back toward her bed.

"Eat more."

"I'm tired," she says in a small voice.

I stand up and grab the pizza box, open it, and hand her another slice. "Eat. Then you can go to bed."

She sighs, but doesn't meet my eyes or argue with me. Dakota eats quickly and gulps down a glass of pop and goes back to her bed. She turns over on her side and doesn't make a sound.

I eat until my greedy stomach is full and bloated, and then I lie back on the mattress and stare at the ceiling until my eyes burn for sleep.

Thirty-three

*T*HE NEXT MORNING IS COLD, colder than I expected it to be. I leave the hotel to get us Starbucks while Dakota is still sleeping. Since I moved away, they built one with a drive-through out by the mall. Living in New York, I forgot how much I've missed drive-through anything. I miss being able to drive through somewhere and get pop, candy, toilet paper. It's convenient and laziness at its finest, but it's one of the few things I miss about the Midwest.

To my uncomfortable surprise, the person who scans my phone at the window is Jessica Reyes, a girl I went to high school with. Come to think of it, I went to elementary, middle, junior, and high school with her. She looks the same, just a little less alive. Her eyes have bags under them, and her smile isn't as bright as I remember it once being.

"Oh my God! Landon Gibson!" she says in a slow, drawn-out voice. I smile, not sure what to say. "I heard you live in New York City now! What's it like? I bet it's just crawling with people every-where, like it is in the movies. Isn't it?"

I nod. "Yeah, it's pretty crowded." I want to turn the conver-sation away from myself the best way I can. "How are you?"

She leans a little farther out of the drive-through window. "I'm good. I got a job here, and they give me good insurance for me and my boy. I have a little one now. I had him right after we graduated. Do you remember Jimmy Skupes? He's the dad, but he doesn't help me any." Her face scrunches up in disgust, and I try to imagine Jimmy Skupes, with his baggy jeans and frosted-white-tipped hair, as a father.

Living around strangers for the last two years has made me realize that not everyone discusses every detail of their lives in a simple conversation. It's weird to be back to a place where over-share is the norm. If I logged in to Facebook right now, I would find out what Jessica had for lunch, or why she and her boyfriend broke up. I would be able to watch her life through a screen. The thought is unnerving.

"I'm glad to hear you're doing well." I can see the drinks I ordered sitting on the counter just behind her, but I get the feeling she isn't going to hand them over just yet.

Jessica says something to one of her coworkers, then turns back to me. "I heard about you and Dakota breaking up." Her eyes turn to a pity-filled green. "You were always too good for her. I never liked her anyway. Her brother was much nicer. Man, why couldn't she have been the one—"

"Jessica." Whether she likes Dakota or not, she doesn't have the right to say such a disgusting thing. "I really have to go." I nod to my drinks behind her.

She nods back and tells me to stay strong. After settling the drinks into the car's cup holders, I tell her to have a good day; the things in my head I really mean aren't something I ever want to say to a woman. Gripping the steering wheel tight, I drive back to the hotel, and when I open the door, I find Dakota pacing across the room from wall to wall, her small body looking like she might fall over any second.

"Landon, where were you?"

I set the drinks down next to the TV and turn to her. "Getting us some coffee. I thought you would still be asleep when I got back. I didn't want to wake you up."

Dakota nods, and I can see the physical change in her body now that I've explained myself. "I thought you left."

I shrug. "Where would I go?"

"Back to Brooklyn," she says quietly.

I push my straw against the table and tear the wrapper off. "Don't be ridiculous. I wouldn't just leave you here in Michigan." I take a sip of my Frappuccino, and Dakota grabs hers. I was tempted to get an Americano, but something about the dreary sky over this town stopped me from bringing my New York drink here, and this choice feels nostalgic.

"Guess who I saw." I turn to Dakota, who's now sitting on her bed with her legs crossed. I make sure I don't keep my eyes on her for too long or think too deeply about her only wearing a T-shirt and pink cotton panties.

"Who?" she asks between sips. Her hair has dried now, in wild waves around her face. I always loved her hair.

I loved the way the curls bounced back when I gently tugged on them.

I loved the way her hair bounced when she laughed. The smell of it, the soft texture.

Stop it, Landon.

I get back on track. "Jessica Reyes. She works at Starbucks. The new one by the mall."

Dakota doesn't have to struggle to remember the girl. That's how this town feels: you can be gone for years, but you'll never forget it.

"She told me to tell you hi," I lie.

Dakota's fingers move her straw around the top of the whipped cream to catch a dollop. "Hmm, I never liked her. Always so negative."

After Dakota talks to her aunt, we finally head out to the hospital to see her dad. He's in Sion, the new facility built last year. With all the residents complaining about the struggling economy in these parts, it strikes me as weird that all this new construction keeps popping up. The new McDonald's and Starbucks I get, but the new one-hundred-store outdoor mall loaded with major department stores and expensive restaurants—I don't get. If there isn't any money in the town, who's shopping there?

When we get to the reception desk, I give one of the nurses our names. She tells us she's going in that direction herself, so with a smile on her lips and a clipboard under her arm, she leads us to his room. I hate the smell of hospitals. They remind me of death and sickness and they creep me out. There's always an odor just beneath the antiseptic cleanliness.

We follow the nurse down a long corridor and I can't help but look into every room that we pass. I know it's rude, but I can't stop my eyes from examining every single person lying on their deathbed. That's what they are all doing in these rooms, dying. The thought is sickening. What if I'm the last person they see before they die?

Man, my mind is becoming a dark, morbid place.

Finally, we get to the room. When we enter, Dale is sitting straight up on the hospital bed with his eyes closed. After a few seconds they are still closed, and a small chill runs down my spine. Is *he* dead?

If he died while we were drinking Starbucks . . .

"Mr. Thomas, your daughter and son-in-law are here to see you." The nurse has a calming voice and thick black hair pulled back into a sleek ponytail. Her dark eyes are serious, and her assumption that Dakota and I are married stings, but there's something I like about her. Maybe it's the lack of sympathy in her eyes when she looks at Dale. When she looks at Dakota, yes, there's some there, but not when she looks at the monster before us. His white skin is blotchy with yellow stains and deep purple bruises and his eyes are sunken into his sockets. His cheekbones are hollow slopes down his face.

Dale's eyes open marginally and he looks around. For a dying man, his room is notably empty. No flowers, no cards, no proof that anyone aside from his nurses have been near this room. I wasn't exactly expecting a welcoming party. When he looks in our direction, his eyes find me first. After looking over me like he doesn't have a clue who I am, he turns to his daughter. He lifts a thin arm and waves for his daughter to come closer.

"I . . ." He clears his throat. "I didn't expect you to be here." His voice is so hoarse, and a wheeze accompanies each breath he draws. His arms are twigs, his bones sticking out like the rocky edges of a cliff.

Dakota puts on a brave face. If I didn't know her better than she knows herself, I would never realize that she was terrified and an emotional wreck inside. She's holding herself together bravely, and for that I lift my arm to her back and caress it.

"I didn't expect to come." Dakota moves closer to the hospital bed. Her dad is hooked up to more machines than I expected. "They told me you're dying."

He doesn't blink. "They told me that, too."

I keep my eyes busy by reading all the signs on the wall. A pain chart, leveling 0 to 10. Level 0 is a smiley face; 10 is a red face. There are no smiles here, so I wonder, what is Dale's level of pain? And if it's anything over a 5, does it make him regret drinking his life away?

Or does it even matter to someone like him? I bet it hasn't even crossed his mind that his death is leaving his daughter alone in the world. Not that he's been of much use ever, but now she is down to no one, and she has to deal with the repercussions of his life choices. She's a twenty-year-old who has to bury her father.

Acknowledging me for the first time since Dakota and I walked into the hospital room, he has the nerve to ask, "Why is he here?"

"Because you're dying and he was nice enough to come here

with me from New York," Dakota responds in a low, cold voice. I hate the way this man makes her feel small. Her voice changes, her entire stature changes when this asshole is around. Whether he's dying or not, I've never hated anyone more than this man.

He looks at me condescendingly. "How nice of him."

I dig deep for something—anything—that will make me feel bad for him.

Dakota and I both ignore his comment, and she sits down on the bed. "How are you feeling?"

"Like I'm dying."

Dakota smiles. It's small, but it's there.

He waves one scrawny arm in my direction. "I can't talk to you in front of him. Make him go."

"Dad." Dakota doesn't turn around to me.

I don't want to be in here anyway. "It's fine. I'm sure he doesn't want to be reminded of the awful shit he's done. I'll go." I walk closer to his bed.

He jerks to the side. Well, as much as he can. "Get out. You have some nerve coming here after you took my daughter from me. You and your mom—" He starts coughing and is struggling to breathe.

I don't care. I push past Dakota and stand over him, feeling all-powerful. I could easily put us all out of our misery and . . .

"Landon!" Dakota pulls at my arms.

What the hell am I doing? I realize my hands are raised in fists. I'm threatening a dead man with nothing left to lose. I can't believe the level of hatred burning inside me right now. Now I understand how it's possible for people, even the purest people, to snap.

I breathe out and step back. "I'll leave the car here for you." I leave the room.

The last time I look at the monster, I take him in as a weak, frail man, and the look on his sunken face is almost enough to erase the image of his beating his son to a pulp. Almost.

I struggle for breath when I leave the hospital, and I sit on the bench outside for thirty minutes. I meet the eyes of too many sick people for one day and stand up. I don't know where I'm going, but I can't sit here anymore. What was I thinking coming here in the first place?

I roam around the parking lot and count the cars. I check my phone. I count the trucks. I check my phone. Finally, I call my aunt Reese. After she yells at me for not telling her that I was coming—that I was the reason Dakota no longer needed a ride—she meets me at the new Starbucks. Jessica has gone home for the day, which I'm more than okay with.

After an initial hug hello, my aunt sits down and immediately sees that something is wrong. "So, what's going on, Lan?" She moves her head but her hair stays still. She has the same hairdo she's had my whole life, and I wonder if her hair-spray company has a lifetime loyalty program?

I shrug. "Dale's dying. Mom's about to have a baby, and I'm going to fail my next exam. Same old, same old."

Reese gives a wry chuckle. "Well, that sense of humor stayed intact. How are you? Do you like the city? I miss you, and your mom. How's that husband of hers? Do you like him? How's his son? What's his name . . . Harding?"

"Hardin. And you talk to my mom all the time." I take a drink of my third coffee of the day.

"It's not the same. She could be lying. She's happy out there, right?"

"Yes." I nod. "She's happy. Very."

"Are you staying long?"

I shake my head. "No. Only two days."

I talk to my aunt for three hours. We laugh, we talk about

old times and new, and I feel much lighter than I did this morning. I didn't mention Nora, not once. I don't know what to make of that.

When I get back to the hotel, Dakota is lying in bed. It's still light outside. Her shoes are still on her feet, and her tiny shoulders shake when I close the door. And like that, I know he's dead. He's *finally* gone.

What a horrible thing for me to think.

No matter how horrible, it's true.

I walk over and sit down behind this frail girl. When I gently turn her shoulder, to get a look at her, her face is twisted in pain.

I lift her up and gather her into my arms. She fits in my lap, like a tiny bird.

"I'm sorry," I say, and rub her back, and she sobs into my shoulder. Her arms tighten around my neck, and she cries, "I'm not."

Her honesty is pain-fueled, like mine, and I can't judge her for it. The death of an evil man is hard to mourn, even a father. It seems like people are expected to pretend the dead person was perfect and speak highly of them at their funerals. It's uncomfortable, and the morality of it is murky at best.

I hold Dakota until her tears run dry. She climbs out of my lap to use the restroom and comes back quickly. I'm reminded of the day we buried her brother, and the memories flood over me. Are we ready to leave the past in the past? Everything included? All the tears, yes, but what about the good times? What about all the nights we chased lightning bugs and the days we chased the sun? All the firsts, all the seconds, and the thirds. This woman has been such a big part of my life—am I ready to let her go?

She nods, asking if she can climb back onto me, and with a resolved sigh I open my arms for her.

chapter

Thirty-four

THE ROOM IS QUIET. Dakota is asleep, and my laptop burns bright through the dark hotel room. Today we signed the paperwork to cremate Dale's body. Dakota didn't want a funeral, and I didn't blame her.

It's four in the morning. I check my phone again. Nothing from Nora.

I should have known that she was making her mind up to walk away from me. I should have been able to tell by the slow movements of her hips and the soft kisses to my forehead as I finished inside her. I miss her body, her laugh. It feels like months, not days, since I said goodbye to her.

I pull up Facebook again. I know this isn't healthy and that I won't find anything new this time, but I type in her sister's name again. I scroll to the beach picture, where Nora looks like the sun in her yellow suit and the man next to her is holding on to her waist. If he were able, would he choose her?

I'm able, but am I capable of choosing her?

Why does everything come down to a choice, this or that? What if I want it all? What if I want to spend my days holding her and my nights loving her? I look over at Dakota. Does she think about me the way I think about Nora?

Is it fair of me to think about Nora while Dakota is grieving and I'm supposed to be here for her?

I look back at the screen and put the cursor over Nora's face. A name pops up. Her name. I click on it and it takes me to a profile that I didn't see before. She must have had it hidden from me. I don't know if it makes me happy or sad to know that she doesn't feel the need to hide from me anymore.

She doesn't have a lot of posts here, mostly just random horoscope posts and people tagging her in random chain things and recipes.

"She has an Instagram."

Dakota's voice makes me jump. "Huh?" My cheeks are hot with embarrassment and guilt.

"She has an Instagram page." Dakota shuffles in the dark and, after a few seconds, hands me her cell phone over the space between our two beds. The screen is full of little square pictures. It's a profile. Nora's name is in the corner with an X next to it.

I look up at Dakota, but she rolls back over. She's either wanting to give me privacy or she's hurt that I'm doing this in front of her. I turn the TV on, on mute, so it maybe appears like I'm doing something else as I scroll through the images.

Food, and lots of it, fills the screen. Beautiful pastel macaroons and sprinkled cookies galore. A picture of a cake with purple flowers makes my chest throb. The next picture is Nora and Tessa, a dollop of pink icing on each of their noses and their arms wrapped around each other's back. Tessa's arm is outstretched as she takes the picture, and I laugh at the idea of my best friend, who is so behind on technology, trying to take a selfie with any kind of grace. I scroll on.

My face is there, more than once. There's a picture of us in front of Juliette and another of my scrunched expression as I try to read the menu. There are candids of me in my kitchen, even one of me with Hardin, captioned *Light & Dark*. Hardin's dark clothing and bowed head contrast with my appearance; we walk side by side, my face turned toward him with a goofy smile plastered across it. It's strange to look at, but the picture itself is actually really, really cool. They all are. Each caption is abstract and poetic. Sometimes they're as simple as just a hashtag symbol with no letters, and other pictures have longer captions, such as a paragraph about the beauty of seeing a child laugh for the first time. There's a picture of Nora with lighter hair and darker makeup sitting in a tight dress that looks like it's been painted onto her skin, specifically designed for the full curves of her voluptuous body. In front of her sits a cocktail, and she's holding a little piece of paper up to her painted lips. It reads: *I see light coming toward me and I'll do my best to keep you on.*

There are pictures of her sister, round with a pregnant belly, and others of her before the belly, looking beautiful and regal with full makeup. I see my face a few more times, and my heart rattles inside me; I feel both baffled and remorseful at the same time. I miss her, but I'm angry at her. To say I'm confused would be the understatement of eternity.

There's a set of two pictures of me, looking away from her, with the sun shining bright in the background. The two photos are nearly identical. Their captions are different, though. The first has the same words from her familiar love-note-inspired cocktail. I remember the night I found out that Dakota and Nora were roommates. The night began with some promise but quickly turned sour. Every detail from that moment with her floods my memory.

I've noticed her taking pictures of things before, but I just didn't really think too much about it. Since Tessa has joined the world of Apple products, she's on her phone all the time. I'm even on my phone a lot, checking scores or looking at my work schedule. There's always something to do on the interwebs.

This entire time I'd been focusing on her not having Facebook, or lying about it in one of her many attempts to keep herself hidden from me. But now, here I am staring at an entire collage of her life. Dakota even makes an appearance a few times: she and Nora sitting cross-legged on the floor of their apartment, a board game between them, bottles of wine by their feet. And when I see the pink phone, I remember playing this game with Dakota and Carter when we were younger. It would usually be me and Carter playing while Dakota cooked dinner and their dad slept on the couch—or wasn't home at all.

I need to move my thoughts away from that time in my life. The hole from the loss I shared with Dakota seems to steal the air from every room we're in together. With the loss of so many people . . .

Her sorrow is in control of the room, even though she's trying not to show it. She rustles on the bed and tugs at the fabric of her T-shirt, and I know she's awake. She knows that I know she's awake. She knows that I know that she knows—and so on forever.

I choose to be selfish for once and look back at the little screen instead of at her. The caption on the second picture reads: *You chase the winter and I chase the summer. And, darling, the two will never meet.*

A chill runs through me, and I tap out of the screen and toss the phone back onto Dakota's bed.

A dreadful silence draws a long breath. Her voice is quiet in the dark. "Landon?"

"Yeah?"

She doesn't turn around when she asks, "Do you love her?"

I think about my response and how it may feel for her to hear it.

"Yeah. Yeah, I think I do."

Dakota sighs from her bed. "When did you stop loving me?"

How on earth can I answer that? I don't know if there *is* even an answer to her question. I'm not sure that I ever stopped loving her. I look over toward her and remember how she felt in my arms as she slept. Most importantly, is four a.m.—right after I told her I love someone else—really the time to have this conversation?

And still, I can't hide from this forever.

"I don't know if I'll ever stop loving you, Dakota."

"Stop lying."

Her voice is harsh. Her back is turned to me. I need a moment to prepare an answer for her. I'm too tired to fight, but I need her to understand that she hasn't been in my life for six months. Six months. That seems so much longer right now, in this hotel room with two beds and empty Starbucks cups in the trashcan. She still smells the same, and her slender body has grown into an athletic, toned figure. She works hard, and she looks incredible. It's strange to think about the difference between her body and Nora's—they are equally beautiful and so different; neither is better than the other. I would be the uglier of the couple with either of them. The difference, though, is that it's deeper than their exterior—it's the energy, the connection, the expectations from each woman.

I sound like I'm filling out an application on a dating app.

I wait a few seconds for Dakota to say something about my silence. She's lying still, her back toward me, and the old TV doesn't give much light to this vampire-dark hotel room. I had stepped over a used syringe in the parking lot, so maybe it's just part of the package. When I was younger, it wasn't this bad. This city used to be pretty cool, and I have a lot of good memories from this place. But drugs have taken over because the economy in the Midwest has fallen and there aren't good jobs to soften the blow.

I shake my head even though she's not looking at me. "I'm not lying. I have no reason to lie to you."

Dakota's body moves so quickly that her cotton-candy-pink T-shirt is a blur in the dark. The small television is playing old episodes of *Maury*. Well, I hope this is an old episode and people don't *actually* watch this show anymore. My mom always used to watch it; while I was doing my homework, I heard "You are *not* the father!" too many times to count.

"Yeah? You sure about that, Landon? Because it seems to me that you've been lying to me for quite some time now. And now, here we are, back in Saginaw to watch my dad die, and you won't even talk to me."

Our room is silent as a woman is jumping up and down pointing in her ex's face, yelling something that appears far too gleeful for such a tragic moment between them.

"Did you have sex with her?" Dakota asks, and before I answer, she adds, "I need to know if you had sex with her."

Are we really here? Should I agree with whatever she says and admit to every accusation she throws my way? Or should I take the harder road, the more complicated one, and tell her how childish this whole thing is? We've been through too much, especially her, to be acting like this.

I tighten my armor and step into the battlefield.

She's standing in the gap between our beds, only a few feet away from me.

"Is this where we are?" I move to the edge of the bed and sit with my back as straight as can be. If she moves closer to me, she'll be touching my knees. "Are we these people"—I correct myself—"these strangers, who fight over jealousy and pettiness? Or are we two people who've been through half of their lives together and want to stay civil?"

She regards me. "Just answer the question."

"Yes. I have." I tell the truth because I don't have it in me to lie.

Dakota sits down on the bed a foot away from me and drops her face into her hands.

I don't know what to say to her—or even if saying anything

to her will do any good. I can't apologize, because I'm not sorry. I can't tell her that it didn't mean anything, because it did.

I let her cry as I stare at the TV. Now there's a new woman onstage; her face is stoic as a man jumps in circles around her. He's so happy not to be the father of her baby—it's a sad, scary world out there.

The only way I'm keeping track of the time is from the TV, and the commercial break just ended, so some time must have passed by the point Dakota asks, "If we would have stayed here, do you think we would still be together?"

I nod. "Yeah. I think we would."

Dakota's hands are trembling in her lap, and she doesn't lift her sad eyes to mine. "You're being so quiet. You didn't even try to explain yourself." Her voice is defeated, and her shoulders are slumped. She looks like a doll sitting here, her face as still as stone.

"I don't have anything to explain. We haven't been together for six months, Dakota." I remain as calm as can be. If I let her see the stabbing needles multiplying inside my chest, I'm done for. If we fight—if I raise my voice and actually fight with her— that would mean we'd be crossing the line back into relationship territory.

"When did it start?" she asks.

I glance over at Dakota, and she's looking at me now. Her eyes are already swelling up from her tears, and I force my hand to stay down, gripping the edge of the mattress with both hands. I look away from her face.

"A little while back."

"Before we . . . *tried to* that one day?" Her eyes dart around the room and focus on the clock on the tiny desk.

We both should have known that this wasn't going to work since that embarrassing mishap.

"No. After that," I say, hoping it will sting a little less.

A low noise comes from Dakota's throat.

After a few more awkward beats, she turns her back to me and lies down on her bed.

When I lie back on my own bed for the night, I hear her say, "I slept with Aiden."

The words float to me, and my brain tries to scramble a response to my heart before my mouth gets the message and I say something I can't take back. I'm not exactly sure what to think, let alone to say. My insides are all turned around, and I don't think I'm supposed to be sad about this, and I don't think I'm supposed to feel like a volcano erupted inside me. But again, I'm not the strongest of knights, so it kind of hurts more than I thought it would. It's a little hard to describe the way I feel about her sleeping with a guy I know, a guy I despise.

Out of all the guys in this massive freaking city, she had to be sleeping with the one guy I don't like at all. From his arrogant smirk to his meticulously quaffed white-blond hair, he oozes everything I can't stand. *Why him?*

I look at Dakota's side of the room and close my eyes. I think of Nora's body on my lap, soft and aroused in my arms. I think of the way she moaned when I put my tongue on her. Her hair messy, her pouty lips swollen and soft red, her bright red shirt and sexy black pants. I think of the way she laughs when I nerd out on her and the way her skin rises into tiny bumps when I run my fingers across it. I don't regret a moment with her; it's not fair for me to believe Dakota can't share similar moments with someone else. No matter how hard I try to think of the perfect words for her, there's nothing more I can say to Dakota that will make this better.

Maybe we aren't supposed to live happily ever after with our first love after all.

chapter

Thirty-five

I T'S BEEN A LONG MONTH since I got back from Michigan. Everything in my life has changed. My mom had my little baby sister last week, and I just returned from a weekend trip to visit them. Abigail Scott is the cutest little girl I've ever seen. It's insane the way my family has grown and changed so drastically in the last two years. I would never have imagined that my mom would fall in love again, or that I would ever have another sibling, let alone two. The tiny little girl is easier to get along with than Hardin, for sure. With everything that's happened between Hardin and Tessa recently, the two of them aren't speaking. Which only makes things even more difficult for me as unofficial middleman.

Tessa started sleeping on the couch and is back to hating music again. It reminds me of *Twilight* when Bella Swan rips out the radio in her truck with her bare hands. I can understand how she felt, and I wouldn't blame Tessa for ripping her headphones to shreds. I've signed up for HBO GO and been binge-watching *Game of Thrones,* and with the end of each episode I think of Nora and how incredible it would be to watch it with her and talk about our theories and rant about the latest death. I started the show three weeks ago but now only have two episodes left. During the first few episodes, every time I saw Ned Stark, I wondered what Boromir was doing away from the White Tower. It took me a moment to get reoriented there.

Nora hasn't reached out to me, and I haven't reached out to her. Tessa stays silent between us—a middlewoman of her own sort—but she's so lost in her own pain that I don't even think she knows what's going on between us. Well, nothing is going on between us anymore. Nothing at all.

This morning when I get to work, Aiden is behind the bar. He's pouring a cold brew into a cup full of ice. Surprisingly, my dislike for him hasn't grown since I got back from Michigan. I've tried to focus on his positive traits, but searching those out took too long. Even though he slept with Dakota, I feel indifferent toward him and don't want to bother.

"Hey, bro," he says, and I wonder if he even knows that I dated Dakota at all. The thought occurs to me that she may not want him to know about her past, or maybe they were never emotionally attached enough for her to talk about that. Maybe she just slept with him—the way I did with Nora.

My BS alarm goes off in my head. I didn't just sleep with Nora—I fell in love with her and couldn't stop. Even now, I'm still mourning the loss of her presence in my life. I miss her every time I smell cookies or walk into my kitchen. The chairs hold memories of her straddling me, of me on my knees in front of her, and when I look at the counters, I see her long hair cascading down her back, a seductive smile on her lips.

"Hey," I finally respond to Aiden as I step over a pile of boxes. Of course he didn't put them away. He waited for me to get here because he knows I'll clean them up. Of course I'll unpack the coffee beans and put away the straws. Of course I'll unwrap the cups and put away the bottles of flavored syrups.

I clock in and tie my apron. At least Posey will be here in thirty minutes.

I watch the minutes tick on and on, and after an hour, she's here, the lobby is still empty, and I've gotten around to unpacking the boxes. Lila is sitting quietly at a booth, rolling a little car on the table. Posey nods along to a man in a suit who's talking about how delicious the espresso is in Europe. We're pretty slow today, and I have a paper to finish tonight. My reward to myself for finishing the essay is to watch another episode on my laptop.

I start sweeping, and a few minutes later when a customer comes into the shop, I walk over to help Posey. She stands behind the register, and I stand by the line, ready to take the cup and start the drink. The sound of a familiar voice makes the hairs on my neck stand straight up.

"An ice-blended caramel latte," Dakota says. She looks around behind Posey, and I wonder if she's looking for Aiden. Should I tell her that he's not here?

When her eyes fall on me, she gives me a smile. It's not unfriendly, but it's not the familiar smile I'm used to getting from her.

"Hey," I say, and quickly busy my hands. I grab the cup from Posey and push the ice scoop into the bin.

Posey turns to me, gives me a knowing look, and walks to the back room. I don't know if I should thank her or call for her to come back.

"How are you?" Dakota asks.

I glance up and dump some of the ice back in. I wasn't actually paying attention, and I need to dump out half of the ice I scooped into the blender jug.

How am I? What a loaded question.

Tessa is freaking miserable. I'm nearly failing my Educational Psych class. I miss Nora, and sort of miss Dakota, too. Just because we no longer have a future together doesn't cancel out my feelings for her. Part of me will always care for her. In a few years when she's posting engagement photos, then gets married, then has a family, I'll smile and feel relieved that she has a good life, even without me.

I opt for the short version. "Good. You?"

I pump in two squirts of caramel syrup and switch on the blender. It's loud, and neither of us talks until I hand her her drink.

She takes a long sip. "Same. I just got a callback for a commercial."

I can see the excitement rumbling inside her and smile. "Congrats!" I say, truly meaning it.

Dakota turns her cheek, and I take her in. Her dark hair is straight. It's pinned back behind her ears in a tight little bun. She's not wearing any makeup, and she looks gorgeous.

I ask her what type of commercial she's starring in. She tells me with a shy smile that it's for a gym and that she's meeting with the owner of the chain to possibly host a workout video for them, too.

Diverting the conversation away from herself, she sips her drink and asks, "Can you sit with me for a minute?"

After making sure the lobby is empty enough and double-checking with Posey that she's got everything under control, I go to a back table with Dakota. I can't stop staring at her hair; it looks so different, *so good*. I glance at the kitten on her sweatshirt. It's a little white furball of a cat wearing a pair of hipster glasses. It's a good distraction.

"Nora came to get the last of her stuff from our place this morning," she says.

Please tell me that she didn't come here today to fight about Nora again.

I stare at the door and she speaks up before I do.

"I thought for sure you two would be together by now. It surprised me that she had that driver with her. I don't know why she's living so far from the city."

I haven't really been able to stop thinking about what Nora's been up to in the last month. I feel like I knew she was going to start spending more time in her Scarsdale mansion.

I've found that the more I think about her, the longer the days get.

"Yeah, where else would she go?"

I wonder if Nora has come to a resolution with her husband and his family? Has Stausey had her baby? Is Nora sitting in a big, empty house with him? I'm not jealous; I feel awful for everyone involved. It's such a tricky situation, and I honestly commend her for her strength. I've always thought of myself as strong, but I'm merely aluminum compared to Nora's titanium.

"Good point." Dakota pulls one of her legs up onto the chair. "I've been thinking about you a lot."

Here we go . . .

I smile noncommittally. "Is that so?"

Dakota shakes her head, and I'm so used to her bouncy curls floating around her head that it's sort of weird looking at her with her hair straightened. "Not like that." Then she nudges me.

When I look up, Posey is staring at me from behind the counter. Our eyes meet, and she quickly looks away. I'm going to miss her when she leaves Brooklyn. I was pretty bummed when she told me she was moving to be closer to her aunt. I understand, though. Her grandma's health is declining, and it must be hard for her to take care of an autistic toddler all alone. Posey is just a good person, through and through.

"Are you still seeing Aiden?" I ask before Dakota can elaborate on her recent thoughts about me.

She smiles and leans back against the chair. "Sort of."

"Hmm . . ." If I have nothing nice to say, I shouldn't say anything at all.

"Nora said you haven't called her at all."

Why is Dakota sitting here talking to me about Nora? Isn't this like some conflict of interest? It's also very awkward.

But maybe—*maybe*—we can have this type of friendship. I don't want us to be one of those couples who break up and turn into enemies. I don't want us to have that. I fell in love with her for a reason. No matter how things are now, I loved her at one point. I will never understand those guys who say awful things about their exes—attack their appearance or disrespect them—when just a few days before the girl was "sexy" and their Wednesday Woman Crush online.

Or is it Woman Crush on Wednesday?

"Landon, why haven't you called her?"

A customer walks through the door, and I stand up. "I have to get back to work."

As I lift the partition to get behind the bar, I hear Dakota say, "Call her."

Which just makes me all kinds of confused.

This isn't how this type of thing usually goes. The angry, horrible ex doesn't try to help you with your girl troubles. Especially when she *hates* the new girl.

chapter

Thirty-six

Nora

*L*UNCH IS ALMOST DONE; the timer goes off in the kitchen, and I push Amir down the hall. Jennifer is here again, but I asked her to stay upstairs. I'm trying to get used to being alone with him again. The house feels bigger than it ever did. It's hard to imagine myself as the type of person who would need this massive house in order to be happy. It never felt as big as it does now. I take the corner of Amir's chair and push him down the beautiful dark wooden ramp put in just for him.

The despair and denial on Amir's mother's face was chilling. I felt for her, I felt for Ameen, for their sister, Pedra, whom I was close friends with, but I never took the time to deal with the loss of my husband. It was also hard for me to admit that if the accident hadn't happened, we would have ended up divorced. I believe that we would have happily gone our separate ways, and stayed friends through both of our lives. I would have been happy for him to get married, to have children.

The mention of children makes my stomach burn. I don't like to focus too long on the things he'll be missing out on. It's not good for me, or for him. I would like to think that having me around more is making him happier.

I didn't leave his side for months after his accident. I slept at the hospital until we moved into our house. The house was supposed to be a wedding gift from his family, even though we had already been married for two years.

"I made cabbage and bread," I tell him, unsure as always if he can even hear me. Jennifer insists that can, but what does she know? I think that's more a spiritual hope than reality.

I pull the curtains back and open the blinds. When was the last time he went outside? I need to ask Jennifer.

I pop the maple squares I'm baking into the oven. When I make myself a plate, I wish he could eat with me. I miss the vibrancy that radiated from within him. I like to talk to him about our past, how wild we were as teenagers, and once, I swear he smiled.

Since I've seen Landon last, I've had a lot of time to think about this. Sometimes we just have those people we are tied to for our entire lives. Landon has Dakota, Stausey has Ameen, Tessa has Hardin, and Amir has me.

The aroma of the cabbage immediately fills the kitchen, and I try my hardest not to think about the way Landon kissed me between each bite of the cabbage I made him. I loved every silly, simple moment with him. He made me feel like a better person.

He gave me hope, even if it's hard to explain what the hope was for.

Once upon a time, Landon hated my cooking, which is funny even still because he loved his mom's cooking and she was the worst. The woman burned grilled cheese, for God's sake.

When I take a bite of the cabbage, Landon's face fills my head. He was so cute, so sweet, when I fed him my cabbage.

I throw my plate of food in the trash.

"Let's go outside," I tell Amir. I grab my book from the counter and slowly push him out to the patio. It's colder now, the last week of October is here. Tomorrow is Halloween, and

I've been in hiding for so long that I am debating whether to ever leave this house on the hill.

It's silent out here and no neighbors are close to us. That was my favorite thing about the house. Back when I had a favorite thing.

Amir watches me without expression in his eyes. Is he in pain? Jennifer says he's not, but again, what does she know?

I open my book and read a chapter out loud to Amir. I don't know if he ever liked *Harry Potter*, we never talked about it. I knew a lot of things about him—his family, his favorite shows. But I didn't know half the things about him that I do about Landon.

I read faster to clear Landon from my head.

"Sophia!" Jennifer's deep voice shouts through the garden.

What part of "stay upstairs" does this woman not understand?

Her round body is moving fast through the grass, across the lawn from one of the side doors. "I've been yelling for you!" She bats her little arms in the air. "Someone is here for you. A guy, and he won't leave."

"For me, or him?" I hope that Amir's family has realized not to fuck with me. I got a lawyer, and as Amir's wife, I will protect his land from their greedy paws.

"You, girl. I told him you were out here but he's just sitting in the living room!" She's frantic. I can't imagine her dealing with a patient if she's this frazzled by a delivery guy or whoever.

"Oh, hush, I'll go inside. Watch him."

Jennifer gives me an angry look, as if to say she always watches him, and I roll my eyes behind her back.

Debating whether Jennifer is a good fit for this job, now that I'm paying better attention to everything, I wander into the living room.

Only to have the breath knocked out of me to find Landon

sitting on the couch. He's wearing a confidence that I don't remember him possessing the last time I saw him. And even though I have seen him every time I closed my eyes, I hadn't remembered him properly. He's beautiful, with more facial hair than I realized.

His arms are bigger than before.

Is he taller?

"What are you doing here?" More important, how did he find me?

Then I remember the two missed calls from Stausey yesterday. I'm sure this was her doing.

"Jennifer said you were outside," he says, not answering my question.

"Did she?"

"Yes. And she made me coffee while I waited," he says with that puppylike smile I love.

Of course Landon would get the impersonal Jennifer to make him a coffee. Landon looks so out of place here, in this massive house. He's sitting here so comfortably, like he's been here a hundred times. Why did he come here? How did he know where to go?

"Am I keeping you?" he asks when I glance toward the back door. When I turn back, I take his entire body in again. He looks too big for the couch. His shoulders are slouched, and he seems older somehow, like some of the light has been drained from him. He's wearing a white T-shirt with a blue button-up over it. He looks so good, so familiar. His hair is longer on top. How long has it been since I've seen him? Months? Years, maybe?

"No. I was just sitting outside with Amir."

I changed my routine, Landon. I'm finally going outside today. Are you proud of me?

I wait for Landon's reaction to my words, but his expression doesn't change. He looks at me thoughtfully and runs his hand over the knees of his dark jeans.

"How is everything?" he asks.

I watch his eyes scan the room. The art in the living room is gone now; all the money they once represented is being put into a charity that aids the families of victims of drunk driving. Just one of those expensive pieces could pay all the medical bills of a family. All six of the art pieces are being appraised now.

"I've been busy," I say, clearing my throat. "I'm sure you have too. Tessa said you got promoted at Grind."

He nods. "Yeah."

"Congrats, that's pretty cool. I'm sure you're the youngest manager they've ever had."

He looks at me, and I think about the way my words might sound.

"I didn't mean it like that," I say, struggling to clean up the spilled words.

Landon's lips turn into a half smile, and the timer on the oven goes off. I don't know why I still bake as much as I do; no one eats it anymore. I don't live with Maggy and Dakota, I'm not at Landon's apartment every night, and Jennifer only eats gluten-free cupcakes. The cupcakes just sit there on the granite counter, decorated and delicious, waiting to be eaten, and three days later, when the icing starts to harden, I toss them out.

"I'll accept your apology if I can have one of whatever that timer was for."

That smile that makes my entire soul ache.

I nod, agreeing, and choose not to mention that I got the recipe for the maple squares I'm baking from his mom. She promised me that she won't tell her son how often we talk. I cherish my friendship with her, and there was a point in my life recently that I allowed myself the fantasy of her being a permanent fixture in my life. Who am I kidding? Sometimes in my darkest of times, I allow myself to imagine a better, happier life I might have.

I told Karen about Amir before Landon could. I wasn't entirely sure if he would even tell her, but I didn't want any more secrets between any of us. Karen has been good to me. Ken even helped me find a lawyer to help me deal with the pressure from Amir's family. I don't want a dime of his money, I just don't want to be harassed anymore. I'll gladly move out of this house and back into a shared apartment, and I'll even pick up extra shifts at Lookout if need be.

I don't trust the family's intentions; even my lovely sister has more allegiance to the other side. I'm all alone over here, with only crabby Jennifer on my side, and I'm not 100 percent positive that money wouldn't sway her to work against me. I'd like to think that I would be House Stark and that Amir's family would be the Lannisters, but once the fighting starts, who really knows.

"Deal?" he prods after I'm silent a little too long.

I nod. "Of course. How are you?"

"I'm busy, too."

I look around the room and back at Landon's boots. I don't know if either of us have it in us to keep up this small talk. I decide to take one for the team. "How did you find me?"

He takes a breath and brings his hands to his mouth. I miss touching him. "You're not the only one who's good at stalking."

We both laugh at the same time, and it's refreshing and nostalgic.

"Can I ask you something?" Landon says.

I probably shouldn't tell him that he can ask me anything he wants. I simply want to hear his voice.

"Anything." I run my fingers over my messy braid. If I would have known he was coming, I would have dressed a little differently. My leggings smell like cabbage and syrup, and my shirt has a small red wine stain on the collar. Will he notice? He's staring at me now, taking me in. His gaze seems to stop in places where I'm bare: my shoulders, my face.

"How often were you coming here when you lived in the city?"

My throat tightens up.

"Almost every night. Sometimes I would have a driver and sometimes Cliff would drive me."

"Cliff?" he repeats.

The name is familiar to Landon. Of course it is. Cliff, Amir's closest friend, acted like an idiot and tried to spy on me at Landon's place. When I confronted him, he told me he was looking out for me. He heard I was hanging out with a college guy from that damn Mitch, who was bartending that messy night when I had Landon meet me out.

Me, Landon, Dakota—all in the same room. It was a mess, and the moment I saw Mitch behind the bar, I knew word would get back to Cliff. He still had no right being a creep and checking in on me, and he deserved the fractured hand from Hardin's boot. The thought of Hardin makes my blood boil. I was rooting for him, and he fucked up *again* with Tessa.

Landon doesn't press upon the truth hidden beneath that name; instead he moves on to another question.

"Why did you just assume I would think the worst of you if you told me about Amir? Why did you make that choice for me, and not give me the benefit of the doubt?"

Why does he always ask me questions that require such naked answers? Landon is the only person I know who just says what he means; he has no problem talking about wrongs and rights and admitting faults. The world could use more Landons.

"I wasn't meaning to assume the worst of either of us. I just expected it. I didn't know any better. When I met you, I wasn't at a point in my life where I was looking for anything other than a friendship. I have so much on my shoulders, so much responsibility. I didn't just have myself to consider, so I couldn't stay out at bars until three a.m. I was dealing with problems that I would never have wished upon my worst enemy and trying to do the right thing by my husband, my family. I had no time to fall in love with anyone."

Landon's shoulders flinch ever so slightly, but I notice.

"I told you from the beginning, Nora . . ." His voice soothes a fraction of my need for him. I never imagined I would miss him so much after such a short period of time. "I wanted you to open up to me. I wouldn't have judged you."

He turns his face to me, and his expression slices me to the bone. A face like his wasn't made for sadness. "I would have thought you were brave."

I struggle for breath. I should look away from him, I really should.

"I would have thought you were selfless."

When his words take shape, I feel like they're unraveling me. My muscles are unwinding, and the weight on my shoulders is disappearing.

His eyes don't waver from mine, not even for a flicker of a moment. "I would have thought that you were a strong, incredible woman. I would have tried to take some of the burden from your shoulders and place it onto mine."

"I don't think you can carry any more," I say softly.

"I can try." Landon shrugs, and I try to imagine how this could possibly work.

Does he love me? Are we too far away from that now?

Does my life have room for one more person? Is it fair for me to bring Landon into my life before I've even fully figured out how to handle it myself?

"I would like to meet him," Landon says, standing.

So much is happening. My normal, quiet day has been flipped upside down by this boy's unexpected arrival. Speechless, I nod and stand up. I'm afraid that I won't be able to hold myself up without the support of the couch, but I use every ounce of strength I have, straighten my back, and cross the living, moving toward the door to the patio.

Without a word, he follows me through the massive kitchen and outside. He mutters something about cabbage, but I don't turn around. I don't know what to say or why he's here.

"I was reading to him," I softly explain as we approach Amir, and Jennifer scampers off.

The expansive garden feels smaller with the presence of both of these men. The two of them are so important to me, in very different ways. The flowers around us smell even stronger, look even brighter, now that Landon is here. I've always wanted a garden, which has always been my qualm with living in the city. I love flowers and trees and the smell of pollen and nature, but I love being able to walk to a coffee shop, too.

"Landon, this is Amir."

I gesture to my husband and watch Landon's calm smile stay right there on his face. He looks straight into the eyes of Amir and introduces himself. He doesn't seem to be the least bit uncomfortable. I envy that about Landon, that he can be the calming breath of life into every soul he encounters.

I watch him, studying his face as he smiles and bends down and grabs the book from the soft grass, sits on the bench next to Amir, and cracks it open where I left my little bookmark.

Landon clears his throat and begins, " 'It is our choices, Harry, that show what we truly are, far more than our abilities.' "

epilogue

A summer and a winter later . . .

*O*UR WEDDING CAME AND WENT so quickly. So, so quickly. We went from being the engaged couple who wanted to wait a few years to get married, the ones who thought we had all the time in the world, to us suddenly being in the midst of a whirlwind of preparation.

I'd gotten used to my mom's voice on the other end of the line asking over and over when we were going to start planning, but all it took one day was Tessa bringing home bridal magazines, and that was that. I was fine waiting. My wife-to-be had already been through this once, and I didn't want to rush her into anything. But when the planning started, it took off like a dang rocket.

The sudden haste was her idea, insisting on visiting venues and choosing flowers that matched the cupcakes that would be served. Weddings have way, way more details than I ever imagined. While the two women were planning the biggest day of my life, I tried not to be the stereotypical guy who just nodded along and pretended to know what was going on. I wanted this time to be perfect for her. For *us.*

I helped choose the flavor of the cake, and my bride made my favorite cake and added thoughtful little purple flowers made of buttercream icing that only the two of us will understand. I helped her as much as I could and as much as Tessa, wedding-planner-slash-evil-monster-who-has-taken-over-my-best-friend's-body, would allow.

Just last week Tessa yelled at me when she found out the tailor got Hardin's measurements wrong and the pants to his suit landed right above his ankles. She swore he probably did it on purpose and even called the store in Chicago to try and correct the mistake. I laughed at the pictures he sent, but she just huffed and tossed the phone back at me. I'm a little nervous about how the two of them will get along at the wedding. Tessa has really been avoiding him, and he won't shut up about her in his interviews. Last weekend when I got home from school, I found Tess flipping Hardin off. Only Hardin was inside our TV, doing an interview on his book tour, and Tessa was furious and maybe had had a little too much wine.

Now, here I am sitting at a table full of people I love and admire—and *I'm married*.

I'm in college and I'm married. Married to a beautiful, successful, sharp, and feisty woman. She's sitting next to me, talking to my mom about the whipping cream and gluten-free something or other.

Hardin is seated on the other side of me, and he's looking straight ahead at Tessa, who's standing next to a table filled with wedding guests.

"How's it going?" I ask him. I remove my arm from around my bride's back and take her hand in mine. She turns to look at me, gives me a kiss on the cheek, and turns back to talk to my mom.

Hardin looks up at me and fusses with his hair. "Bleh." He half smiles. "How is it going for you? Do you feel any different now that you're legally bound to one person for the rest of your life . . . well, barring a divorce."

I roll my eyes. "Aren't you a ball of sunshine?"

He cracks a smile for me, and I watch him panic as he loses sight of Tessa in the crowd. He sits up a little further in his chair, and his eyes scan the room.

"She's there, by the door," I say.

He relaxes and rests his eyes on her. Ken hands Abby to her, and Tessa giggles when Abby pulls her hair. I look over to the next table and see Stausey taking a selfie with her wineglass. Todd and Amir are on either side of her. Amir is dressed in a suit, and the color of his tie is the color of Nora's eyes. I wonder if that's why Nora chose that tie for him. I hope so.

Things have been slowly working themselves out since the divorce. She stayed executor of his estate and in charge of the legal and medical parts of his life. He's become a pretty big part of my life, too, and through her stories about their adventures, I feel like I know him as well. Helping take care of him has also made me consider doing a master's in Special Education after I graduate. It will mean more college, more student-loan debt, but I have a feeling I would be great at it.

Stausey straightens out Amir's tie, and I turn my attention back to my stepbrother sitting next to me. "What are you two going to do?"

Hardin sighs, and I tighten my grip on my bride's hand. My mom laughs, and Hardin brings his fingers to his mouth. Tugging on his lips, he says, "Get married."

"Really? Does *she* know that?" I ask, raising my brow.

I'm positive that Tessa doesn't know much about this plan. I heard her practicing what to say to him in the bathroom last night before bed. I feel bad because she has no privacy now that the three of us live together, but the two women seem to love the arrangement. I had asked my wife—I still can't get over how that sounds—if she wanted me to ask Tessa to move out since we were getting married soon, but she told me over and over that she loves having Tessa around.

I sort of suspect that both of us just know that she doesn't have anywhere else to go.

"Yep. Why not? You two did it, and you haven't even known each other as long as I've known Tess."

He has a point there. "Yes. But you two aren't even dating. I think you're skipping a step, perhaps."

Hardin grins at me—his plotting grin takes over his whole face. "The order of the steps isn't important. Either way, we end up the same place."

He lifts his glass and I raise mine.

A few more summers and winters later . . .

"Mommy!" Addy's voice is always high-pitched when she wants something.

My wife strides into the room with her hands full. Her face is flushed, she has the phone to her ear, and I feel sorry for whoever is on the end of that call. But her voice changes from irritated to soothing when she talks to her mini-me. "What, baby?"

My little monster crosses her arms over her chest. "Daddy said I can't have any more cake."

Nora looks at me, unable to keep a straight face. "How much did he let you eat? You know we have dinner with your aunt and uncle in two hours, and you still have homework to do."

"Well"—Addy's pouty little lips turn up—"you shouldn't make so much if I can't eat it."

I burst into laughter and try to cover my mouth when my wife glares at me.

Then the little devil tattles on me. "Dad said so, too."

"I did not!" I lie.

Both girls ignore me.

"Addy, no more cake." My wife's tone leaves no room for negotiation. "Go brush your teeth and finish your homework."

Addy saunters off and disappears down the hallway, her long, wavy brown hair swishing back and forth.

When I look back to my wife, her hands are empty and she's

reaching for me. I pull her into my lap and she straddles my waist.

"Stop feeding her sugar before every meal." She kisses my lips.

"Stop making so many cakes if we can't eat them." I shrug, and Nora playfully slaps at my chest. Her hair is so long that it brushes against my legs when she shakes her head.

Her mouth presses to mine and she wraps her arms around the back of my neck. "I missed you today." She tells me this every day during the school year.

"Someone has to teach our heathens," I say against her mouth. "I missed you, baby."

She takes my face between her open hands. "I'm filming again tomorrow. They just told me they need another take."

I sigh, trying not to throw a tantrum. She's been working so much lately, and I feel like I barely see my wife. "What happened now?"

She taps her index finger against my lips. "Someone dropped the cake before the last few frames. This is what happens when they use real cakes for commercials."

"Isn't that the point?" I remember the faux cupcakes from last weekend. The wedding cake was real and so was the couple on the screen. But when they called "Cut!" and the shoot was over, I grabbed one of the stupid cupcakes and nearly chipped a tooth. The director made Nora decorate the fake cupcakes and everything. Then again, they pay her more for one day than she makes doing two weddings.

"One day, I'll quit my job and you'll homeschool all of our babies, and we can do this all day." She rubs her breasts against my chest.

I softly push her back. "And what would that teach our babies?" I tease my tongue along her jaw. She pushes her breasts to me again, begging for me to touch them.

"Not yet, little one," I whisper behind her ear, and she squirms in my arms.

"The kids would learn how to love their spouse. And to bake. We will have the perfect little army of loving chefs behind us." Her eyes light up with amusement, and I run my fingers through her long silky hair. "That's it! We can travel the country baking and teaching. We would never have to work in an office again."

I kiss at her neck, imagining her in the middle of the country, only dirt and wind around us. Somehow, I don't think she is thinking too far in advance about this.

"Shh." I kiss her cheek. "Shh, my city girl. You wouldn't last a day out there in the land of no offices and corn."

She begins to challenge me, but our daughter comes barreling down the hallway with a pink hairbrush matted into her hair. "Mommy!" she screams.

Nora jumps off my lap. "Your turn," Nora says to me, biting at my lip just as our daughter enters the room. Between the chaos of my daughter growing up too fast and my wife trying not to laugh, my heart swells and I am the luckiest SOB in the world.

Sometimes it's tragedy that binds us with another. The bond feels unbreakable, but sometimes in between the tears and the ache of a dull knife carving the painful memories into you, you can find a spark of light. The tiniest of sparks can ignite to fire with just a touch of happiness. The light can burn out the darkness, and when there's nothing but ashes and a fire, you learn a new kind of bond. One that blazes brighter than the sun.

acknowledgments

$\mathcal{S}$ OOOO, WHEN I FIRST TOLD my readers on Wattpad that I was going to write a book about Landon (Liam back then), I was almost finished with *After 3* on Wattpad. I wrote Landon's wedding scene, but his bride didn't have a face. It was the weirdest thing. No matter how many times I tried to force her to have a face, she refused. I kept thinking about how he met her, who she was, how they got there—but still she had no face. Details started to fall into place, but not her identity. It drove me crazy, and I couldn't wait to find out who she was. But when I started to write it, my head got more and more cloudy. When I finished *Nothing More*, there still wasn't clarity. The characters took control of my story, like they always have, and I love that. So, just like you, I didn't know who she was until I typed the words. Thank you all for loving Landon the way I do.

Adam Wilson: This is our sixth—well, seventh with *Imagines*—book together, and with each book you continue to amaze and impress me with your patience and willingness to try new things and let me do things (somewhat) my way. I am so grateful to you for being so willing to help me figure out what was missing, which I saw was Wattpad, and you went to bat for me and trusted me to do something different. I feel like all of these acknowledgements are always the same, but you should hear these things more often than just in the back of a book. Good luck with everything, and I'm excited for Gallery 13 and all the awesomeness I know you'll continue to trail-blaze.

Kristin Dwyer: Dude!!! You're the best, and I really, really, really appreciate everything you do for me. You keep me on track and make me laugh. I heart you a lot.

Ashleigh Gardner: Thanks for helping me navigate through the massive publishing world. I'm still not getting an agent, unless it's you ;)

Aron Levitz: My unicorn friend, I'm happy to be your bunny emoji friend. You're awesome and fancy and you made me fancier than I was. Thank you for being a friend and keeping me grounded *eye roll* and for always being there to brainstorm and conquer with. I know you're only using me to get to my husband, but I'm okay with that.

Paul O'Halloran: Paul! I don't even know where to start. I feel like you work harder for me than even I do. You do so, so much, and I really appreciate you being on top of the world, literally. I wouldn't be able to keep up with all the traveling, the translations, the madness, if it wasn't for you!

Chels, Lauren, Bri, and Trev: You guys were so essential to this book and my life in general :P I'm so lucky to have the four of you as my closest friends. You mean so much to me, and I love you for sending me Nick Jonas gifs.

Ursula: I feel like this is always the same :P But you are still my BFF, my assistant, and my brain. We've made so many amazing memories this year, and I can't wait for more. Thanks for not trying to steal Miles from me lololol.

Sales and Production: Thank you for working so hard on such short deadlines! I owe you all a drink—or nine.

My readers are the most important thing to me, and I still thank you every day for my life being what it is now. Now that I know how it is to be able to live my dream, I never ever want to stop.

Connect with Anna Todd on Wattpad

The author of this book, Anna Todd, started her career as a reader, just like you. She joined Wattpad to read stories like this one and to connect with the people who wrote them.

Download Wattpad today to connect with Anna:

 imaginator1D

wattpad   www.wattpad.com

THE INTERNET SENSATION
WITH OVER ONE BILLION READS—
NEWLY REVISED AND EXPANDED

Book One of the massively popular After series
#HESSA

1 BILLION READS ONLINE—NEWLY REVISED AND EXPANDED!

A NOVEL

AFTER

ANNA TODD

wattpad SENSATION IMAGINATOR1D

∞

Pick up or download your copy today!

GALLERY BOOKS
A Division of Simon & Schuster
A CBS COMPANY

Because the best conversations happen after dark . . .

XOXO
AFTER DARK

*Visit **XOXOAfterDark.com** for free reads, exclusive excerpts, bonus materials, author interviews and chats, and much, much more!*

XOXO**AFTERDARK**.COM

LOOK FOR

Once Upon Now

A collection of
modern tales with a
fantastical twist!

by the **wattpad** authors